THE BOLLYWOOD AFFAIR

THE BOLLYWOOD AFFAIR

GAURI SINH

HARPER
BLACK
An Imprint of HarperCollins *Publishers*

First published in India in 2021 by Harper Black
An imprint of HarperCollins *Publishers*
A-75, Sector 57, Noida, Uttar Pradesh 201301, India
www.harpercollins.co.in

2 4 6 8 10 9 7 5 3 1

P-ISBN: 978-93-5422-366-2
E-ISBN: 978-93-5422-374-7

Typeset in 11/13.6 Minion Pro at
Manipal Digital Systems, Manipal

Printed and bound at
Thomson Press (India) Ltd

A Note to My Readers

The second wave of the pandemic here in India has been brutal. As I write this, I am all too aware of the grimness around. Unlike the first wave, the virulence of this one feels more potent, because everyone I know has been affected—either directly or indirectly.

How does a writer manage to cocoon herself from the manic, oft-traumatic present, to concentrate on her craft despite the physical/psychological weight of the misery and despair surrounding everyone? No matter the number of consequent waves one might live through, never before has the struggle to fight a virus been so universal. And the experience so gutting.

This is what I tried to do—focus on the better. If we are not there now as I write this, we soon will be. To believe in it and live by it—this is fundamental to fighting free of the brain-freeze. And then, despite everything to the contrary—try to channel joy.

This book, set in the late 1990s, hearkens to a simpler era where joy was perhaps easier to come by. Reading it allows nostalgia, the permission to skip to a lighter, less complicated moment in time when we still had the luxury of wallowing in our pleasant pastimes. Among them—the poster child of the big, beautiful world of Indian cinema—Bollywood! Larger-than-life auras, the absorbing thrill of a make-believe world.

I do hope reading my book brings you some happiness/relief, especially if the turbulence around us has not passed, or moved only to return in third or subsequent waves. I cannot predict as I pen this, whether our lives will return to what we once knew. But I truly hope this book can be for you what it was for me throughout the publishing process—a little world of my own to disappear into, a make-believe comfort cushion buoying me, when the reality of the pandemic, of the forever-seeming lockdown, threatened sanity.

And as you read, my continuing wish for you: May my book, in embracing B-Town's hyper-bombastic late 1990's vibe in the telling of a detective tale, also become what commercial big-budget Bollywood always stood for to the great Indian theatre-going public—a temporary escape. As very much—a solace.

Gauri Sinh
April–May 2021

Prologue

The room was dim. The afternoon sunlight from the huge ornate windows did not serve to illuminate, only increase the severity of the shadows already at play within.

A face and form of classic beauty appeared at rest on the giant four-poster bed, perhaps even more beautiful here than it seemed on-screen to his crazed fan following. The man slept.

The cat rested with the man, its bulk obscured by the pillow in the crook of his arm. The tableau was one of tranquillity. Not even the familiar chime of the century-old grandfather clock in the hall precisely on the hour, every hour, disturbed the surreal calm of this picture.

A siesta of enviable peace. And then, after the lull—the shattering. The sleeping man leapt up as if badly startled, the cat with him, spluttering and hissing at the disturbance. A noise, relentless and manic, pierced through the quiet of a moment ago. A scream of such unhinged proportions, it extracted an equally hysteric dread from its listener.

The man was no hero, but he tried. His panic was utter, yet he grabbed the cricket bat casually placed at the corner of his bedside and lunged at the door, towards the source of that scream. The cat mirrored his movement. Their combined weight swung the heavy wood outward, to reveal the contents of the great hall beyond. And then the momentary panic settled like a full-blown fever in the man's brain, clamping dank fingers round his heart, obscuring his physical vision even as he peered into the darkness beyond his doorframe. As before, as countless times in the past few weeks—*there was no one there.*

1

‘Do you know who this is?’ The voice at the other end was vaguely familiar. I couldn’t place it at first. Nor the sharpness of unease that followed immediately after.

Without waiting for my response, as if confident that I would indeed know who it was, the speaker continued.

‘Can we meet at, say, 4 p.m. today?’ This was when it came to me, where I’d heard that voice. On two occasions, actually.

The first one—a memory trawled from the depths of my subconscious—at a national beauty pageant, almost three years ago. But more recently, while listening to a radio talk show featuring superstars of the silver screen. Yes, that voice was certainly familiar.

Saurav Roop Kamal, actor and Bollywood superstar, was at the other end of the line, demanding we meet. How could I possibly refuse?

First things first. You might be familiar with my name. I’m Akruti Rai, one half of the Akruti–Parvati Private Investigators duo, the central (the media prefers ‘celebrity’) detectives in our global firm currently. But this is 1998 I’m telling you of—the kind of reputation and trust we enjoy at present was yet to be established as firmly as it is now. We were still finding our feet as investigators in the India of the late Nineties. And we were so young.

It was true, our first case at solving some particularly gruesome murders at the nation's biggest beauty pageant, Miss Glamour Princess 1995, had propelled us into the limelight overnight. It had given our fledgling venture unbelievable momentum and a rather high-visibility public profile. Add to that my partner Parvati Samant's RAW connections (her father was chief of the national security agency, her brother pretty high up on the chain too). And my own erstwhile career as a supermodel with the 'right' contacts, no wonder we were being singled out so, for both attention and advice.

That first case had gotten us the credibility to attract a cross section of clients, among them those from the nation's upper strata who valued discretion and privacy to showmanship. Their business had cemented our reputation over the intervening years in a way that allowed us to grow in both stature and merit, in a relatively short timeframe.

Indeed, we had done well by most standards, in procuring the more baffling and darker cases of the day. Also, having solved them to our patrons' satisfaction in the three years leading up to this curt phone call by the superstar, we enjoyed an unshakable trust in certain circles.

But I was uneasy, had felt so the moment I heard Saurav Roop Kamal's well-practised baritone drawl out that confident query, 'Do you know who this is?' Such was the level of his blinding fame at the time, he seemed absolutely assured that anyone in India would most certainly recognize his voice in an unannounced phone call. In fact, back then his celebrityhood was riding the crest of such a wave, he had adoring fans slit wrists and build temples in his name.

'Yes, indeed I do, Mr Kamal,' I had replied, making sure to keep the wariness out of my voice. 'Who wouldn't know

Bollywood's reigning superstar Saurav Roop Kamal—or as the rest of the world often says, SRK?'

'Actually, I prefer my second name, Roop,' he had drawled out. 'Don't go by the other, less familiar colloquialism. The abbreviated name is RK, as the Indian mainstream media calls me!'

'Fine, RK then,' I had indulged him, but the unease persisted, despite my light-hearted tone.

So why was I troubled when I should've been rejoicing at this call from so very famous a potential client? Our cases up until then, barring our first at the beauty pageant, had been of the more discreet sort, even if the clients involved had been illustrious. The incredible publicity wave that followed us initially had calmed after the first few months. In fact, our current reputation was built on our deduction abilities, more than any overt press attention.

However, RK's business, if it came through, promised tremendous visibility, never a bad thing for a profession like ours. If this meeting he wanted turned him into a client, it would be the first high-profile case of its kind in our business together. (Our first case at the beauty pageant had been high-profile too, but we weren't full-fledged detectives then!)

In fact, our initial case had a connect to him in a bizarre manner—I won't go into details here, because I've written about it and I don't want to give out spoilers to those who'd like to read that and haven't yet got around to it.

As I finished that 1995 pageant story (for those who have read it), I wrote of how our chance meeting with RK at the time lead to RK's calling us now, omitting to elaborate more. I cursorily called it our 'first' case, rather than our first 'high-profile' case as detectives, given the focus then was not RK.

But now—three years later—it most certainly was, and my present wariness at RK's call went deeper than the oddity of that past career connect.

Now, looking back, this case seemed ominous from the very beginning. I've always had a sense for what is seemingly out of place—call it a sixth sense if you will. Despite the practised charm, and that artless, unthreatening query, in that very first call his voice seemed … foreboding?

Regardless, I went ahead and accepted the 4 p.m. appointment. I was a detective, this was my profession. I had handled a number of complicated cases with Parvati till then. He was a megastar requesting a simple audience. In spite of any shadowy misgivings and the prickle of disturbance I already felt—how could I refuse?

2

We had agreed to meet at RK's home that afternoon. Those familiar with Mumbai and its bombastic, hyper-wattage Tinseltown of the Nineties would undoubtedly know RK's vast mansion, the one nestled on a hillock in a leafy South Mumbai bylane, an enduring landmark for locals and gawking tourists alike. And its evocative name, *Taqdeer*—'fate'—channelling many a legend, stories about how it came to be his. Fact and fiction so deeply entwined, they could not be separated, true to the tradition of authentic Bollywood myth-making around superstars.

I could not but help feel a pang of nostalgia for my old life as we approached his house. The glitz and showmanship and sense of importance accorded to mega stardom. It was evident in the regalia, the fans in wait, just outside the mansion—I too once had all of it, as a supermodel.

My face on hoardings and massive ad spreads, much like the dark-haired Sunsilk lady I woke up to, her bouncy locks spread across the entire bottom half of the morning newspaper. Or my face on magazine covers—I missed out on the big international ones, having already quit glamour town for my current profession by the time *Elle* arrived here in December 1996, with *Vogue* and others following within the next decade or so. But I remembered the feeling. Maybe not as overreaching as a Bollywood star's fame, but there, all the same.

My journey to the past was momentary; I snapped out of my fugue state almost immediately. I much preferred my present life, with its twists and turns and the thrill of solving inexplicable mysteries. And the delicious sense of heady satisfaction after, when a case was solved and a client appeased.

Parvati had accompanied me with some reluctance on this trip. We tackled cases as a team, but it wasn't always that we met our clients together. In fact, as our business grew, we had often split up to save time and maximize our effort.

'You meet him, that world is more familiar to you anyway,' she said when I told her. 'I can meet the next appointment.'

But something about that call had got me uneasy, I couldn't quite put my finger on it. And I insisted Parvati go with me. 'Fine,' she had relented, giving me a sharp once-over. Maybe she sensed I was a bit edgy, without knowing why.

Her presence on this trip was a sign of solidarity. We were good together, picking up on non-verbal cues from each other, like my out-of-character disquiet today. And we supported each other unquestioningly, when needed.

Parvati seemed cool and unflappable now, as always, her clear brown eyes surveying the mansion placidly as we entered, past massive gates, clearing security at the entrance. 'Quite a setting,' she remarked, dryly.

Anyone who knew Parvati would've understood her comment as a deliberate understatement. Because the sprawling mansion and its almost terrifying grandeur harkened to India's majestic colonial long-ago.

Imposing towers and turrets, gargoyles nestling within awnings and arches high above, complete with rolling manicured lawns, their expanse checked at intervals by gothic-seeming, intricately designed lamp posts and fountains. The entire spectacle was geared to summon up necessary and instant awe.

But also, enough superstition to channel every creeping terror in a gothic horror movie. An overwhelming and intimidating bit of Mumbai's historical architecture, this place. And a cunning piece of real estate, its expanse deftly obscured by tall palms, and tangled shrubbery at its boundary walls, a world away from the bustling, manic city just outside its gates. Well hidden, indeed, from prying eyes in overcrowded Mumbai.

Taqdeer stood immense and proud before us now, its seeming personality as portentous as the connotation conjured up by its name—fate. Listed under the city's prime heritage properties, it was witness to centuries of evolution and, now, central to Bollywood's myth-making—also, to its superstitious nature. But to think of it as a home seemed rather daunting.

But home it was, for the lucrative Indian film fraternity's most popular poster boy. And RK had lived there for a while now. We were admitted inside by a lone, uniformed help, and ushered past a cavernous corridor to his inner sanctum—what appeared to be his study.

'I'm not a stickler for punctuality,' the superstar drawled, upon sighting us. 'But I needed to speak with you on an urgent basis.' We had already been waiting an hour in his study by then, but with the authority accorded to celebrity perspectives, he absurdly seemed to believe he was very much on time.

'Things are happening,' he continued without preamble, the smoothness of his perfect features at odds with his words, which came out hesitant, as if unsure of telling us his concern.

As he spoke, he seated himself in an oversized leather armchair facing us, the light from the bay window behind throwing his face in shadow. The darkness of the room seemed unusual for a hot Mumbai late afternoon, for despite the huge windows all around us, the inside of this study was decidedly dim.

'What things, Mr Kamal?' I asked. Parvati was silent, a cool though intent spectator today, her gaze appraising him speculatively.

'Things,' he repeated, almost to himself, then looking up at us with a glimpse of his on-screen disarming charm for a moment. 'Things that shouldn't be happening ...'

If it had been three years ago, this would've been an awkward moment for us. But now, with a considerable repertoire of solved cases and countless dealings with clients who were reluctant to share misgivings initially, we knew how to draw out information from him.

'It's a strange world,' Parvati spoke up, her voice and face the picture of forbearance.

'Yes, yes,' RK turned to her, immediately in agreement. 'It wasn't always so. But now ...'

We waited at the pause, expectant. A pin could've been heard, had it dropped, such was the unnerving silence. A silence seemingly stretched by the long length of the teak-lined corridor of that vast study.

A sudden, low murmur then. Parvati and I, we semi-started at it, then turned to face its source. A massive cat was ambling in, its green eyes aglow in the dim light of that setting. It padded up to RK and rubbed itself on his trouser leg, then arched in satisfaction as he bent to scratch its head.

'That's a fine fellow.' Parvati nodded her head appreciatively at the cat. I knew for a fact that dogs were her obsession, so I figured she was helping RK find his voice.

Certainly, the cat's presence and maybe Parvati's immediate and vocal admiration for his pet gave RK the succour to finally blurt out what he'd been struggling to say.

'The truth is, I believe I'm being haunted!' he choked out the words. His expression, while saying this, seemed almost comical, I recall thinking, because it didn't fit in with all the tough-guy scenarios his features were most famous for, on screen.

It was now that I partially recognized the source of my unease all this while. Saurav Roop Kamal, superstar, had been deeply frightened by something. As an actor, he had masked the depth of his fear effectively, hidden it under that blustering, confident front he put up in his phone call to me.

But my unerring sixth sense had picked up on the searing panic bubbling underneath, even though it had been so skilfully covered—hence my awful disquiet about meeting him at all. *There was something unquantifiable at play here.* And I didn't like it.

Parvati's face was expressionless. I believed her to be highly amused, probably holding it in to have a hearty laugh in private later, because, unlike me, she was the practical, sensible sort. But her manner in dealing with RK was artless in its tact.

There was no denial or disbelief in her voice, in fact, quite the opposite.

'The house certainly lends itself to it,' Parvati said softly, as if in sympathy with RK's wild notion.

He looked up, focusing on her properly for the first time, grateful for her words.

'You think so?' he asked, almost childlike. 'This house is ancient. And I've had it a while. But it never happened before. Only now ...'

'Why don't you tell us about it?' Parvati said softly, looking at him, eyes bright in sympathy. Only I, having worked with her for the better part of three years now, understood the intentness behind her current expression. Parvati had sensed something important in his manner, was on the prowl to discover the source of his tension.

'Y'know, I'm doing a big-budget movie right now,' RK spoke up. 'It's a film about a haunted house, strangely enough. It's a romantic musical with a supernatural thriller angle. And I like to do my research ...'

'Go on,' Parvati encouraged him.

'So, we're almost halfway into the shooting of it. And I'm a person who isn't scared of such things, but I wanted to know more, to be authentic to the character. So, I decided to try and speak to spirits. I used an Ouija board.'

'And ...?' I could almost hear the impatience in Parvati's voice as she prodded RK to come to the point faster.

'Since that day—about three weeks ago—I'm experiencing ... *a difference*.'

RK's expression was sheepish, almost anguished, as if he couldn't bring himself to trust his own words.

But he soldiered on. 'Here, in this house. I bought this house around five years ago. I've never felt any sort of disturbance, much less a presence in it. Even though it looks the way it does. Anyway, I'm not the kind to believe in these things.'

'So, what has made you change your mind now?' Parvati asked softly.

'I'm hearing things,' RK blurted out, visibly embarrassed at his confession. 'Awful things ...'

'You mean like voices?' I had been silent so far, but I simply could not contain my incredulity.

'Like—' RK was cut short by a sudden entrance.

'Guests! Why, Roop, why didn't you tell me? I would've come earlier ...' The eagerness of the words spoken was not in keeping with the tone they were delivered in. The new entrant strode in, his manner bristling, hostile. His sudden entry had changed the cosiness of the room, the ease of RK's confidences. A chill seemed to settle in the room, even though it was warm outside.

'Ladies, I seem to know who you are!' the man announced. 'The question is—why exactly are you here?'

3

RK seemed to have shrunk back into his earlier hesitance at the arrival of this person. His expansive nature didn't appear dimmed, but it seemed more than a touch restrained.

'Shashi—this is Akruti, you remember we were considering her to star opposite me three years ago, during her stint at the pageant? Of course, post-pageant she turned high-flying detective!' RK introduced me first, with the typical aplomb of a Bollywood personality singling out one of his own for attention first, before the rest.

Those familiar with the workings of any old boys' club would know this immediately—the in-group solidarity, not just typical to Bollywood, where who you were and who you knew counted more than what you brought to the table. I hadn't realized I was in the running for a film role opposite the superstar.

How this information would've gladdened me a few years ago, as I took part in the Miss Glamour Princess beauty pageant. But that pageant had altered my world view and changed the course of my career and my ambitions. I was no more a jet-setting supermodel looking for an entry into Bollywood. Now I was a detective, making my mark in the world of sleuthing, and the crème of Bollywood was coming to me for help!

'The glamorous Akruti Rai—who wouldn't know you!' The man called Shashi mouthed, his sharp eyes meeting mine, searching for more than the obvious in my face.

'And this is Parvati Samant,' RK continued. 'She's the detective who works with Akruti.'

Parvati seemed amused rather than offended at RK's description of her role. She was an equal partner, in fact, the person responsible for bringing me into this line in the first place. But here she was being introduced as a secondary credit. *Bollywood for you*, I thought to myself. Always those you know first, rest be damned!

Parvati had taken the hand this Shashi proffered, drawling out, softly, almost lazily, her eyes hooded, 'And who do we have the pleasure of meeting, Mr Kamal?'

'This is Shashi. My best friend,' RK said, as if that childlike qualification was enough by way of introduction. Then, as if remembering the professional nature of our presence, he added, '… And my manager.'

'Shashi Sunder,' the stranger elaborated. 'I look into all of RK's affairs. Oversee, generally offer advice. Look into his publicity too. And I can tell you, meeting two well-known detectives, that too in the intimacy of your own home, not in the necessarily impersonal setting of an office—very bad for publicity if it got out!'

'It won't get out, you worry too much, Shashi.' RK became a charmer instantly, though his annoyance was evident underneath. 'And to answer your question, put to them earlier—they're here because I needed to get to the bottom of this *haunting*.'

'But you could've told me you wanted to hire someone—I would've looked into it, arranged it,' Shashi persisted, insistent in his displeasure.

Some clarity, for readers in 2021 and beyond, here. There was no internet savvy in the 1990s. There was barely any internet yet, in India. So social media and public profiles hadn't happened in Bollywood. Neither had media-savvy managers like today.

But each star had a secretary, a precursor to today's manager. The secretary oversaw dates, schedules, publicity—a sort of jack of all trades. Including providing emotional support to temperamental, oft-isolated superstars, whenever required, though often without acknowledgement.

In keeping with that last sentence, RK, at present, was taking great pains to clarify that Shashi was important to him, much more important than a mere secretary. He hadn't used that term earlier either, preferring the more expansive 'manager' during introductions. And he hastened to stress that further.

'Don't get the wrong idea—Shashi is not my secretary,' RK interjected, seeming conciliatory now. He was trying to appease the clearly displeased Shashi. 'He's a good friend, who now helps with all I do. He's always there for me. And I turn to him for advice first.'

'*Most* times,' Shashi said, only half-appeased. 'Not always, as you can see. Besides, it seems these ladies have already been told of your … *imaginings*?'

'You don't seem convinced, Mr Sunder?' Parvati swooped in on his comment.

'Call me Shashi, please,' he said, before answering, rather vehemently, as if irritated. 'Of course I'm not convinced. Are you?'

'We haven't heard the whole story yet.' Parvati's reply was smooth, courteous.

'Then let me fill you in,' Shashi continued. 'Roop believes he's hearing something. Some*one* apparently. And this person chooses times when no one else but Roop is around to make herself known. Interesting, don't you agree? If I didn't know Roop better, I'd think he's hiding a secret love affair!'

As he spoke, Parvati was watching not Shashi, but RK.

'Is it a "her", Mr Kamal?' she asked gently.

'I think so,' RK mumbled, a little subdued at the dismissal in his friend's tone. 'I can't really tell because the person is screaming maniacally. But it appears to be a woman.'

'Screaming?' I joined the conversation. 'Just screaming? Like some harpy in a horror movie?'

'Yes, exactly like that,' Shashi answered for RK dryly. 'It seems this has happened now for the last three weeks.'

'It has, Shashi.' RK turned to his friend, stubbornly insistent. 'And it is because of this attitude of yours, this dismissiveness, that I had to take matters in my own hands. I had to call these two ladies. I cannot take it anymore.'

'Suppose you tell us exactly what happened,' Parvati said quietly. 'Begin from the first instance.'

'I told you I'm doing this movie.' RK ceded to her request. 'And I wanted to get into character. But the Ouija board I consulted stayed silent. I tried this at my office, not here. However, that same night the screaming began—*here*.'

'Why am I not surprised?' Shashi muttered, not quite sotto voce.

'Are you saying Mr Kamal is easily spooked?' I asked.

'No, he's actually *never* been fazed by such things. This is his third big romantic musical with a horror twist. The horror angle is not new to his work or his life. So, if you ask me, I'll say this reaction isn't that. But he's isolated at the top, like all superstars. I think he picks up energies, internalizes them.

He's far too sensitive. Do you know, on that Ouija board, he tried to call his mother who had passed away tragically long ago in an accident, to see if it would work. It didn't. But now he *imagines* he hears a long wail … You get where I'm going?' Shashi said. 'It's why I absolutely refuse to indulge him in believing this. Best not to further this nonsense.'

'How many times do I have to tell you—you know it's not that at all,' RK spat out, angry now. 'I am not *imagining* my dead mother's final agony. It's true, using the Ouija board I had tried to contact her, thinking it better to call a familiar spirit, but it didn't work. This is different—and it isn't even her voice. It's a long, loud, desperate wail. Frankly, it's unnerving.'

'Where is it coming from?' Parvati asked.

'That's just it—I can't tell. This house is so big it seems to be from one direction one time, and another, the next. And it doesn't have a particular time to manifest either, it happens anytime. Once it stopped for three whole days, I thought it was done. But then the fourth day it returned, more unnerving than ever. I told Shashi, but he just wouldn't believe me …'

'Does the help know about this?' I asked.

'They live in a separate section—another wing of the house entirely,' RK said. 'They don't come here unless summoned. I'm hardly at home most of the time, always shooting. They serve me meals when required. Clean in the early mornings. But they're not here otherwise.'

'So, they've not heard anything,' Parvati persisted.

'No—by the third week, I'd asked all of them,' RK said. 'Not one of them had.'

'Do you actually believe it's a haunting?' I spoke up, practical now.

'Honestly, I don't know what to believe.' RK turned to me, his deeper feelings surfacing, now that he'd shared the full story. 'But what else to think? I've begun to keep a cricket bat next to me for protection. I tell you, I'm not easily spooked, but this screaming has got to me. Which is why I called you.'

I saw before us a pragmatic man, not easily scared, reduced to a doubting, nervy self by an inexplicable, repetitive occurrence.

'And what do you make of it, Shashi?' asked Parvati.

'I told you what I think,' said Shashi. 'Roop has been working too hard of late. Then this Ouija board nonsense, which we both accept didn't work. He's a sensitive man, a great artist. But he needs rest. And that's all it is. His mind telling him to rest, *imagining* things to slow down his physical work ethic.'

'Did you ever try and help him get to the bottom of this?' I asked.

'You mean did I encourage him with his "I'm being haunted" stories? Of course, not!' Shashi snorted. 'If I cater to his whimsy on this, it'll only get worse. So, I never indulge him.'

'You know I'll do anything for you, Roop,' he turned to the superstar here. 'But I won't do that. It's for your own good.'

'I only meant to ask, did you ever stay here with him to see if there might be truth to his tale,' I continued. 'Given that he says it's been going on for three weeks?'

'No,' Shashi looked a bit taken aback, contrite even. 'It didn't even occur to me. Because the whole thing seems so far-fetched. In the five years he's lived here, there's been nothing like this. Despite the hugeness of this house. And three or four of the bigger rooms are soundproofed as well, done so Roop could view movies or practice dialogues in peace without disturbing others. What he's saying seems unrealistic, given that fact …'

'Also,' Shashi continued, his eyes narrow now, 'Even if I had thought of it, I couldn't stay with him. He's been filming on location mostly. In these last three weeks that he's returned to film in the city, he's been getting time off at odd hours, whenever the shoots wrap—hence coming home to rest. But nothing is pre-decided, so I can't come to stay over, I don't know exactly when he'll get home. I do know his broader schedules, being his manager, of course, so I tend to drop in when I know for certain he's home. And let me tell you, he says this screaming has no fixed time, and I too come by at any time, but I've heard *nothing* whenever I've been here. I don't want to give this importance, really. Besides, as I told you, I believe he's overworked and stressed, internalizing stuff he shouldn't, which is the heart of the matter, not some imaginary *haunting*. It's his delicate nerves. And then there's Alena.'

'Who?' Parvati and I both said it together.

RK now looked seriously upset.

'Give it a rest, Shashi.' His voice was terse. It was not a request.

But we had already heard Shashi speak the name.

'Do you mean Alena Palekar?' I asked, incredulous now. 'As in the movie star?'

'She's the new lady in Roop's life,' Shashi said sarcastically, ignoring the spark of anger and what looked like sudden, abject misery in RK's eyes. 'Or shall I say the lady who has lasted the longest till now ...?'

'But isn't she married?' Parvati spoke up softly. 'And isn't she supposedly also in a relationship with Saddaq Haque?'

Alena Palekar, the firebrand movie star who reigned the silver screen and the city movie magazine news cycles in the Nineties with her chutzpah and her acting histrionics both—

what a match, her and RK. Both blessed with good looks and such startling success in their careers at present.

The only two flies in the ointment to a red-hot romance, on-screen or off—her double liaisons. Alena had a husband according to a recent and shocking magazine news scoop. I was surprised Parvati, who didn't follow Bollywood gossip greatly, should be so clued in on Alena's life. But Parvati tended to surprise me still, on many fronts.

And then, of course, there was that *other* superstar, Saddaq Haque, who Alena was currently linked with, also according to the filmi gossips. Which may or may not have anything to do with drumming up publicity for the currently running blockbuster movie both were a part of.

'I really would not want to speak of my personal life here …' RK began, then stopped short noting Parvati's expression.

'Mr Kamal, this is a matter that is causing you intense anxiety. Your state of mind is disturbed. All of this is happening in your very home. To address its source, to get to the bottom of it, to tackle it, how can we not get personal?' Parvati spoke gently, but her words were firm.

'Fine,' RK looked weary and distraught. 'Ask away, then. But as detectives engaged by me, you will need to sign a confidentiality agreement.'

'We haven't decided if we will take up the case,' Parvati said smoothly. 'But if we do—that goes without saying. Even if we don't sign an agreement.'

'Ah, so you too think this is all much ado over nothing?' Shashi spoke up, a canny glint in his eyes. 'You're not confident about taking up the case of the harpy's wail because *there is no such thing*, isn't it? You feel that too … it's a figment of Roop's imagination, manifested so strongly because of the stress in his work and his personal life!'

'That remains to be seen.' I was suddenly annoyed at this supposed friend of RK's who was so intent on getting rid of us, he was ready to spill RK's secrets about his private liaisons, though he claimed to want to 'do anything' for RK.

'Won't you please help me?' RK spoke up softly, addressing us, the weariness in his eyes evident for all to see.

I was struck by a sudden pity for this man, a superstar, fawned over by adoring fans in public, but unable to get any rest or, indeed, sympathy because of the unsupportiveness in his immediate circle, his best friend, in private.

'We'll be in touch,' Parvati replied to RK. Having worked so much together, I knew she felt as I did, that apart from the supposed screaming he spoke of, there didn't seem to be much to this case. Was it worth our attention at all, despite RK being such a high-profile potential client?

'I'm willing to pay what you need, for my peace of mind,' RK's tone was pleading now—we both realized he wasn't willing to concede to Parvati's non-committal leave-taking. 'I really *need* you to do this. Won't you *please* help ...?'

As RK was speaking, I mentally examined the facts before us. The nagging unease I'd felt since the time of his call had refused to abate, and though I believed I understood why now, I wasn't sure if his fear of the supposed supernatural in his house was the only reason for my discomfort.

On the one hand, there was nothing more tangible to this case at present, no puzzling mystery or Machiavellian plot to unravel, as we thus far had been doing. Just a superstar battling his demons, real or imagined.

And yet ... even though we had so little to go on, I felt that there was more at play, something as yet hidden, but no less present for all that. Something I *sensed,* more than experienced. Call it my overactive sixth sense, now that we were here, I wanted to get to the bottom of this supposed 'haunting'.

It wasn't just the attraction of the money he was offering or the trappings of his celebrity stature or even the desperation in his voice as he requested our intervention, though all of these were tempting enough. It was *me*—my inner voice telling me this might be worth our attention after all. And despite not having much to go on, I was all for heeding that voice.

I looked at Parvati with a pleading face, but with typical prescience, she had guessed my leaning and pre-empted me already.

'Yes, Mr Kamal,' she said clearly and emphatically, glancing at Shashi, meeting his eyes firmly, before turning to RK in deliberate warmth. 'I think we will help.'

4

It was late morning, the day after our meeting and we had arranged to meet RK once more. The previous evening had ended rather abruptly, with RK's 'best' friend Shashi sulking magnificently at our decision to take up the case of the mysterious screaming in the superstar's home.

'You'll regret this,' he'd said mystifyingly, before walking off in a huff. That last, almost caricaturish statement from Shashi had RK looking torn—unhappy about his friend's temper, yet glad we'd said we'd help him in sorting out his woes. Parvati had indicated we'd return on the morrow to delve further into this.

'Better in private,' she'd voiced quietly in RK's ear as we'd departed. In other words, better if there were no Shashi around to distract us.

'What do you make of Mr Kamal's situation?' Parvati asked me as we hung about our office prepping to leave for his home.

It was a comfortable office, mainly wood, with minimal decor. Interesting without being overbearing, we had felt, whilst decorating it. A client could admire it, yet feel at ease talking to us here. I had loped my legs along the sidearm of my desk chair, a position I often employed whilst seated alone. It helped me think better.

'I know what *you* think!' I was in a mood to tease Parvati. 'He's cuckoo ...?'

'Not at all,' Parvati was not in the same mood clearly. 'Mr Kamal seemed filmi and overly dramatic, sure. But he also seemed sincere, a man deeply worried. I actually believe he is telling the truth.'

'*You think he's being haunted?*' My jaw dropped at Parvati's words. Sensible, pragmatic Parvati—such words never came from her.

'I didn't say that,' Parvati smiled at me, being irritatingly Parvati. Enigmatic, yet utterly not. But she wouldn't elaborate.

'What do you make of Shashi Sunder?' she asked instead.

'The "best friend"?' I mused. 'Yesterday he didn't seem very "best friend"ish, did he? Telling us about RK and Alena, right off the bat. That too, after RK warned him to keep quiet. And then walking off in a huff like a spoilt child when we said we're taking the case ...'

'No, he didn't seem like one,' Parvati said. 'But that doesn't mean he's not a best friend.' Again, she was speaking in riddles, confusing me entirely.

'What do you mean, Parvati?' I asked, exasperated.

'Things are not always as they appear to be.' Parvati looked at me and smiled affectionately at my pique.

'It could be that there is a simple explanation to Shashi's antagonism towards us.'

'Which is?' I asked, in annoyance still.

'He's possessive of his friend,' Parvati said simply. 'So possessive that he doesn't want anybody to get close to Mr Kamal, not even in an insignificant, casual manner. Not us. Nor Alena, naturally—didn't you pick that up?'

Once she said it, I saw it. Of course, that was true. Shashi's behaviour from the moment he'd spotted us till the end—it was about *ownership*. Ownership of the one he considered very precious, the one he seemed to know all about—affairs, moods, stressors, all. The one and only people's prince: RK. All the rest of his behaviour was resentment towards anyone who got in the way of that ownership!

Shashi hadn't liked that he wasn't in the loop when RK had invited us over. He hadn't liked us going over to RK's home, rather than meeting at an impersonal setting that perhaps he could control. Most of all, he hadn't liked that we'd taken the case, because he hadn't been consulted when RK called us! And put together all at once, it seemed to point to an almost obsessive preoccupation with RK.

'I see now,' I told Parvati. 'It's simple, put like that. He appears *too* possessive though, don't you think, Parvati? Not exactly enchanting for RK, who might need space ...'

'Despite Shashi's grumpiness and reluctance to have us on board, I do believe he's Mr Kamal's friend,' Parvati mused. 'And a lot to do with friendship in Bollywood has to do with protecting your friend's personal space. Especially if he's a superstar ... So, one could even say that his possessiveness stems from his *loyalty* ... couldn't one?'

She looked askance at me, her eyes twinkling, teasing almost. She knew quite well that I hadn't taken at all to Shashi Sunder's attitude to us. And no matter how *transparent* he appeared—gruffly dismissing RK's fears as 'imaginings', or childishly warning us we'd regret taking up this case, or petulantly bringing up Alena despite RK's clear disapproval—I wasn't ready to overlook him as a suspect, acting against his friend's interests just yet.

'Things are really not as they appear to be,' I echoed Parvati's earlier words. 'Not just with Shashi but with this entire case. Maybe he's too transparent, so as to make us look the other way, *not* suspect him in this screaming business? I keep getting a feeling that we don't know a larger *something* here. It's unsettling me. Shall we chart out our plan of action towards tackling this case?'

'Yes, indeed,' Parvati positioned herself near the board over my desk, marker tip in hand. 'We'll try and uncover this hidden element you're sensing. Let's detail how we go forward. Longer meeting with Mr Kamal, where we get more information on these screams. Then quiz him on vested interests, hidden agenda, enemies, and the like. We've already spoken to Shashi, who claims Mr Kamal's "imagining" noises. We need to speak to his house help too, though he says they heard nothing. Interviews with all the key players that come up after that, of course—including Alena, and anyone connected to the two of them … Then we see how it develops and plan further.'

Since our first case, where Parvati's meticulousness had her using her now-famous diary to plan our investigation process, we had progressed to a board in our office to chart game plan and developments in our work.

Basic POA done, Parvati finished her furious scribbling on the board, then grabbed her bag as I mirrored her move. 'Let's leave. We'll be late otherwise.'

As we left, I made a mental note to call Jehaan, my significant other, who worked as a journalist at *Bharat 360*, one of the nation's leading dailies. He was a sports writer (full byline: Jehaan Warrior), heading the sports bureau now, but could always be counted on when we needed background information on prominent people. He would consult the news archives available to him, or put us in touch with other journalists who could help. *Maybe he could help with information on the players in this case too*, I thought to myself.

Meanwhile, when we got to RK's home, he was already waiting for us in his study. Surprising, given that the last meeting was graced by him an hour late.

'I couldn't sleep,' he said, as soon as we came in. His manner was nervy; he kept pacing the floor. He was still in his dressing gown. I noticed a drink in his hand, though it was barely noon. His calm composure from the day before had clearly slipped greatly in the intervening time.

If he had been stoic for three weeks, letting us in on his demons the previous day had brought home their realness to him. And the release of his secret had him unravelling now, at a rather furious pace.

'Something's happened,' Parvati pronounced, looking at him.

'Yes, it happened again last night,' RK muttered. 'The screaming. It made Mr Pickles go wild!'

'Mr Pickles?' I asked. RK was seeming increasingly bizarre to me. But he was only talking of his cat.

As if on cue, Mr Pickles sauntered in, his immense yellow-golden bulk moving smoothly towards RK's leather chair, the one RK had sat on the previous day. As RK wasn't on it, the cat jumped up and settled himself there, fixing his intense green eyes on me.

I stared right back at him. 'My eyes are equally green,' I taunted him telepathically, removing my sunglasses and placing them within arm's reach as I communicated. Just an amusing diversion with this fellow light-eyed creature, then I turned my attention back to RK. The cat was quite a character, I thought. Big enough to be a dog, and showing guests how much RK's home was actually his.

A monogrammed collar rested beneath the fur, which was thick at his neck. There was even a bell attached to it, one that didn't tinkle when he moved! Soundless, but elaborate—a designer brand no doubt. Evidently, Mr Pickles was one pampered creature. And a handsome one too.

'Did you get enough rest?' Parvati addressed RK, her manner one of calming a distraught child.

'You don't believe me …' RK murmured, swigging his drink in one go, turning his bloodshot eyes on me from Parvati. 'Akruti—how about you? Do you think I'm making this up?'

'None of us thinks you're making things up,' I assured him heartily. 'Why don't you sit down?'

'My anxiety—it's because of this damned movie. I need to get into character properly. I'm not being able to concentrate. It's a night shoot tonight, so I won't be home later,' he mumbled, still unable to stop his nervous pacing. 'I need to concentrate. And to rest. But I can't rest.'

'Tell us about Alena,' Parvati intervened smoothly. 'What's her part in your current state of mind?'

'Alena …' RK began. 'She's actually the best part of my life right now. The only one who isn't behaving oddly.'

'Why? Who is behaving oddly?' I asked curiously.

'Shashi for one,' RK voiced, darkly. 'He wasn't thrilled about Alena, but he's never been thrilled by any of my girlfriends. And he's even less pleased, now that it's serious. And then, when he saw you both yesterday, he was absolutely furious. I hadn't consulted him—he didn't like it at all! But what was I to do? He wasn't even willing to agree that I might actually be telling of a real experience, not some stupid imagining. How long has he known me for? Doesn't he know I'm not that person he spoke of—"sensitive" and delicate? What utter CRAP!'

'Tell us about Alena,' Parvati repeated smoothly, sending me a warning glance. RK telling us of the oddities of his entourage could wait. At present, he needed to calm down drastically.

'Well, what do I say about Alena's beauty that the movies she's been a part of don't showcase already?' RK said, stopping for breath. 'She's young, much younger than I am, as you know. She's a powerhouse actor as you can see. And after all this time, struggling in so many relationships, I'd like to settle down—I think she's the woman for me. We're serious enough about each other to be talking marriage, you see.'

'When did you two start seeing each other?' I asked. Mentally, I was thinking, *but she's already married, what about that part?*

'About three and a half months ago, maybe?' RK mused. 'She entered the industry about two years back and was an instant success, as you might be aware. There was talk of us being paired, but till this movie, it didn't happen. It's strange, our paths never crossed before, not even at a premiere or a party, though there were so many opportunities to bump into each other. The first time I met her was on the set of this film. She's doing a double role in it—she plays my ex-wife in a former life, killed by mysterious circumstance. And then my daughter, imagine, reincarnated in a haunted house. It's funny to think I'm in love with a lady playing my daughter in this movie. But there it is!'

'The first time I saw her, it was against the backdrop of the set—a home aflame. She was in character as my daughter, waiflike and vulnerable, her long hair loose, swirling in the breeze created by those set fans, fighting the fake fire around her. I took one look at her and it was like being struck by a thunderbolt. I was lost.' RK's mood had changed, he seemed like a little boy, confessing his first crush to his mother. 'I know I'm taking a big risk with this role, allowing an adult star to play my daughter when my career is at its height. Anyone else would not. But I've done so much of the conventional; I wanted to get creative, to grow as an actor. I thought, why not? Little did I know it would lead to—romance?'

Watching his face, it was clear he was serious about Alena Palekar, no matter his erstwhile playboy reputation. 'Love at first sight—not just in the movies!' he laughed wryly, lightening the atmosphere considerably, all of a sudden. 'I know it seems very abrupt, just three months or so into it, to be talking marriage. But I love her and I want this to happen.'

'I see,' said Parvati. 'And Alena feels the same?'

'As you know that recent magazine article went to town on her being wedded. She is indeed married.' RK had switched back to moodiness, appearing not to have registered Parvati's query. 'But you shouldn't believe everything you read in these filmi gossip magazines. A college affair, which was impulsively legalized. It barely lasted a month. He left her long ago. Then she found fame as a movie star. And he returned by way of talking to a movie magazine. Disgusting! And he won't let her go, now that she's a star. He wants her money ...'

'This husband of Alena's—does he know about your relationship with her?' Parvati spoke up, letting her earlier question slip.

'I can't say,' RK said. 'We've managed to keep the extent of our involvement an open secret of sorts for now—limited to the movie cast on the closed sets of this film and our immediate friends. In the wider world, and this is important for the movie's publicity, we'll be linked, naturally, when the movie releases. And hopefully married by then, with the ex divorced and out of the picture, obviously. But for now—there's the matter of Saddaq.'

'Saddaq Haque?' I asked, to be sure, though we already knew, given all the gossip surrounding Alena and Saddaq's ongoing film. Saddaq's popularity at the box office was almost at level with RK's, and the former was younger than him, to boot—if Saddaq Haque's connect to RK's already complicated love life wasn't enough, they had professional rivalry too.

'Alena and he were an item last year. Plus, now that their movie has been released she's meant to continue that liaison till necessary, for publicity's sake,' RK spoke, his expression dark again. 'He won't let go of her either.'

'Does he know you're in the picture now?' It was my turn to ask that question.

'Yes, Alena's told him,' RK's reply was terse. 'He's unhappy about it. But, excluding what's being done to publicize their movie, Alena and he are over, really. It is she and I who are very serious about each other now.'

A rather painful picture was emerging to us here: A dramatic, if furtive, love triangle, between three public figures, further complicated by the requirements of publicity in their career. To add to that, a bad marriage to a different party than the two fighting over their lady love … the kind of anxiety felt in this situation would be enough to unhinge many. It was increasingly becoming evident that there might have been a grain of truth in Shashi's words about the strain on RK's nerves, after all.

There was the pressure of a mega movie riding on RK's shoulders, and supposedly having to contact the other world to get into character for it. Alongside that was the strain of a lightning *affaire de cœur*, which was complicated and convoluted. All this put together might have made RK believe he was hearing things when, in reality, there was nothing to be heard. RK's best friend, Shashi, may have had hit the nail on the head when he said RK had internalized the stress he was currently going through.

'There is so much going on right now. Could you at all be imagining these screams?' Right on cue, Parvati asked RK, voicing what was in my head too. He turned on her, his eyes furious, almost splashing the second drink he had poured out and cradled thus far.

'I am not a paranoid person, please understand!' he vented his frustration, his face thunderous. He might have said more, but with a sudden volte-face, as if forcing himself to regain control, checked his words. 'I'm tired now. I haven't been able to rest, and I don't want to show you an unfavourable side of me when feeling like this. Maybe we could meet later?'

My years in the glamour world had prepared me for sudden mood swings from fellow celebrity colleagues and Parvati had always been a quick study.

'We'll take your leave then,' she said artlessly, not wasting another word, gliding towards the study exit in a smooth movement with me following as quickly.

'That was rather abrupt,' I said as we walked out of the front door, squinting in the sudden sunshine. The heavy wood of the door's ancient frame creaked as it swung ponderously, taking its time to close behind us.

'We won't get anything out of him if he's in that frame of mind,' Parvati nodded, concurring with me as she spoke. 'Better we visit him again, when he's more agreeable. We can also speak to the help then.'

As we briskly tackled the path leading to Taqdeer's main entranceway, I realized I'd left my sunglasses in RK's study.

'I was making eyes at Mr Pickles when I removed them. Come with me, it'll only be two minutes,' I told Parvati, who seemed reluctant to make the trek past the rolling lawns back to RK's study.

Dragging her with me, I got to the front door, which miraculously, being so old and cumbersome, hadn't managed to swing shut fully, post our departure.

'No need to ring the doorbell again, see,' I chirped, pushing the heavy frame inwards, and stepping in.

We approached the study, catching the eye of an astonished RK as we entered, shutting the door behind us firmly, as it had been closed post our departure.

And right then, before he could utter the words of surprise forming on his lips at our reappearance, we heard it.

A shrill screech, arising low, as if from the pits of someone's stomach and then moving to a full-blown crescendo—a shriek as unutterably terrifying as sudden. My blood curdled at its commencement, my hair standing on end as it intensified. It was coming from just outside the room.

Both Parvati and I turned to the study door we had closed a few seconds ago, flinging it wide open in our mute panic, in our haste to help the person making this agony of a sound.

The corridor beyond yawned before us, dim despite the long windows it was lined with. A light breeze fluttered the gauze curtains, almost mocking in their movement. *Empty,* the space seemed to say.

5

We turned back to face RK in the study, Parvati and I, badly shaken by what we'd just heard. The shriek had my nerve ends ringing while it lasted, a sound so pained, so intense, it was almost animal-like. RK hadn't moved at all. He turned to us as we faced him, something akin to triumph in his expression. The glass rattled with the tremor in his hand, ice clinking against it, devoid of the liquid, which was inside him once more. Even if he hadn't moved, the scream had unnerved him, as before.

'Shall I say "touché"?' he prodded Parvati. 'Or will "I told you so" cover it?'

Mr Pickles hadn't been as sanguine as his owner. The noise had him sprinting to the door and up the corridor, hissing and spitting, to investigate. Now he padded to his seat, jumped on it, curling up once more.

'Funny, the cat doesn't like the scream,' Parvati mused, collecting herself from the shattering experience.

'Who would?' I turned to her, incredulous, still rattled by what had transpired moments ago.

'You misunderstood,' Parvati said. 'I meant—animals may get startled, run either to or from an unexpected sound. But they don't necessarily get hostile. Mr Pickles isn't as much startled as he's angry ...'

'I didn't realize that,' RK's brow furrowed. 'He does that every time he hears it. He's always been with me, so I know. What does it mean?'

'It cannot possibly mean it's a real ghost!' I said, much too loud. The scream had shaken me badly, I can tell you that.

'Whatever it is, the cat doesn't like it.' Parvati's brow was flurried in concentration. 'He was hissing badly at it.' She addressed RK immediately at this point: 'I think we owe you an apology, Mr Kamal. We were sceptical of what you were telling us earlier ...'

'I don't lie,' RK said curtly, not mollified, and still drinking hard. He had swigged a third drink very fast, and was now cradling a fourth. 'Why did you two come back anyway? I had said we'd meet later?'

'I forgot my sunglasses,' I hastened to explain, before RK's moodiness returned. 'It's very hot outside ...'

'Well, well, well, and here you are again,' a familiar, disgruntled voice wafted in from the corridor just outside the room. We had left the door ajar, and now the low light from the windows lining that corridor was blocked by the form of an irritated Shashi Sunder.

'Every time I turn my back, these two happen to sneak in,' he shot out, tartly, striding into the room. His manner was overbearing and his face set in grim lines. 'I know they're now looking into this "haunting" of yours,' he addressed RK. 'But I was not told of their appointment with you, not yesterday, not today. Tell me Roop—why is that?'

Parvati seemed preoccupied looking at him. It struck me too. The scream was heard seconds earlier. There had been no one in the corridor. And now, almost as if he had been lurking somewhere close by—Shashi appeared? Convenient, or perhaps, *too convenient*, his entry?

'They wanted to speak with me,' RK drawled, his annoyance at Parvati's earlier query, about whether he'd imagined the screams, forgotten now. His words were a bit garbled, the stiff drinks were beginning to tell on RK. 'In private.'

'Please continue.' Shashi's voice was pleasant as he turned to us, but his expression said otherwise. 'Nothing is private between me and Roop. I know all there is to know about the man. Isn't that so, Roop?'

He had been offended by not being included in any of our meetings and was making it clear to his friend. We could sense the challenge in his words, daring RK to contradict him.

RK didn't reply. He shrugged casually and sauntered to the minibar, as if busying himself, pouring yet another drink.

'It is this regular?' Parvati asked Shashi in low tones, gesturing to RK's glass. She was making an effort to mollify Shashi, conspiratorially going along with his present displeasure towards RK.

'It's his day off. He's allowed to relax a little,' Shashi said, his eyes cool, appraising her. He wasn't about to become our confidant against his friend, even though RK's behaviour concerning us had scarcely pleased him.

'Did you hear anything as you entered?' Parvati continued, addressing him pleasantly, unfazed by his hostility.

'Why?' Shashi looked at her sharply, his eyes alert. 'Why are you asking me this? I've told you I hear nothing when I'm here, so why should today be different? Because you both are here?'

So intent was he on showing his displeasure at our presence, he didn't actually wait for Parvati to answer his question, but continued on in a similar vein.

'I came in via the garden,' Shashi droned on. 'It is a longer route than the main passage connecting to the corridor just outside. It involves passing other rooms, some of which Roop had soundproofed as I told you before. They are his TV- and movie-screening mini-theatre spaces, and those adjacent to them, he uses for dialogue practise at times. Because of the way the house is designed, he had to soundproof all three or four in that line—he couldn't do just the one alone.'

Looking at Parvati's expression he stopped, then, as if collecting his thoughts, repeated, 'Why do you ask?'

'No reason,' Parvati said. 'Just wondered.'

RK was not so drunk that he didn't catch on to her deliberate omission of what had transpired before Shashi's entry. We both gawped at her in surprise. Why not tell Shashi we had heard the awful scream too?

But the inscrutable Parvati stayed mum. Following her cue, neither of us spoke up.

'That cat is spoiling all the furniture,' Shashi said sharply, as he searched for a place to sit. 'Shoo, shoo,' he waved at Mr Pickles, who was startled because he had just settled back into RK's chair. He got up hissing again, his tail upright, swishing from side to side in displeasure.

The interchange wasn't lost on either of us. Not only was Shashi's entry too close for comfort to the strange wail we'd just heard, but Mr Pickles clearly wasn't thrilled by his presence in the room. The cat didn't like the scream. More importantly—*the cat didn't like Shashi.*

'I wish you'd keep a dog,' Shashi dropped himself into the chair Mr Pickles had vacated and addressed his friend. Parvati's eyebrows shot up. She was a fanatic dog lover, but I guessed she couldn't quite reconcile this dour and aggressive man with the image of a pet-friendly person at all. Especially going by the manner in which he had just shooed Mr Pickles off that chair.

RK chose not to respond to Shashi's comment. He stared moodily into his umpteenth drink (I had stopped counting, he was downing them so fast) still preferring to stand, though the frantic pacing had stopped.

'So, what is this private conversation you were so keen on having with Roop?' Shashi addressed me now. 'Or did I miss it entirely?'

'We were discussing varied things,' I spoke evenly. 'We needed a bit of background on Mr Kamal's life thus far …'

'Why not ask me?' Shashi said his eyes still on me. 'Sometimes another perspective helps …'

'Indeed, it does,' Parvati said smoothly. 'We're happy to have you fill in the blanks. Tell us, Shashi—what's your take on Alena in Mr Kamal's life?'

'The lovely Alena,' Shashi looked at her, emphasizing every syllable. 'What's not to like? Right, Roop?' He had said this casually but there was a charged depth to his words, not lost on RK.

'Do we have to go over this, Shashi? In front of my guests?' he said the words wearily, as if they had been repeated before without resolution. But RK wasn't done.

'Shashi thinks Alena is after my money. And this house.' He addressed Parvati, his words definitely slurring badly now. 'As if she needed either!'

'She's a huge star in her own right,' I concurred, turning to Shashi in the chair. 'Why would you say that?'

'She is just a couple of years into this industry.' Shashi's tone was measured. He wasn't saying this out of emotion, as his words before—he seemed to really believe it. 'And though she's been very lucky in her choice of films, not so much in her personal life. A vagrant sponge of a husband who refuses to go away. The temperamental, rumoured-to-be-abusive

Saddaq Haque who won't go quietly into that good night either, even though Roop is on the scene now. And her own financial troubles, perhaps as a consequence of the wayward husband. Don't tell me if you were facing these kinds of issues you wouldn't welcome the strong, silent and loyal support of someone like Roop. With a heritage-status house, to match!'

'I didn't know she had financial issues,' I mused.

'This is Bollywood,' Shashi replied, looking at me as if surprised. 'So many live beyond their means, to give the impression of being larger than life. Why not her?'

RK made a disconsolate noise, as if unable to bear the weight of Shashi's words. He bent down to pet Mr Pickles curled nearby, who wasn't in the mood and stalked off, tail in the air, out the still-ajar door, disappearing into the far corridor.

'Shashi is my closest, dearest friend,' RK slurred unhappily. 'That he dislikes and distrusts Alena brings me no peace …'

The atmosphere in the room was despondent, the two friends tense and irritable, which wouldn't have helped us probe much further. Also, RK was appearing progressively more drunk and likely to become volatile if we kept on with this topic. We knew we had to change tack.

'How many people live in this house along with you?' Parvati asked, switching to a more general line of questioning. We did, after all, plan to interview the help; it seemed prudent to get all the information we could now. And it seemed RK was ready to give us a fuller picture.

'It's a huge house,' RK mumbled. 'I shoot most days, even nights as you know. I like having a full house, so I encourage family visits on my rare days off, but I haven't had a holiday in maybe, two years …? My family doesn't live in this city anyway; it's difficult for them to travel all the way to spend just a day with me. So, they've not come for around two years. I visit them, of course, when I shoot in their hometowns. In this house, the help lives in a separate wing, as I have told you before. They only come here to cook, clean or when summoned, which is not often. And then there's Alena, who has been with me on location for this movie, but not stayed here yet. It's only been around three and a half months or so since we began seeing each other, but it seems like so much longer. We're talking of her moving in very soon. I want her near me, living here ...'

'Aren't you forgetting someone?' The ever-dour Shashi remarked after RK finished his rambling address to Parvati.

'Me,' a bright voice spoke up, as if on cue, from the open doorway. As the person stepped in from the dark corridor behind, we caught a glimpse of a wiry frame, casually dressed, with twinkling eyes, as light as mine, though they were grey in colour. An easy smile, revealing deep dimples and even teeth. Not a film star, but certainly, this man could well have been one, given his looks and evident charm. Though he was speaking to RK, his stance was such that it appeared as if he was addressing everyone in the room. 'You forgot your only house guest!' he said, jocularly.

6

'Aman, you're finally back!' RK had moved from the bar to the door smoothly, and with a florid gesture embraced the new entrant, unselfconsciously and heartily, into a bear hug.

The stranger grinned conspiratorially at us, from over RK's shoulder as he was being folded into the drunken embrace of his host. Parvati was watching Shashi's face, as was I, for any emotion over RK's open fondness for the new entrant. But for once, Shashi didn't appear hostile. Clearly, he was familiar with this person.

'This is Aman,' RK slurred, but with a new vigour in his voice. Aman's entry had brightened the earlier mood, we saw that at once. It appeared that he was liked very much by RK, and certainly tolerated by the over-possessive Shashi.

'Aman Azad,' the stranger smiled, utterly at ease in this gathering though he knew only RK and Shashi yet. 'I have the good fortune of having been offered this home, to live with RK for some time. Till I'm better, that is ...'

He turned to me as he spoke. I noticed he was having trouble with his left leg as he turned. A very slight limp, a shadow of pain on his face. Then it was gone.

'The beautiful Akruti,' he said, revealing his dimples as he smiled at me. His charm was unmistakable. I smiled back immediately. '1995's Miss Glamour Princess winner!'

'Aman, she's a detective now,' RK said, continuing, 'and this is Parvati, who works with her.'

'Call me Aman, please,' he continued easily, pre-empting any formal addressal by his last name, appearing unalarmed at the professional introduction. Our being detectives often fazed people on initial meetings, but he remained unperturbed.

Parvati offered her hand to Aman, a quizzical look on her face.

'You live here. But you weren't here yesterday …?' she asked casually.

'Aman's been travelling,' RK, who had come to her side, spoke before Aman could. 'For the last three weeks, in fact. I allowed him a little break because he looked like he needed it!'

'What RK means is that he sponsored my holiday,' Aman said to Parvati brightly. There was no self-consciousness or embarrassment at the fact that RK had provided the funds for his vacation. His relaxed vibe was disarming.

'You missed much drama in your absence,' the taciturn Shashi said, finally entering the conversation. 'I'm glad you're back though.'

He said this gruffly, but we could see he meant it. I guessed he was glad RK would have company in his home now; he had caught on to how shaken and nervy RK appeared at present. Perhaps he had been feeling guilty at my words earlier on, when I asked him if he had stayed with RK to verify his friend's fear of the noises in his home.

'What did I miss?' Aman asked, moving to the minibar slowly, his limp evident, before pouring himself a drink, as RK had earlier. It was not lost on any of us how at home he appeared to be in RK's mansion.

'There have been sounds,' RK was clearly struggling to express his experiences of the intervening weeks without sounding fanciful or drunk. 'Screaming. As if a person, a woman, I think, is hurt or in mortal danger. At odd hours these last three weeks. They began just after you left. You know I wanted to try out the Ouija board for the movie? Since then. I didn't try the Ouija board here though; it was in our office, and it didn't work. But these sounds began here. And when I try to follow them—there is no one there.'

'That's odd,' Aman looked concerned as he sipped his drink. He did not appear dismissive or irritable at RK's narrative, the way Shashi had been earlier. 'Did you get to the bottom of it?' he asked.

'Only Roop has heard these screams,' Shashi informed him shortly. 'In three weeks, I haven't, though I'm here quite often. Neither has the house help. I think Roop is stressed. A lot.'

'You don't think the screams are real?' Aman guessed, watching Shashi's face. He turned to RK. 'I'm here now. I'm in the house. So, when the screaming happens—I'll be around.'

I noted how in one word he had indicated he believed RK and was on his side, rather than with Shashi. He said 'when' the screaming happens, not 'if'. It was clear he was offering RK both comfort and the assurance that he was there for him, should the screams reoccur.

RK had understood this, even in his drunken state. He looked considerably brighter than before.

'Aman, you've just arrived,' he said, ruffling the younger man's hair in a further gesture of affection. 'Go freshen up. There will be plenty of time to talk later.'

Aman stood up, dimpling as he finished his drink. 'Yes, my bags are just outside. I wanted to say a quick hi before I went up to my room. I didn't realize we had company. Glad we met though!'

His wide smile was for both Parvati and me, a flirtatious, casual grin, expansive, as if to indicate admiration for our appearance and presence, both. *This house guest of RK's is rather charming*, I thought.

'So how is it you forgot Mr Azad?' Parvati became business-like the moment the door shut behind Aman. 'And, who is he?'

She was addressing RK, but it was Shashi who spoke up.

'I think Roop was immensely stressed,' Shashi said, his face worried. 'I didn't realize the whole thing had affected him so. He has managed to hide from me how tense he was feeling on account of the goings-on, I think … I got fooled into thinking he was fine. Roop? This drinking isn't healthy.'

'It's true,' RK mumbled softly, ignoring Shashi's comment on the liquor. 'I had actually managed to forget all about Aman in my anxiety with this business over the last three weeks.'

'Well, can you explain to us *in detail*, please,' I intervened. 'How is it that you have a house guest at present, yet you omitted to mention him to us completely, until Shashi reminded you, minutes before he actually appeared in person? How do you know him?'

'I told you.' RK looked wearier by the minute, his eyes bleary from either stress or lack of sleep. 'This business with the screaming has unnerved me enough to overlook all else. Also, Aman isn't a loud or intrusive guest. Most days we barely meet, though he's been staying here for the last six months.'

'*Six* months?' Parvati's tone was incredulous. 'And yet he didn't come up *once* in our conversation yesterday?'

'What Roop says is true,' Shashi hastened to intervene. Again, I noticed his earlier hostility was held in check now. The RK before him appeared confused, even frightened, and strangely vulnerable, even though he was a tough-looking man. To my mind, Shashi hadn't seen RK like this before, and it was worrying him.

It was evident his friend had used his acting skills to mask his very real fear of the unknown deepening over the last three weeks, and Shashi hadn't caught it, till it came to this point. I trusted Parvati's insight. She believed Shashi was a genuine friend to RK, though the previous day it hadn't seemed so. And now that his friend was agitated, it appeared that Shashi, putting aside his own misgivings, wanted to help him as best as he could.

'This house is very big, it has a lot of rooms,' Shashi continued. 'You could have someone stay and not cross paths with that person for a very long time if you keep separate schedules. Which is what has happened with Aman and Roop. No wonder Roop forgot he was staying here! As frankly, did I, in all this business of hauntings and, now, detectives visiting. Till you asked just a while ago, about how many people lived here ... then it came to me.'

To someone who didn't understand celebrity lives, the fact that RK forgot Aman's presence in his home would seem extraordinary, as it had at first to Parvati. But I was from the glamour world, and knew enough about hectic schedules and intense self-absorption to realize RK's state of mind wasn't too different from many in similar professions. And such glamour-world-personality behaviours also included RK's possessive, single-track minded manager Shashi, whose existence solely centred on RK, it would seem, despite his hostile exterior.

At this point, RK shuffled to the restroom located within the study. Obviously, the constant downing of drink had brought on the urge to relieve himself speedily.

'I noticed Mr Kamal is very fond of Aman,' Parvati said to Shashi, using the opportunity of RK's absence from the room, immediately. 'But Aman is not as demonstrative. There is a formality in addressing Mr Kamal, too. He doesn't use his first name or the familiar "Roop", as you do. He used the colloquial abbreviation: RK. Why is that?'

'I must say you are extremely observant.' Shashi appraised Parvati for a while before he elaborated, 'Roop is addressed so, only by his dearest and oldest coterie of friends. He won't allow its use by a random person, or even a recent friend, no matter if they are ardent well-wishers. You have to be extremely special to him if he allows you to call him "Roop". To all others, he's RK or Mr Kamal or then they use his first name, Mr Saurav. Aman is a new entrant in his life. And you know by reputation, and now by observation, how affectionate Roop can be, as a person. In Aman's case, Roop doesn't hesitate to show how fond he is of him. But in truth, he's only known him properly for six months. And Aman understands, I think, that he should not overstep any boundaries, so he's always a tad formal. Smart fellow, Aman.'

'RK's known Aman properly only these last six months, yet he offered him his home?' I was most curious at this point.

'Shows you Roop's generous nature,' Shashi turned to me. 'The story is rather interesting, but not unusual, given Roop's expansiveness. Roop, as you know, is going through a phase of heightened fan interest. But they don't just write to him to praise him. Many write to him asking for help with their problems. Aman Azad was one such.'

'He was a *fan*? RK is having a fan stay in his home?' I was incredulous now. 'How long does he plan to have him stay?'

'Well, it happened by accident,' Shashi continued. 'Aman had been writing to Roop for maybe ten years or so? He was only ten or eleven years old at the time he began, writing from some little place in India. It started out as fan mail, but then they struck up a bond. Of course, this happened because Roop, once upon a time, read all his fan mail himself! He wasn't the superstar he is now; it was in the beginning of his career. And somehow, he was drawn to Aman's innocence, his simple life.'

'The sentimentality of Bollywood,' I said to myself. Huge fortunes could be made or lost in the span of a weekend; the opening of a new movie generally dictated the trend and its fate. In a world that was in such a state of flux and upheaval, insecurities and superstition were bound to run rife.

No wonder its denizens tried to hold on to any bond that allowed positive regard and unadulterated admiration from a rooted place, independent of their own insecure circus. The unspoilt adulation of a small-town boy for a budding movie idol—what could be a better antidote for box-office blues?

No wonder Aman Azad's boyish notes had struck a chord within the raw and hungry-for-success RK as he began his fateful journey towards becoming the Master of the unpredictable B-Town Universe, ten years ago.

'So, even if Roop didn't know Aman well till these last six months, they aren't really new to each other in a sentimental sense,' Shashi went on. 'This bond is ten years old, kept aflame via the trusty Indian postal service. Aman stayed in a small town, somewhere in India's heartland, I forget the name. Roop used to offer encouragement to his boyish angst, I suppose? And Aman buoyed his ego in return. Anyway, Aman's journey to finally meet his idol began on his twentieth birthday. By then, of course, Roop had become who he is now—a mega celebrity.'

'Herein lies the tragedy in this tale,' Shashi changed tack, sitting up in the chair he'd been lounging on, whilst narrating this. 'Listen. Aman journeys to meet Roop. Roop didn't know he is coming, mind you. It was impulsive of Aman, really, to try this. Regardless, fate had other plans. En route, heavy and unexpected rains in Mumbai's suburbs, courtesy of a freak hurricane out over the seas. Aman's rickshaw is involved in an accident. It overturns after being hit by a speeding car. *He nearly loses his life …*'

Both Parvati and I were transfixed at this point, as Shashi continued his narration. We didn't notice that RK had re-entered the study quietly.

'But he didn't,' RK spoke up suddenly, causing us all to startle at the sound of his voice. 'He didn't lose his life, thank God.'

'Instead, he lost the partial use of his left leg.' RK, now that he had our attention, was in full-sozzled flow. 'And he came to meet me not that day, but after he had recovered a little. I hadn't known. Of course, trying to meet me is another story, because I'm so distanced from the fan junta physically. But he got through the security and other blocks finally.'

'Is that why you offered him a room here? In your home?' Parvati was looking at him speculatively.

'We've been corresponding for ten years. He was hurt trying to reach me. And he had nowhere to stay …' RK trailed off.

'There are good hotels, service apartments …' Parvati persisted. 'You could've sponsored those and footed the bill, as you did his holiday. Why ask him to stay?'

'He was with me in the beginning,' RK looked at her. He wasn't sober, but he was alert, fey. 'I used to read his letters and feel confident in my dream of becoming a success as a movie star. He helped me with his belief in my acting even though some of my movies were failing at the time. He was there for me from boyhood, when I was at a low point, though I'd never met him, not even seen a picture. I thought I needed to be there for him at his low point. He had no money when he came to me, either ...'

'He speaks wonderful English.' Parvati was not done. 'You wrote to him in English?'

'Courtesy of a missionary school, the only one in his tiny town, he learnt the language, worked very hard. This, he told me when he arrived,' RK said. 'Our letters, though, were all in Hindi. He wanted to surprise me by his presence and his English, both, when he came!'

'RK is generous and impulsive,' Shashi spoke up. 'These qualities have always been highlighted in the media—all his fans and the greater public are aware of them. RK took one look at Aman and decided he would help him find a footing here.'

'I see,' I said. Aman was a charmer, no doubt RK had been taken by him from the first. Aman had that je ne sais quoi quality—it meant admirers would be many and varied throughout his life, no matter his circumstances. But something was still unexplained.

'A footing here?' I asked, puzzled. 'Not just a recuperative stay till he's fully functional in his walking?' So, he's clearly staying for a while, I made a mental note to myself.

'Did Shashi not tell you, right at the beginning?' RK turned to me. 'Aman told me, when he arrived here, that he wants to become an actor. And since he's injured and a bit unsteady on the left side in his walking—I want to help him become one.'

'So, you took him in, and …?' Parvati was relentless I could see.

'I took him in. I'm making sure he has all he needs, to rest and be well again, in mind and body, both. The best doctors, food, a good holiday just now—all of it,' RK addressed her query. 'He has made tremendous progress staying here from when he first arrived. When the leg is recovered completely, I will start introducing him to film producers. Till then, my house is his own. The only thing is, I can't spend any time with him. My earlier movie was being shot when I took him in. And we started this one, with Alena, almost immediately as the one before wrapped, around four months ago.'

'Does he know about Alena?' Parvati asked brightly.

'Yes, he does,' Shashi intervened. 'Roop introduced them just two weeks before Aman left for his holiday, I believe. A casual introduction I think, Roop?'

'Well, we haven't seen much of each other, Aman and I. And I'd been on location, shooting a couple of months before,' RK said, still slurring heavily. 'Aman walked in on me and Alena here, actually! On one of our rare evenings off. It was really funny! I introduced him to Alena then, said she might become the lady of the mansion soon enough, and he'd have to ask her permission if he wanted to stay on!'

'And what was his reaction?' Parvati asked.

'He was surprised, I think,' RK's eyes, though bleary, looked amused. 'Because over the years in my letters I've spoken a bit about my girlfriends, but it's been nothing serious. He didn't know I was thinking of Alena as girlfriend, forget marriage material. But he rose to the news marvellously! He praised Alena, said he was a big fan!'

'And you,' Parvati turned to Shashi. 'When did you meet him first?'

'When Roop called to tell me he'd invited him to stay,' Shashi said. 'That was six months ago. I knew of him over the years; Roop had mentioned his letters, on and off. But I didn't think he'd ask him to live here.'

Parvati met my eyes. Obviously, for all of Shashi's relief at having Aman return from holiday to stay with RK at present, he wasn't exactly happy about it as a long-term arrangement. Typical Shashi, we were beginning to realize.

'And now that he does stay with Mr Kamal?' Parvati probed. 'How do you feel?'

'Right now? That he might help my friend.' Shashi's voice was firm, his eyes serious. Though he was addressing Parvati, his gaze followed RK, who, inebriated beyond his tolerance threshold, was now unsteadily trying to hold himself upright. His attempts, however, were unsuccessful. He had drunk so much, his legs buckled. He toppled heavily, pulling the nearby drinks cart he'd used for support along with him. The crash was deafening.

'Roop!' Shashi's shrill scream rent the air as he dashed towards his fallen friend. *The superstar wasn't moving.*

7

'Roop, Roop,' bleated Shashi, his intense distress stark on his face as he tried to lift RK's inert form from the floor where he had crashed heavily in drunken stupor, pulling the drinks cart along. The cart had been empty, but he had knocked against it badly as he fell, dragging it down along with him as he collapsed.

The drink glass in his hand had smashed to the floor on the other side of him, and shattered. A sodden mess surrounded the star on that side, full of shards of broken glass. Shashi, it appeared, wasn't strong enough to lift the dead weight of the inebriated and now passed-out star off the floor.

Parvati had, in the meanwhile, run to the bar, grabbed a bottle of ice-cold water and returned in a trice. She bent low over RK, even as Shashi, evidently desperate, was pleading with him to awake, without success. Giving no warning, she flung the contents of the bottle on to RK's inert face. The shock contact with ice water was enough to rouse the superstar from his sozzled stupor.

'Um,' he mumbled, his eyelids fluttering open, his face shiny with water droplets, despite the dim afternoon light in his study.

'Roop, thank God, oh Roop.' Shashi's relief as his friend awoke was palpable. The urgency in his worry had had us all out of sorts, just minutes before. Parvati stepped away, calmly replaced the empty bottle on the bar and returned. Her expression was inscrutable as she watched Shashi's emotions play on his face as he gazed at his friend, now awake, but confused.

'Um—what's this,' RK murmured, attempting to sit up, rubbing his sides because the cart had done its number on him. There would be purple, angry bruising on the morrow, he would tell us later.

'Roop, you passed out and fell. Oh Roop, what if something worse had happened,' Shashi scolded him in a tone used for a naughty but beloved child. 'Why are you drinking like this?'

RK had understood his impossible predicament in his still-dazed condition. He sat up, then gingerly hauled himself to the sofa nearby, laying himself across its length.

'I'm shorry,' he slurred to us, just before turning over and curling up. 'I don't usually drink like this ...' Incredibly, and almost immediately after that—RK dropped off to sleep.

'Best to let him doze it off,' Parvati addressed the still-concerned Shashi as he moved towards the sofa. 'Is it true, he doesn't drink like this normally?'

'That's what he said, didn't he?' Shashi turned to her, his antagonism back suddenly. 'Roop never lies.'

Then, almost to himself, Shashi muttered, 'He must really be in a dark place. I've never seen him like this. So weary, so tense ...' He moved to the sofa and drew up a stool close to RK's face. He pulled a cushion from a nearby settee and lifting RK's head, gently slid it under the sleeping star. He turned, mumbling still, 'I need to find him a blanket ...'

We both watched this display of concern, feeling as outsiders do whilst witnessing an intimate domestic tableau play out.

'We'll take our leave, Shashi.' Parvati's manner was brisk and cool. 'Do let us know how he's doing when he wakes up ...'

Before leaving, we did have one more task. We got Shashi to round up all the domestic help in RK's mansion for us, and spent a few hours grilling them, but to no avail. They had heard nothing, not once, not one of them. So that was a dead end. Had we spoken to them before that afternoon, we would have had more reason to doubt RK's words. But providentially for RK, we had heard the scream ourselves. There was no question of disbelieving him.

The next day, we had our answer as to how RK was doing.

'I'm so very sorry,' he began, without preamble, the moment I answered his call. 'You must believe me. I don't drink like that under normal circumstances. But all that's been happening to me these last three weeks—it's far from normal. And it really got to me ...'

'How are you feeling now,' I asked, knowing he had hurt himself when he fell alongside the drinking cart.

'I'm pretty sore.' I could hear the sheepishness in his voice. 'I took a hard knock when that cart fell along with me. My one side is black and blue.'

'I'm sorry to hear that,' I told him, then asked, curious, 'Did you shoot for your movie last night? You said you had a night shoot yesterday ...'

'I did,' RK was brighter now, in his reply. His work excited and fulfilled him, of that there was no doubt.

'Dear Shashi—he sat with me when I fell asleep,' RK continued. 'All that evening, then woke me at around 8 p.m. so I could go for the shoot. He's such a gem, I'm so lucky to have him.'

'... and Alena,' RK went on, the excitement in his voice even sharper. 'Akruti, I told Alena about you two. She wants to meet you both!'

'When?' I asked cautiously. We certainly had plans to speak to Alena. But we had expected a long-drawn-out wait, her playing elusive, perhaps putting on airs, the way many stars behaved. We hadn't expected her to want to meet us so easily.

'She's heard of both of you from the media,' RK was speaking still. 'She's really eager to meet with you!'

Maybe we are underestimating our influence, I suddenly thought. After all, we had solved a good many cases, attracted the right buzz, even if discreetly in the past few years. No wonder big stars like Alena might have heard of us from certain inner circles or then the media blitz after our first case. I felt gratified by her reaction. It saved us the wooing required for reluctant witnesses.

'How about tomorrow?' RK asked me. 'It's a shoot not at our usual location, but at a constructed set in the city suburbs. I'll ask someone from my entourage to send the address across. The setting is a carnival. We're shooting a song meant as a dream sequence. It's a gypsy dance. Come—it'll be interesting for you both to watch, too!'

'Why not?' Parvati said when I informed her where we were going on the morrow. 'It's one more interview off our checklist. We can get a sense of Alena in her own territory, also see the vibe to their interaction in a setting familiar to them! Much better, I believe, than asking for a formal interview at home.'

'And guess what?' I added, a trifle unkind in my mischief. 'A closed set, isn't it—so no Shashi!'

Parvati half-smiled at me, her gaze preoccupied when I mentioned Shashi.

'Did you notice how very attentive he is to Mr Kamal?' she mused.

'Yes, of course,' I told her, a bit put out at the memory of the previous afternoon. 'He says Aman is RK's big fan. But honestly, the way he fawns over RK, it's as if *Shashi* is RK's fan numero uno!'

Parvati didn't answer. But I had recalled something else.

'Tell me, Pari,' I asked her, using the nickname that demonstrated our familiarity of ease with each other. 'Why did you not mention to Shashi that we'd heard the scream yesterday?'

'He thinks RK is making it up, that it's all in his head,' I continued. 'Meanwhile, RK is a nervous wreck, and has seen no support on this from his best buddy, thus far. Why allow that to continue? Especially now that we know how ghastly that sound is, and how it can affect even the toughest among us, forget supposedly "sensitive" stars like RK. He's been bearing it for almost three weeks, you have to hand it to the fortitude of the man. I was almost ready to run yesterday when I saw no one there outside that door!'

Parvati knew I was only half-joking about that last line. The scream we both had heard had been nightmarish, and the fact that it seemed to come from nowhere, extremely disturbing.

'Shashi might be thinking Mr Kamal is making it up,' Parvati mused, practicality personified, despite all. 'Or he might not. He emphasized to us that Mr Kamal only hears the scream when no one else is around. Why? If he is hanging around his friend as often as we have seen him in the last two days—*he might have heard it too.* If he did—*why hide it*? On the other hand—if he is telling us the truth, if he was passing through one of those soundproofed rooms and thus heard nothing, even yesterday when *we* heard it—best we not disclose too much at this stage. There is so much unanswered. Why show our cards so early? Let the whole picture reveal itself.'

I looked at her speculatively. We had been thrust into this profession at a young age. I was barely twenty when I won the nation's premier beauty title, Miss Glamour Princess, three years before this case. Parvati was even younger, at nineteen, when she took part with me, a stranger at the time. With characteristic determination and cool-headed tenacity, she had convinced me to help her get to the bottom of some gruesome murders, which led to our coming together to form a detective agency.

Now, years later, we had fallen into an easy camaraderie as private investigators, a pattern that allowed us to read each other's mannerisms without the need for words. We trusted each other absolutely. I certainly preferred her efficient practicality to useless panic, especially in the face of the unexplained, as we were now having to deal with. But, I found Parvati maddeningly cryptic at certain moments.

As for our chosen vocation, remember that this was India in the late Nineties. Twenty-something might seem very young now, to be as self-aware as we both appeared then, but at the time it was an age in which one got settled squarely on one's life path. Many of our peers had already had their first child or were on a serious career route by age twenty. In today's Roaring Twenties and beyond prototype, one can still be 'in search' at forty, whether for a career or love, but the society of the 1990s (and earlier) was more exacting on the whole, shall I say.

So, we were both at the start, career-wise, and at our peak, age-wise, to becoming a part of something both exciting and fulfilling. But being 'young and glamorous' (a media term, not ours!) investigators in the India of the late Nineties still came with its share of pitfalls.

Among them—men such as Shashi, I thought darkly. He seemed chauvinistic without actually having done anything to appear so. And I felt he grudged every bit of our journey towards helping his famous friend, though it was certain he cared deeply for him. *We* were the problem, it would seem. I was very pleased to believe he wouldn't be on RK's set the next day, and I hoped Parvati shared my sentiment. But she was busy being her inscrutable self at present.

'It's lucky we heard the scream, Parvati,' I told her. 'Just the day after we took on the case. Shashi keeps saying that he hasn't heard it once, which as you say might or might not be the case, but it didn't allow us to favour RK's version of events when he first told us. The help hadn't heard it either. We took up this case despite there being nothing really to go upon, but now what we do know for sure is that RK isn't lying.'

'But I always knew that,' the redoubtable Parvati smiled at me. 'I told you so yesterday, remember? We hadn't heard it yet, but I believed Mr Kamal.'

'Yes, you believed him,' I echoed. 'About the screams. Not necessarily about the hauntings … *Things are not always what they appear to be.* I remember your words.'

Parvati grinned at me, then, at her practical best, got down to business. 'Let's do some research on Alena.'

'I want to know more about her and Saddaq Haque,' she continued. 'We need to go through the back issues of cine magazines, dig up what we can, Aku, before we meet her. And what was the name of her wayward husband?'

When Parvati asked that, with a start I remembered I had not managed to pick Jehaan's brains on any of the players in this drama thus far. There had been too much going on, but I knew I'd need to get to it soon.

Meanwhile, I smiled affectionately at her for using my name in its familiar short form. And then answered, as she knew I would, 'Samuel Rodrigues. That's Alena's husband.'

'Yes, Mr Samuel Rodrigues,' Parvati echoed my words, rolling the R in the last name as she looked up from the cine magazine she had picked up and begun going through.

I thumbed my nose at her ruefully destructive pronunciation of his name, then got to work reading up on Alena and him. If covering all angles helped get us closer to the source of that maddened scream—well then, I was not going to shirk my duty!

8

The next day dawned, overcast.

'We might be heading into rains early,' Parvati said to me, casting a glance at the skies as we prepared to leave for the far suburbs of Mumbai. Point to note: it would be an hour's journey, much longer if there was traffic, even more so if it rained. Remember, we had no Sea Link connecting North and South Mumbai in the 1990s! And rain slowed everything down—then, as now.

'But we need to go,' I said, determined to not let the weather play spoilsport to our timelines. 'Even if it rains.'

We got to the set late afternoon. The sky was still overcast and cloudy but there was no actual rain yet. RK beamed as we entered his vanity van, herded through by the junior production in-charge. He had left word about our arrival, else we wouldn't have been allowed in—this movie was a closed set.

And I must mention here that vanity vans in the late Nineties were not familiar sightings around Bollywood sets as they are now. In fact, they had been introduced to Tinseltown quite recently—before which actors used makeshift areas allotted on pucca sets, or then, often, just changed behind curtains made of sarees or dupattas, or some such, at outdoor shoots. To have a vanity van, and a rather swanky one, spoke of RK's superstar status more than words could.

'My dears,' he said effusively, none of the panic or the drunkenness of the previous day visible on his face, as he greeted us. 'I'm so glad you could make it. Alena is dying to meet you both!'

Clearly, RK was an able chameleon, transforming from a troubled man to a cheery superstar at will, or when his career demanded.

'Where can we find her?' Parvati asked, business-like in the face of his stubborn bonhomie.

'She's getting ready,' RK said expansively. 'You can meet her as soon as her make-up is done. Would you like a tour of the set in the meanwhile?'

'Yes, please,' I said. The more we learnt of his craft (because it was what he spent most of his time doing), the better we'd know the man.

'Is today mainly an outdoor shoot?' I asked, curious, even as he gestured for a production in-charge to take us around. 'Because it looks like rain, soon enough.'

'It is,' RK said to me, then smiling as if heartily amused, 'But if it rains, it will actually help us. Midway through today, a rain scene was scheduled! We dance in the wetness!'

We left him in his vanity van, where he said he'd bring Alena later, and proceeded with the production junior he'd requested to help show us around the vast outdoor set. Just a little away, a tableau out of a child's fairy tale awaited us.

'It's rather lovely,' I said to Parvati, most caught up by the scene constructed in front of me.

An outdoor carnival seemed to be in progress, everyone around appearing busy and the scene bustling with activity. Exuberant dancers, dressed as Harlequin clowns, rehearsed their steps in energetic moves, their loud claps and bounding leaps at regular intervals adding to the high-octane atmosphere.

They were dancing in tune to melody from a massive sound system which kept stopping at a particular note and replaying over again, as they exerted repeatedly to get their steps absolutely right. A dance director was shouting in pidgin Hindi into a conical loudspeaker, counting down their exact cues, demanding perfection in huge bellows while simultaneously offering glib encouragement.

Colourful buntings interspersed with huge pastel balloons crisscrossed high over the fake lamp posts erected down a quaint cobbled street leading from this scene towards where we stood. In the distance, behind the dance troupe, a massive Ferris wheel rotated by itself, fed by the strong wind gusts in the damp air. An ice-cream van colourfully striped in candy cane hues rested just upfront of the street. In the face of such gaiety, even if only on a movie set—I was a child again.

I clapped my hands, charmed—I couldn't help it, I was so taken by Bollywood's ability to stream a setting straight out of my childhood books, then make it their own, with typical filmi showmanship.

'Wish *my* moves could make those green eyes dance so!' A familiar voice spoke up behind me. Startled, I whipped around and in doing so, fell back, right into the arms of, well, Jehaan! The significant other I had mentioned earlier! But what was he doing on this set, was my first thought. And today, of all days, the day I was visiting.

Jehaan and I, we were serious about each other, and we had been together for more than a couple of years now. But we understood the demands of our careers and gave each other plenty of space whilst at work. So, it was surprising to see him on set, especially given that I hadn't mentioned I would be there myself!

'This is a closed set,' Parvati spoke up, her eyes twinkling as she bent forward to accept his affectionate peck on the cheek as greeting. 'No journalists allowed!'

'Ma'am, I'm not here strictly as a journalist.' Jehaan's tone was equally mischievous, matching Parvati's in its light-heartedness. 'I'm here to support a sports star who's making a guest appearance as a celebrity dancer in this movie! I was invited! But if it should lead to a "colour" story later ... well, who is to say, now?'

I observed the two banter, matching my light-hearted mood, fuelled mostly by this bright, colour-infused set. Only Jehaan's playfulness could have Parvati behave as she did—few ever really saw this impish side to her. I, very rarely. It was nice to relax, wallow in the unexpected thrill of bumping into Jehaan, pretend like 'everything's okay' in this make-believe setting, even if just for a bit. But reality lurked close by, in the shadows, as always.

'Jehaan,' a voice from the group of Harlequins called out. 'Over here!'

'I must go,' Jehaan gave me a quick kiss, nodded courteously at Parvati, then sauntered over to his sportsman friend. 'Good luck with your sleuthing.' He knew we had been engaged by RK for a case, of course, but I hadn't been able to fill him in on the details. Yet, meeting him here was joyous, if unexpected.

'Well, that was a surprise,' I told Parvati as he left.

'A pleasant one,' Parvati smiled briefly, then her face turned impassive. 'Here comes the unpleasant one, for you, I think ...'

For walking towards us, unbelievably, was the omnipresent and currently scowling Shashi Sunder.

'Hello, ladies,' he snapped as he got close. 'How's the preparation going?' His words were pleasant, his tone not so much.

'... preparation?' Parvati asked, quizzical.

'To meet the dazzling Alena,' Shashi answered her query. 'Are you still waiting?'

'Well, we're getting a tour of the set,' I remarked, then, because I couldn't resist. 'How did you know we would be here?'

'Did you think I wouldn't?' Shashi's sharp eyes appraised me evenly. 'This may be a closed set, but I am Roop's manager, allowed to be present. And I am in on all of Roop's affairs, remember? Nothing goes through without me knowing ...'

You didn't know of the two times when RK met us earlier, I thought darkly, but didn't voice it. Why antagonize the man further?

Our tour and any information we might have hoped to gain from it, though, was cut short by the reappearance of the junior production in-charge. He had materialized to escort us back to RK's vanity van.

'She'll see you now,' he said to us, so we understood we were to follow him back immediately. The 'she' he had referred to, who needed no name, as if royalty, was Alena, naturally.

As we returned to the van, we noticed that Shashi had tagged along behind us as well. But he was stopped at the van door by the junior hand.

'She's not fully ready,' the boy insisted. 'Only the ladies may go in.'

Shashi gave the boy a venomous look, but he stepped away from the door, allowing us to pass him on our way in.

'Hello ladies,' said a sparkling voice from within the van as we stepped inside. 'I've been absolutely *thrilling* to meet with you!'

9

Alena Palekar was striking in person. This was my immediate thought as we set eyes on the silver-screen heartthrob of the late Nineties. In fact, to me, she appeared even more beautiful here than she did up on the big screen.

RK had told us she was getting ready, but she didn't appear as if she had any make-up on, at all. A clever trick by her make-up man, I knew—the 'no make-up' look also required make-up, even if minimal, which really depended on how good or bad one's skin was. I knew this as someone who used to be a part of the fashion and beauty industry in my supermodel avatar.

Alena had perfect, unblemished skin and her make-up artist had used his potions effectively to enhance its dewy, natural hue. Her brown-gold hair was up in a semi-pony and ribboned, curling ringlets fell about her shoulders, framing her face. She was in an oversized dressing gown, appearing small and vulnerable to me, just as she had to RK as he'd recounted, when he first set eyes on her.

'It's the look,' Alena had laughed, a tinkling giggle, noting our expressions upon sighting her for the first time. 'I'm in character as his daughter today! I'm supposed to look young and pretty, for my dream sequence gypsy dance! Much younger than he, which I am,' she dimpled at RK, unselfconsciously pulling him closer to her as she spoke. He turned to her, his face alight. She knew her power over him, that much was clear to both Parvati and me, revealed in the very first few minutes of our meeting.

'You little minx,' he let out as she pretended to melt into his arms, then bit his shoulder playfully.

'But you adore cats!' she gazed up at RK, from under long lashes. 'I'm the Miss Pickles in your life!'

Parvati and I, we watched this little interchange silently. We both knew there was plenty of attraction; the air was charged with it. But a romance of three odd months and a love of a lifetime were two different things—how strong was this bond in actuality? Would it really translate to wedding bands as RK had let on he wanted it to? Was this waif of a lady in front of us as much in love with RK as he undoubtedly appeared to be, with her?

Irrationally, I felt a tug of pity for Shashi. I wasn't sure why I felt it—there was no apparent trigger here to think of him in the exchange we just witnessed. But I did. I dismissed the feeling firmly, as Parvati spoke up.

'Alena Palekar, in person,' she said, pleasantly laconic. 'How nice to meet you.'

'And you,' Alena dimpled prettily, then turned to me. 'You're my idol I think,' she said unexpectedly. 'You know while you modelled and before I was a movie star, I followed your career obsessively. The magnificent, emerald-eyed Akruti Rai. You're an icon to so many!'

'I'm glad you think so well of me,' I said, a trifle taken aback at the high praise. 'I didn't realize you knew of my work.'

'I wanted to get into this line,' Alena said to me. 'How could I not? You were everywhere once upon a time.'

'That is not to say you're not everywhere now,' RK hastened to correct the immaturity in his lady's words. 'Only, in a different profession than before.'

'Oh, I'm not offended at all,' I turned to RK. Bollywood lived so fragilely, a sentence could trigger high-strung egos the wrong way. I could see RK was worried, believing I too lived by filmi rules. I hastened to disarm him with a wide smile.

Jehaan had once mentioned casually in that offbeat way of his that my smile had his colleagues actually swoon in sheer longing. I always took Jehaan's comments with a pinch of salt, he was such a jester, but I kept the intent of his words in my mind's eye. My smile had some effect here, I was gratified to see. RK's worried look dissipated, he turned in relief, then, to Parvati.

'I'm so much better when I'm around Alena,' he said.

'Do you know of his worries?' Parvati addressed Alena, smiling encouragingly at RK before she did so.

'Yes, yes,' Alena said, as she turned from us to check herself in the mirror, unselfconsciously once again. 'The continual screaming in his home. I didn't hear it while I visited, but I've barely been there a couple of times since we returned from location. But he says it's loud and long-drawn-out, and he can't rest. Imagine, just a few months after meeting me, now his future wife-to-be, all this supernatural activity occurs. You do know we're getting married, right? It's been *such* a whirlwind courtship, but Roop is sure I'm the one for him. Anyway, I'm as superstitious as everyone in this industry. So tell me, how am I supposed to take this screaming business?'

I looked at Alena. It was clear that she already regarded RK as hers, with a powerful sense of ownership. His home too, for that matter. And the fact that she was still legally married to another hadn't fazed her plans one bit. Like most divas, she was claiming what was hers in front of us, confident all would go her way. But the self-absorbedness of that last comment was undeniable.

That RK regarded her as his one true love was evident, but she didn't seem to have understood the layers to his feelings, or even his extreme reaction to the screams. It was all about how *she* felt, how superstitiously the screams would be viewed by the industry given their newly formed bond, rather than what was actually happening. Did Alena realize just how troubled RK was by the noise? Or had he hidden the real depth of his fears from her as he had from Shashi initially, thus her inability to recognize his glaring need for support?

'How do you mean, Alena?' RK had caught the last sentence and wanted an explanation.

'Well, if we go by Bollywood superstition, this screaming could well be some scary spirit wishing our new union harm,' Alena's musical voice masked the harshness of her words. 'Then it is inauspicious for me to be in your house at all. How do I live in it, post our wedding, if the house hates me? Or say the spirit of your dead mother hates me—remember, you said you were trying to contact her in the first place with that Ouija board? Best we think of selling the house, once we're married. It's heritage property. Imagine the money you'd get for it.'

Parvati and I stood silent, struck dumb by Alena's words. RK looked so grieved, he appeared ill.

'But Alena,' he said, looking both desperate and heartbroken, 'I love this home.'

A commotion outside drowned out her reply. There were voices raised, as if in anger. Then a hammering on the vanity van door, loud and insistent.

'Alena,' a man's voice called out, bold and loud. 'Open up. I know you're in there!'

Alena had gone white as a sheet, her pale face in keeping with her dressing gown colour. She clutched her throat miserably as she murmured. 'Why? Why here? Why now?'

We didn't understand the cause of her distress, but RK's face lost its desperate look and instead turned obdurate as he strode up to the door. He opened it forcefully.

But it was only Shashi who stood outside, his expression inscrutable and grim, behind him the overcast sky looking as heavy and angry, framing his darkened silhouette. He stepped past RK and entered, motioning to Alena to go out.

'They're calling you for your shot,' he said shortly, his voice tight, as if holding something in check. 'You have to leave now. The weather won't hold much longer.'

Alena peered past him, then realizing he was alone, shot us a quick glance. Whatever she might have wanted to say, even to RK, she did not. Wordlessly, she slid past Shashi to the set outside.

Shashi began whispering to RK in low, urgent tones—we couldn't catch what he was saying. Despite the sombre, rather forceful nature of this hushed conversation, RK was courteous enough to realize he had cut us off.

'Go on outside,' he gestured to us. 'See her dance. I'll be right with you.'

Something had been nagging me, I couldn't place what. It was about that voice outside the door. But there wasn't much for us to do inside, so we followed his instructions. We stepped out. And walked the short distance to the set area.

The speed at which the buzzing, chaotic set of a while ago had transformed into a scene of pure symmetry was uncanny. The carnival had come alive, the dancers positioned, in marvellous costume and at the ready. No doubt Alena had also shed the dressing gown masking her costume for this dance and had taken her place.

'Rehearsal shot before take,' the man standing in front of us called out, authoritatively. We had no idea if he was the director. 'Silence! Action!'

And before our eyes, another world opened up. It was pure thrill, the lights, the colours, the Harlequins moving as one, leaping, clapping, dancing, in high fervour to the dramatic, charged song.

Such energy, such rhythm, I could've cried from the pleasure of watching it. The scene stands out as one of this case's most memorable moments, a dream scene, not just Alena's in the movie, but somehow, mine too. In front of me, a glorious gypsy dance, sensuous, bold, vibrant and ablaze, ripe in a riot of colour.

Then, in the centre of it, contorting as if she belonged there—the ingénue Alena, in a shimmery gauze, off-shoulder wrap, as colourful as the carnival, slithering and winding her way through the Harlequins. Her dance as we watched—at once seductive and innocent. She was veiled, as a gypsy would be—only her eyes showed, burning passionate, as if on fire. An Arabic headdress, a flat turban of coins sat on her curling locks, and a belt of coins glittered at her exposed waist. She wore harem pants of blazing gold. And how she moved!

She had me mesmerized, I barely noticed when the director yelled, 'Cut!' Alena stopped casually at his voice and strolled off the set to the side.

'Make-up touch-up,' someone yelled. 'Rolling in three!' The skies looked ominous, clouds dark and ready to burst. As if on cue, a thunderclap sounded in the distance.

But Alena wanted to go to RK's vanity van for a moment. She walked off, and we followed, though we had no reason to. It was still niggling me, how oddly familiar that voice sounded, the one belonging to the person hammering at the vanity door.

In the distance, we saw Alena turn the door handle of RK's vanity van. She was about to step inside, still attired like a gypsy princess in her gold harem pants and multi-coloured gauze wrap. Before the van swallowed her, however, a jingle-jangle of the coins at her waist, a tight scream.

We rushed forward even as the skies opened up. Through the heavy sheath of rain, through the abrupt distraction of the thunder that crashed like cymbals overhead, I suddenly remembered why that voice earlier had sounded so familiar. But I was late in my realization, much too late.

As the deluge lashed the van, we saw in the blur up ahead the form of a soaking Alena being struck repeatedly by a burly muscled figure who held her tightly as he smacked her. Then, lightning completed the drama of this moment by streaking across. As it cleaved the sky, it lit up the man's features in its jagged path. Raw, tormented but undeniably good looking. I had heard that voice so often in the movies, I knew it was him before I saw his face. *The face of Saddaq Haque, superstar.*

10

'Stop, stop it at once!' Parvati, fury writ large on every inch of her taut face, dashed the last couple of metres to the limp and moaning Alena, as she was being battered by Saddaq. She reached them in seconds, then extended herself to her full height to grasp at Saddaq's fist in order to halt it midway through the pummelling.

As former beauty pageant contestants, we were both taller than average. But none of us was physically equipped to combat the testosterone-heavy, bulked-up mass of Saddaq. Parvati might not have had the strength had not he, caught off guard by our arrival, checked himself abruptly in mid-motion. He let go of Alena, who crumpled to the ground, splattering blood as she fell. It flowed from her face without pause, joining the rain rivulets on the already wet earth.

'Step away from her,' Parvati said, her tone even, low, but so cold it sliced through me, an ice sliver. I had never seen Parvati so angry, angry such that her body was trembling violently even though her face was obdurate, inscrutable.

Saddaq blinked at her, then at me. He seemed zombie-like, as if he couldn't get control of his body.

'I … I …' he mumbled, but Parvati wasn't listening. She was down on her knees in the wet earth trying to help Alena up. The rain pelted down, ferocious, soaking us all to the skin though the whole interlude had only been seconds long. Saddaq stepped away, shuffling backwards awkwardly till the heavy downpour blurred him from our sight.

I helped Parvati support Alena to the van. We opened the door and stepped in, dripping water, Alena dripping blood from her head.

RK's face turned a bleached white through his make-up tan when he saw Alena like that. The fury of the rain and the violent thundering had prevented him from hearing all that had happened just outside his vanity's door. Parvati didn't bother to explain, she simply got on the walkie-talkie in his van to alert the production team on the set outside. They would need to arrange an ambulance for Alena. Rain or no rain, this shoot was definitely over.

It was only on the next day that we finally had some time to discuss the events that had transpired before us. Seated in our office, the cool monochrome of its wooden interiors seemed a far cry from the drama and colour and terror of the previous day.

'Alena will recover, that's a relief,' I said to Parvati. She had just got off the phone with an agitated RK for the umpteenth time, as he wept for Alena and railed against Saddaq in turn.

RK had known Saddaq was on the set. It was indeed Saddaq who had banged on RK's van, demanding Alena open up. His superstar status had granted him access to a closed set, but the aggressiveness he had shown hammering on RK's van had been checked almost immediately. He had been asked to leave at the time, instantly, by Shashi hovering just outside the van's door, and of course, the production team.

Shashi had confided the same to RK, in low, urgent tones, the very whisperings we had heard in the vanity van and were purposely kept out of, as RK urged us to go see Alena's dance that afternoon.

Saddaq's voice as he called to Alena, so familiar, but one I could not quite place then, though I had heard it often enough on the silver screen in my model avatar. A time when my dreams of becoming a Bollywood star were still alive, and I devoured Indian cinema in preparation for those dreams.

But back to the case at hand. RK was now distraught, for he had believed the situation had been handled when Shashi asked Saddaq to leave. He blamed himself for not seeing to it personally that Saddaq, for all his superstar status, was removed from the set then. Parvati had been trying to calm him down ever since.

'It was close,' Parvati said to me quietly. 'No man should ever lay a hand on a woman like that. Or on a child. No human being should attack another as he did, for that matter.'

I couldn't agree more. 'Saddaq seemed out of touch with reality,' I said to Parvati sombrely. 'The way he looked and behaved, after ...'

RK had mentioned Saddaq's possible drug abuse the previous day, after the incident happened. We had already read rumours of the same from blind items in film magazines much before this occurrence. We could see that he had not been in his senses when he attacked Alena. But that did not absolve him of the fact that he did attack her, and mercilessly at that.

'No one saw him hit Alena that day, except us,' Parvati looked suddenly frustrated. 'And Alena doesn't want to press charges, or even speak of his violence.'

Despite the serious nature of Saddaq's attack, no one had called the police to the set either. Alena had been taken to the hospital, strings pulled so there would be no awkward questions from the doctors or the law regarding how she came to be beaten up quite so bad. The shoot had wrapped quietly, with no one except those present any wiser as to why. And Alena wasn't ready to speak against Saddaq even now.

'That's terrible,' I told Parvati. 'It might happen again, and we might not be there to prevent it—he might take her life the next time. Does she understand that?'

'The dark underbelly of Bollywood.' Parvati looked straight at me. '*Things are not always as they appear to be.* Aren't you glad you decided to shift gears, become an investigator, rather than a movie star?'

I didn't quite know how to answer that. It had been my single-minded dream, entering the movies, once upon a time, till meeting Parvati changed my world view and my ambition, both. I couldn't help but think—if these three reigning superstars of the day despite their success were yet so intensely fragile, each battling their own demons—what chance did the rest of ardent hopefuls entering the movie business have, at a normal existence?

Parvati was watching my expression, and decided to let me off the hook by changing tack.

'Don't let this distract you from what we had originally signed up for. Do you think Saddaq is behind what's happening at Mr Kamal's house?'

'He could be. He seemed unhinged enough,' I said to her, disturbed. 'We need to find out the reason for his fury, why he hit Alena as he did. Does it have to do with RK and her being together now?'

'If he'll actually admit to touching her, ever, that is,' Parvati looked sombre again. 'We need to find out from Alena, at least. When she wakes up, and is free of the medication.'

'Speaking of Alena—we can't rule her out, even if Saddaq beat her up,' I mused. 'Did you hear how she spoke to RK earlier?

'Yes, she wanted to sell his beloved home,' Parvati mused. 'Possible motive in attempting those screams. He may not part with his home easily, so maybe scare him into it? Yes, most definitely, we ought to keep an eye on her too, apart from the private drama in her life.'

'That's Shashi, Saddaq, Alena—almost everyone in RK's immediate circle,' I said. 'Any one of them could have tried to scare him for different reasons. Shashi's motive is unclear right now, but he was the one who appeared just after we heard the scream at RK's home. And Mr Pickles doesn't like him either. The last one left in this is the fanboy, Aman, who says he was travelling the entire duration of RK's ordeal.'

'Yes, he was, I got that checked with the airline Mr Kamal booked him on,' Parvati said. 'Aman Azad did fly out to Bali and back.'

'So, he's the only one who was not around from those close and connected to RK in this time span,' I said. I have to admit, I was relieved; I had been rather drawn to Aman's languid charm. But Parvati's sensible voice mocked my susceptibility to Aman's obvious magnetism.

'To me, that's actually a point to keep in mind,' she said looking at me, her gaze piercing in its directness. 'The mysterious house guest who is close to Mr Kamal ... *yet was never there* ...'

I had to agree with Parvati—we could discount no one till we were completely sure of their innocence.

'You mean Aman could've used an accomplice to scare RK, even if he wasn't here himself,' I mused. 'But why? Why would he want to scare RK, his mentor and host? There seems no motive for Aman to do so. No motive for Shashi too, for that matter, as we know.'

'Yes, but we don't know all the facts still. Anything is possible,' Parvati replied. 'It's early days yet in this investigation. And it's so different from our other cases, a supposed haunting, based on random though blood-curdling screams. We're only investigating demons—real or imagined—in a superstar's home!'

'I'm glad we have a complete list to begin with, at least,' I told her.

'Actually, the list of people connected to Mr Kamal is not complete yet,' Parvati said to me. 'We're forgetting someone vital.'

I glanced at her, puzzled. As far as I knew, we had covered most of those RK spoke of.

'Think about it, Aku,' Parvati said. 'Mr Kamal wants to marry Alena. And she clearly thinks of him as hers. However, they cannot exchange vows in the future, something stands in their way ...'

'Yes, of course!' How could I have missed such a fundamental fact, especially when it kept coming to my mind. '*She's already married*. She would need to divorce her earlier husband.'

'The unknown quantity in this convoluted conundrum.' Parvati met my eyes. 'We will need to track down Mr Samuel Rodrigues.'

11

Mr Samuel Rodrigues wasn't that difficult to track down. Actually, he was handed to us almost on a platter, courtesy of Jehaan's journalist contact. One of Jehaan's colleagues who worked on the desk at *Bharat 360* was married to a journalist from *Cine So Fine* magazine.

This was the film magazine that had broken the story of Alena being married, just a little while ago. Jehaan cajoled a meeting with the subject of that story, Mr Rodrigues, upon my request. Jehaan had a way with people, his colleagues adored him. Before we knew it—we had an appointment set up for us at a local coffee house.

'It's so nice to have Jehaan around for such things,' I said smirking at Parvati, en route to our meeting, a couple of days post our film set visit. It had taken those two days to get this meeting set up. Parvati smiled indulgently at me. She too was very much a member of the ever-expanding Jehaan Warrior fan club.

'It is, though,' she said. 'When you need the right information—go to the source. And who could be a better source in this case than the hidden husband? Was truly wonderful of your Jehaan to swing this for us.'

We reached the coffee house well in time, and settled for a discreet table in a corner, hidden from any curious eyes. Seconds after us, Samuel Rodrigues arrived.

'I wouldn't have gone to any other table,' he said, the moment he reached us. I had been wondering if we would be able to identify him in the packed place, but it looked as if he had found us first and immediately. An oily, ingratiating sort of persona, this was my first impression of Samuel Rodrigues.

'Your face is not one easily missed, Mees Rai,' he continued meanwhile, by way of explanation.

I have avoided making much of myself in the telling of these events, but I would have to reveal there was truth to his words. My beauty pageant days might well have been over for me, but not for the rest of the nation. When I travelled to public places like this one, more often than not I had fans walk over for autographs or a chat. Remember this was way before mobile phones became the byword that they are now, so no selfies existed, thank God.

'This is Parvati Samant,' I introduced Parvati to the fawning Samuel, gesturing for him to take a seat.

'So, tell us.' Parvati was not one to waste time or words. 'Mr Rodrigues—how does it feel being known as Alena's missing husband?'

'Call me Samuel, please,' he grinned at her obsequiously, flashing ugly, tobacco-stained teeth. 'And I was never missing. Just because she forgot my existence doesn't mean I didn't exist. You know?'

'She forgot your existence! How is that?' Parvati prodded, pleasantly.

'Well, I might not have been there in the beginning,' Samuel let on, carefully. 'We were so young, and it's hard to support a wife when you're still in college. You know? But I'm here now.'

'Anyway,' he continued. 'Shall we speak business? That's why I'm meeting you, na? Tarini from *Cine So Fine* told me you wanted to confirm that I was indeed her husband, that's why I came here personally to meet you. I have a marriage certificate, a legal document. And you are detectives. So, now say—you can help me get what is mine from Alena?'

Parvati and I exchanged glances. Samuel Rodrigues had been very willing to meet us because he had a clear agenda of his own. And it had nothing to do with our case.

'Tarini is that the journalist, Jehaan's colleague's wife from *Cine So Fine*?' Parvati asked me softly, and I nodded in affirmative.

'What is it you want from Alena that is yours?' Parvati addressed Samuel.

'Why, my share of her earnings, naturally,' he looked amazed, as if wondering how Parvati could be so obtuse. 'She's my wife. We pledged a life together. I must be having a legal right to what's hers, isn't it?'

'How come you didn't remember that you pledged to a life together before she became a movie star?' I asked curiously. This ingratiating little man with his oily features, stained teeth and slick talk repelled me. How could Alena ever have found him attractive enough to marry him?

'Akrutiji,' he added the inevitable Bollywood suffix of *ji* to my name, an appendage of such flexibility, it could convey many things just by how it was uttered: respect, formality—at times, sarcasm. 'I was younger then. And young people make mistakes. I'm not saying I was a saint. But I discovered the error in my ways. I'm ready to repent. I'm ready for Alena to take me back into her life. And her home. You know?' The last bit was mouthed with a cunning glint in his eyes, as if he and I were co-conspirators in this ambitious endeavour of his.

'We're detectives,' Parvati spoke up, as yet pleasant but short. 'We're not lawyers, nor are we legal experts. We cannot help with what you are asking.'

'Arre, then why ask to meet me? I was thinking you would be perfect to help me.' Samuel's face fell, even as his cunning eyes continued to appraise Parvati. 'So then I must not waste any more of your time. Achcha, see you, namaste.'

As he got up to leave, I played my last ace, hoping to get a reaction. 'Thank you for meeting us. By the way, have you seen Alena's latest movie yet?' My words found their mark as I'd hoped they would.

'*Mehfil*? With Saddaq Haque?' Samuel's face had darkened, his gaze transformed. He looked malevolent. 'Don't talk to me of that man. He actually threatened me. *Me*, her husband!'

Samuel was getting up to depart, but the memory had triggered something animal in him. He sat back down heavily and leaned across towards us menacingly.

'I will deal with Saddaq Haque my way. He cannot have Alena. Anyone who wants my wife will need to go through me. You know?'

That sentiment was so chauvinistically put, it sickened me, but that was not the only thing wrong with it. How could this man speak about another getting to Alena *through* him—as if she were a property to be lent out on a whim? *His* whim, that too.

I couldn't stomach this ridiculous being any more, but I had to stay silent. We needed to find out if he knew of RK's presence in Alena's life. That was the crux of our reason to meet him, after all.

'Why target Saddaq alone?' Parvati asked smoothly, her face a mask. 'There must be so many co-stars around Alena.'

'You are right,' Samuel turned to Parvati, his lower lips curling in fury. 'There is that Saurav Roop Kamal. He is filming with Alena now. And they think I don't know about their little love game. They want everyone to believe that it's still Saddaq who is with my wife, but they're such stupid creatures. Do they believe I don't have my spies around? I know.' His tone was threatening, he leaned further into Parvati's face and repeated his words. 'I *know.*'

I nodded at Parvati grimly. We had got what we came for. Samuel letting on that he knew about Alena and RK revealed his role as possible mischief-maker and therefore suspect in RK's scream saga.

He may have 'known' that his presence played a vital role in RK and Alena's continuing story. But now, by his confession—so did we.

12

'I'm handling this Saurav Roop Kamal, this RK as he's called,' Samuel leaned further across conspiratorially, his face fox-like in craftiness or bluster, it was difficult to tell. 'I'm handling him so he can never go near Alena again!'

We heard Samuel out in silence. Though his intent in these revelations was clearly boastful, the disclosures of this man were getting dangerous, and we realized how close we were to a possible breakthrough now.

'How exactly are you handling him?' Parvati said. Her expression was neutral, even admiring, as she said this. I marvelled at her capacity for acting, though neither of us was the filmi ones in this sordid Bollywood saga at present.

'Why on earth should I tell *you* how?' He smirked at us both, not a pleasant smile, with the stained teeth glinting hideously. 'But he'll be sorry for carrying on with *my wife* the way he is doing.'

'How did you say you knew about him and her?' Parvati was still continuing her barrage of admiring questions, despite his sneering statement. 'I heard it's a closed set, where they're filming ...'

'Nothing is a secret when you offer money to junior spot boys for information on your wife. You know?' Samuel was so taken in by his own cunning, or Parvati's admiring looks, or both, that he seemed to be spilling vital information without pause. 'And best of all, it's Alena's money I'm paying him with, hah, hah, hah!' Samuel seemed so deeply pleased with himself, he had dropped all discretion. 'But then, I'm her husband, it's mine too!'

'She's been giving me money, naturally.' His eyes glinted as he went on. 'I'm her husband, she ought to. Every time I ask, she pays up, as I expected. But she's also been begging me to grant her a divorce. Why should I? I told Tarini to write this in her magazine, like I'm telling you. I want the publicity to scare Alena into submission. But Tarini said the marriage part was more sensational, and she wanted to keep writing on that for longer.'

Obviously, discretion was not Samuel's strong point, or was there a reason he was telling us, the two detectives he's only just met, all this? Unless he was just a coarse loud-mouth, a braggart by nature, exactly as he was coming across now.

'Anyway, each time I ask Alena for more money, I tell her I'm considering her request for divorce, so she falls for it and gives me my money. Ever since the interview in the magazine hit the stands, it's been like that. I wanted it to cause a sensation. You know? To make everyone know I'm her husband—let the world see that the beautiful, talented Alena Palekar is married, not single! I went to the press first. So, she couldn't hide me away, pretend I didn't exist!'

'You really are quite thorough,' Parvati said to him, still in character. Then she tried, once more, to get him to talk about what we needed. 'How exactly do you plan to tackle your issue with Mr Kamal?'

'Why would *you* like to know?' The bragging we had just witnessed gave way to suspicion in a trice. Samuel Rodrigues, finally realizing that he might have told us too much, stood up abruptly, his face dark.

'Since you can't help me with what I want—I don't need to be here, do I?' he muttered. Then he moved away, rapidly, without so much as a backward glance.

'Such a cultured creature,' I said to Parvati, the sarcasm brittle in my voice. I couldn't help it, this Samuel Rodrigues with his wheedling, obsequious nature and oily outpourings had unsettled me.

'You know, they say like attracts like.' Parvati, unconcerned by my mood, looked as if she was trying to figure something out.

'Yes?' I said, mystified.

'Well, what if the puzzle is not Alena marrying someone like Samuel?' Parvati said. 'What if the real puzzle is Alena looking to marry someone like Mr Kamal?'

I understood at once what she was getting at. Samuel seemed a grasping, greedy creature, not above using dubious means to procure his wife's fortunes—fortunes which didn't exist when he had quite remorselessly left her to fend for herself.

Alena seemed quite lovely on the outside, tinkling voice and fine-boned features. But we had heard her tell RK that she wasn't comfortable in the home he was describing as possibly haunted. We had heard her breaking his heart, in discussing a possible sale of the house, instead of offering succour. We had even heard her remark on the fortune it would fetch, being a heritage home. What if it was not RK and Alena but Alena and Samuel who were similar in their thinking, which is what had attracted them to each other in the first place?

Alena on the inside might actually be exactly the same as her husband: opportunistic, greedy—vengeful, if crossed?

Then the anomaly, as Parvati pointed out, wasn't that a person like her had married a person like Samuel. *The anomaly would be that a person like her was looking to form a union with a person like RK*—disturbed by present circumstances, but at heart, open, expansive and generous.

'RK might be in for more trouble than we realize,' I said softly, meeting Parvati's eyes as we both pondered on this epiphany. Our thoughts, it seemed, turned out to be a portent. When we reached the office from the coffee house, the phone was already ringing, loud and insistent. The secretary we had employed for such matters was out for lunch.

'It's RK,' I mouthed to Parvati as I picked up the receiver. What I wasn't prepared for was the hysteria in his voice.

'It's Mr Pickles, Mr Pickles …' RK kept repeating, as if stuck in a loop on a broken record. His voice sounded unlike anything I had heard before—listless, panicky, and somehow, hopeless.

'What is it? What has happened?' I asked, deeply anxious. I knew whatever it was, it was far from good news.

Then RK did something so out of character, I became helpless in my uncertainty. He broke down, sobbing; I could hear his anguish over the phone line.

'He's crying,' I whispered to Parvati, out of my depth in incomprehension. But Parvati had apparently understood immediately. She grabbed the phone receiver from me, listened to him mumble incoherently between sobs, then addressed RK in a voice that seemed at once authoritative and maternal.

'Mr Kamal? Don't touch anything. We'll be right there,' she said.

'Don't bother to sit down,' she told me, immediately after. 'We're going to his home right away.'

'But what is it?' I was bemused at his grief in the call, as at her reaction. I believed something had terrified RK even further than what he had let on up until now. I certainly wasn't expecting what came next.

'Mr Pickles, Mr Kamal's beloved cat …' Parvati's voice was flat, grim. '*He's been murdered.*'

13

How does one react to intentional and fatal harm done to an animal? Would a cat's murder elicit as much gravitas as, say, a man's?

I am of the view that a life is a life—animal or human. Pain is pain, how to quantify which type is worse or better? Perhaps only an animal lover or a person with genuine empathy towards all creatures would be able to fathom the pain of losing a beloved pet. It is not dissimilar to losing a vital member of one's family.

That Mr Pickles, RK's cat, had been murdered—a strong word, stronger than 'killed' or 'done away with'—that was abundantly clear from the very beginning. And it was a brutal execution too, enough to leave RK distraught, hysterical, utterly undone in wild misery.

When we arrived at his home, RK was at the door. We could tell how spent he was. Shashi, he let on listlessly, was on his way, stuck in Mumbai traffic, having chosen this day to run errands in the far suburbs. Alena was still in hospital, recovering from Saddaq's beating. And the charismatic houseguest Aman Azad—he had a doctor's appointment for his leg injury that morning, and hadn't returned yet.

In effect—all of those who could've supported RK in this traumatic hour of need were not present by his side. Instead, fate's vagaries had deemed that Parvati and I be the first ones on the scene to attend to his inconsolable grief.

He led us silently into the home, in the direction of the study. RK, in his searing grief, had obviously not called in his staff as yet. Not even the lone uniformed house help, who'd ushered us inside on the first day we had come to Taqdeer, seemed to be around.

Mr Pickles lay by the study door, a yellow-gold ball of fur, curled up, as if at rest. From a distance nothing seemed off. It was on approach that the picture changed horrifically.

For the cat's belly had been sliced open end to end, such that along with his blood, part of his insides too were spilling onto the floor. A gruesome sight, it had us both shuddering and a bit nauseated instantly.

This was no merciful poisoning. Nor was it a sharp hit by a blunt object in the hope of putting an end to something bothersome, once and for all. No, this was a gruesome, purposefully vengeful act, as if a signal to RK that he ought to be afraid, very afraid. And whether or not it had found its mark, it had certainly turned RK crazed with grief at this moment.

'My Pickles, my Pickles …' he wept, his anguish uncontainable. I could barely watch, for the desperate sadness of it. Parvati, though, was cool-headedness personified.

'Have you called the police?' she asked RK gently.

He shook his head through his tears, a weak negative gesture.

'You need to,' she said, firm in her conviction. 'And you need to tell them everything—it isn't about a "haunting" anymore, is it? This is an open, intolerable act of aggression against you.'

RK was looking at Parvati, but we weren't sure if he was actually listening, wrapped so, in his all-consuming grief.

'I suspect Shashi is the one who takes care of such details,' Parvati said to me quietly. 'But we need to call in the cops since I'm not sure where Shashi is, at present.'

'I'm here,' Shashi stepped up, as if by magic. None of us had heard him come in, he had been so quiet. 'The man has a gift for these stealthy appearances,' I thought to myself, watching him as he moved past the cat's carcass to the grieving superstar seated next to it. 'Wonder if that's because he might be a part of what's sinister here …'

We watched as he enfolded RK in his arms, rocked him as one would a child. No words were exchanged, Shashi's expression was enough to show us how RK's tearing grief had affected him too. We weren't sure if the cat's death had, though—our last observation of Shashi's interaction with Mr Pickles had shown us they weren't fond of each other.

I suspected Parvati was thinking along the same lines as I, watching this tableau. Whatever irritation Shashi might have felt towards the cat—could it have been strong enough to lead him to possibly kill it?

Could he be the one driven to such a gruesome act of vengeance in his dislike of the animal? Would he actually do such a thing, knowing his best friend's fondness for Mr Pickles and the kind of outpouring of grief that would and did come later? Or then, could there possibly have been some sort of trigger that might have forced him into perhaps doing what he normally would not have? *Was Shashi a murderer*?

'I've called the local police station,' the subject of our speculation looked up at us and mouthed quietly. 'They'll be here soon. Roop needs to rest, to stay calm till they arrive …'

'I'm not leaving Mr Pickles,' RK said dully. 'I'm sitting right here.'

And so, we stayed on in silence, waited with the mourning RK till the police arrived. They didn't take long. I had wondered if my old nemesis, the Additional Commissioner of Police (Addl CP), Crime, Dipankar Mhatre would arrive today. He was senior in the hierarchy and, under normal circumstances, would not be present at the apparent killing of a cat. But I knew that he tended to make his presence felt when the city's high-profile citizens were involved, and Mr Pickles had been no ordinary cat by those standards—he was Bollywood's reigning superstar RK's cat.

I wasn't disappointed. Shashi had managed to make sure he got the top brass of the law enforcement machinery in attendance, to help address his friend's troubles.

And the sunshiny Addl CP (forgive my utter irreverence) was high on that list.

'Ms Rai,' he said the moment he entered, his familiar dour look firmly in place. 'How interesting to find you here.' The Addl CP had been the one in charge in our first and, of course, high-visibility case at the beauty pageant. You could say we shared a chequered relationship, he and I.

Mhatre had accepted our help for that one, and yet, unbelievably, we had been included in his list of suspects alongside, as well. Or rather, I had—I wasn't sure if Parvati had, given her family's RAW credentials. We hadn't managed to run into him for our cases in between that time and now, oddly enough. Maybe because the cases we took on, post our first, required more discreet handling. Also, the police force being vast, other officers had been on the scene for those. Given all this, today was a reunion of sorts, between us and Mhatre, though once again, under tragic circumstances.

'And Parvati Samant too,' Mhatre continued, inclining his head in Parvati's direction.

'If we could get down to business,' Shashi spoke up, impatient. RK was clearly not in a good place, and Shashi, being the empath I recognized him to be around RK, was feeling as acutely for his friend.

Mhatre had two policemen accompanying him. They went about the sorry business of detailing Mr Pickles' abject condition. Then, once done, they covered the poor creature in a cloth Shashi provided, most probably from the spare linen cabinet in the corridor outside.

RK sat quiet through the entire business and would have continued in this manner had not Mhatre decided to get down to the facts about this case.

'Was there anyone in your immediate surroundings who had access to your home, who disliked your pet?' Mhatre began neutrally enough, sensing RK wasn't quite up for starting with the difficult questions.

'My staff have been with me since I've lived here—around five years now. There have been no issues around Mr Pickles,' RK spoke, so low we could barely hear him.

I had that sensation of déjà vu, the unease I had felt on our first meeting repeated now. The strange sense of something amiss, but unable to pinpoint exactly what. Immediately followed by the conviction once again, oddly enough, of RK's vulnerability. I once more felt a wave of intense pity for him surge within me.

Here was a megastar, powerful, rich, successful, his profession allowing him an immense reservoir of adulation. And yet he was being targeted by something or someone so malicious, so evil, it had left him with a crippling loss. *And it was still not clear what this thing was.*

'What about the members of your family? Your friend circle? Your neighbours?' Mhatre continued.

'My family hasn't visited me here in the last two years—I have no reason to believe they want Mr Pickles dead,' RK said, curt and low.

'And the others I mentioned?' Mhatre persisted, unruffled. His job was to get to the bottom of this, no matter RK's mood.

'Not that I know of,' RK looked up at him for a brief moment. 'I have no neighbours; the place is a heritage property, built between two public gardens. Access to it is blocked by the trees and grounds as well.'

'So, this is an inside job—someone who knows how to get in, or someone who has studied how to break in. Staff, friends—all would fall under this,' Mhatre said placidly.

'Mr Pickles was not an aggressive cat,' RK mumbled. 'He never went after my friends.'

'Nonetheless, I need to know the names of all who visited today and in the recent past.' Mhatre was emphatic.

'I will get that for you,' Shashi spoke up.

'Indeed,' Mhatre glanced at him, taking in everything. I had been subject to that trick of his last time, myself. I understood that Mhatre missed very little in the course of doing his job.

'Mr Shashi Sunder, I take it. You called us,' Mhatre said, continuing immediately, without waiting for Shashi to speak. 'How many people actually live here?'

'The staff and a houseguest. Aman Azad,' said Shashi. 'The staff stay in separate quarters and rarely visit, unless needed, because Roop is shooting constantly. Aman is recuperating from an accident and doesn't venture far from the room he's been given. I doubt the cat cared very much about either the staff or Mr Azad.'

'And what about you?' Mhatre asked Shashi. 'Was the cat a bother to you?'

'I don't think my best friend would go after the very creature I considered very, very precious.' RK's voice from the floor where he had been sitting was ominous, guttural. 'I want you to stop this at once!'

I met Parvati's eyes over his head. We both knew Mhatre had been spot-on in asking Shashi about Mr Pickles. We knew there was no love lost there. But perhaps now was not the best time for him to get this information, not with RK so raw and agonized.

Mhatre was astute enough to sense this too, he changed his line of questioning abruptly.

'Where is Mr Azad?' he asked.

'He's with his doctors,' RK replied wearily. 'He'll be home soon.'

'I will be speaking with him, of course,' Mhatre informed RK. 'What I want to know now is—*where were you*? Was it you who found the cat?'

RK looked up, the misery in his eyes reflecting as two shimmering beacons of tears. He nodded acquiescence. 'I was preparing for my role in the study, going over today's lines. Then I heard it.'

'Heard the cat?' Mhatre didn't look at RK, he was busy writing his statement as he spoke.

'No,' choked out RK, the tears now falling freely. Something in his voice made Mhatre look up at him, as we all were doing now, everyone in awful anticipation.

'I heard the screaming first ...'

14

It was late evening by the time Addl CP Mhatre took his leave. By then RK had finished repeating to him all that he had told us the first day regarding the 'hauntings' at Taqdeer. Mhatre now knew that RK was deliberately being frightened on a scale that went beyond a regular prank or a show of bad blood from a disgruntled type. This was intimidation with intent to cause grievous harm—the cat's death had made that absolutely clear.

'Whatever it is … real or a spectre, it has taken Mr Pickles,' RK's voice was gruff in pain as he spoke to the Addl CP.

'This large cut on the animal's belly is very real,' Mhatre said to RK. 'Made by someone who isn't a spirit. I don't believe in ghosts …'

He then made a surprising gesture before he left—he put his hand on the superstar's shoulder, as if to offer succour.

'Neither should you,' was all he said. Then he nodded at us and left.

Whatever that was, and especially surprising too, coming from the dour Mhatre, it seemed to lift RK's dismal mood a little.

'He said he'd be in touch,' RK told us. As Aman hadn't returned, Mhatre would be following up with him when he was available. The policemen with Mhatre had already questioned the help before they left, with no leads.

There was nothing more to be done that day. No weapon had been found near the unfortunate Mr Pickles, and the extra policemen who had been summoned to search the vast premises had gone away empty-handed as well.

'You should get some rest,' Shashi said, his gaze on the spent-looking RK. 'Aman will be here later, of course, but if you wish I can sleep here too, tonight?'

'There is no need,' RK said shortly to Shashi. 'I want to be by myself anyway.'

Shashi had turned away looking anguished and crushed. But he knew better than to cross the already troubled superstar.

'We'll take our leave too,' I had said. 'Call us if you need anything.' We left the pair in the room together. Aman hadn't arrived yet, but it was pointless to wait. Shashi would fill him in, we knew.

On the way back, Parvati was silent and brooding. To break the depressing mood, I tried to converse.

'So there goes any chance of discretion on this. If the police are involved, the press will soon be too,' I said to her.

'Perhaps not,' Parvati looked at me. 'Mhatre is a quiet sort, remember? I think Mr Pickles might be in the papers, but not the other part. Not the scream.'

'It was nice of Mhatre to say he didn't believe in ghosts,' I continued. 'Given that RK is really falling apart.'

'Do you blame him?' Parvati turned her clear eyes on me, eyes filled with a deep sadness today. 'A lady love who wants to sell his home. A home that has turned so scary, it's driving him to destructive drinking. The fiasco on the film set recently with his rival Saddaq. And now, *this*—his beloved pet *murdered*? To kill an innocent, defenceless animal like that—how macabre can evil get?'

'Very, I guess,' I returned her look, a deep despair settling into my bones. It was true what she said. Whatever issues with RK anyone had—why kill the poor animal?

We had heard the eerie scream ourselves, seen no one outside the door. Could this home really be haunted? My pragmatic self refused to allow that theory. *There has to be an explanation*, I thought to myself. For the screaming, for the murder of that little cat …

Not 'little' actually, I mused, deciding silence was best for the rest of this drive. Quite big. And beautiful—majestic, was the word, what with that branded collar and that proud bell …

Something stopped me short.

'Parvati,' I said to her urgently.

She turned to me, expectant.

'The bell,' I said, my voice rising. 'The bell that was attached to his collar always, that bell I had thought was such an indulgence, because it didn't tinkle, it was just there for show …'

'Yes?' she said impatient, waiting for me to come to the point.

'*That bell wasn't there*,' I said. 'He had his collar on still, even with his belly slit like that—*but the bell was missing* …'

'I didn't notice a bell,' Parvati was staring at me with interest. 'But your powers of observation have always been commendable, I know. Do you think, maybe it fell off? Earlier, or during the killing?'

'They would've found it in their search if it had,' my conviction was growing stronger suddenly, a surety I didn't completely understand taking hold of me. 'The police I mean. They searched the entire ground, not just for a murder weapon, but for clues.'

'You think it didn't fall off?' Parvati looked at me.

'It was a branded collar. Expensive, made to last. He wasn't a cat that was scrappy. It wouldn't just fall off in a movement. I think . . .' I said, then stopped short. Why say something that I had no proof of, just a conviction from deep within? *The killer had the bell*, my gut was sure of it.

Parvati understood I didn't want to say any more. She let me leave it at that. I could always count on her to gauge a mood correctly.

'Aman wasn't there,' she changed the topic. 'He hadn't come in at all—his doctor visit took so long?'

Obviously, it had, but what really was there to say? Till we verified it wasn't otherwise, we had to accept each player as being where they claimed they were. Including Alena in the hospital, Samuel plotting her lovers' downfall (where?), Saddaq (whereabouts as yet unknown) and Shashi—supposedly running errands in the far suburbs, but arriving most speedily to commiserate with his friend. How did he get to RK's mansion so soon? Questions we would need to examine later.

In the meanwhile, our true attention was on the crime we had witnessed. An innocent animal had been torturously killed. A beloved pet. The sadness we felt was profound, more so, inexplicably, than if we'd discovered a human so brutally murdered.

And this case had turned, we both knew it, into something far more sinister than disembodied screams in a superstar's home.

It was a shared grief, that day, a grief for the brutalization of innocence. Something, some*one* pure and blameless had been casually done away with, as part of a larger web of evil. We weren't in the mood for more casual conversation, no matter that it was connected to the case. Tonight, all we wanted to do was mourn.

15

The next day dawned grey and overcast, as it had a few days ago. Coincidentally, we were due for a visit to RK's movie set once again, similar to our last visit under cloudy skies. RK had decided to throw himself heart and soul into his movie, so as to dull the immense sense of loss he felt, whilst at home.

He told Parvati this the night before, in a heart-breaking call, one that she had made, to check up on him when we returned to the office. She realized that no matter how he felt, and no matter that Alena was still recovering from her battering in hospital—the show would go on.

RK was to shoot his scenes on the morrow, without Alena. And Parvati and I, we decided to be there too, not just as a show of support to RK, but to be around in case he remembered something he might have missed in the immediate trauma of his cat's murder. Also, we could have a longer conversation with Shashi, though so far, he had had nothing of significance to tell us.

It was a mystifying business, this conundrum RK had led us into. Given his reaction to the screaming at his home—it was unclear why the cat had been killed. If the objective had been to terrify him, he was already uneasy, even before Mr Pickle's death. Why take a life in the process?

And why the cat's life? How was Mr Pickles connected to the screaming in RK's home? They seemed linked, both occurrences—it would be naive to think of both as separate, though we were keeping open minds. So many questions, and we had no answers yet to any of them.

The set we went to was the same as the previous time—because of what had happened with Alena, they could not finish the scene. So, they had decided against dismantling it. Now RK's parts were to be shot in that location, he had informed us. We got there around noon, and made our way to RK's vanity van. We didn't need the junior production in-charge to show us the way this time.

RK was sitting morosely on a chair waiting for his make-up to begin when we entered. His face, unlike the previous time, showed his feelings. His chameleon tricks had deserted him clearly. And the grief was unmistakable.

He got up and spontaneously hugged me and Parvati as we entered. We were a bit taken aback, but we understood his need to reach out for support in this difficult time.

'I'm not doing so well,' was all he said. We nodded, acutely sympathetic. The make-up man entered, and we decided to let RK get ready in peace.

'We'll find you after,' Parvati promised. We needed to locate Shashi. Before sitting for make-up, RK had confirmed he was on set.

We got down from RK's van and strolled the short distance to the set. The carnival-themed set looked the same, it had to be, for continuity. The Harlequin clown extras were sitting around eating an early lunch before their dance sequence shot.

I noticed among the Harlequins, the guest-appearance dancer who was the celebrity—the sportsman who had called out to Jehaan the other day. He was the more animated among the rest, laughing loudly, cracking jokes. He seemed to enjoy being here, there was a relaxedness about him, missing from the others.

'Maybe because he's not doing this for a living, he can afford to fool around,' I thought to myself. 'The rest have to work hard, this is their bread and butter. He, meanwhile, is here in his "celebrity sports star guest appearance" capacity.'

We strolled further along the set.

'Akruti,' a familiar voice called out. I turned, pleasantly surprised at being directly addressed, unlike earlier meetings, when sarcastic comments preceded every conversation. I had recognized Shashi's voice, before I saw him.

He emerged from behind a set lamp post, and today there was no trace of hostility on him. All he did was look apprehensive, deep hollows under his eyes, as if he'd not slept.

'He's not eaten,' he confided softly, showing us a state of despair similar to his friend. 'Roop. I'm worried about him.'

'Give him time,' Parvati spoke softly. 'He's just lost a beloved member of what he considers his family.'

'But he needs his energy,' Shashi spoke up. 'He needs to give a 100 per cent. If he doesn't get his shot right, we could be here all night. He needs energy to do it right.'

It was good we had found Shashi, or rather, he had found us—we could talk to him as we'd planned to, see if he said anything that could shed further light on our investigation.

The Harlequins were preparing to rehearse again as we spoke. They were forming their groups—the choreographer had materialized. Jehaan's sports star was in the centre of the group—the token celebrity 'special appearance' in this song, no doubt.

The dancers were stretching, preparing to perform. The sports star broke from the centre for a bit, went to the far side of the set, where the manmade carnival met the actual line of natural greenery around. A form stepped out from behind a tree. They were not so far away that we couldn't see the features of the new entrant. That oiliness was unmistakable to me, even at this distance.

'What's Samuel Rodrigues doing here?' I asked aghast. 'This is a closed set!' Parvati, her lips set, was hurrying to them, but Shashi beat her to it, racing forward angrily.

'What do you think you're doing here,' he almost screamed, roughly catching Samuel's collar as he reached him. Unfazed, Samuel slid out of his grasp and tidied his shirt.

'Why, I'm here as a guest of our celebrity,' he smirked, dusting down the part of his collar Shashi had grasped. 'Don't you know I'm allowed?'

I realized with a sinking feeling that Samuel was right. It may be a closed set, but guests of actors were most certainly entertained. That was how we were here today, and earlier. That was how Jehaan had been here the last time, guest of the same celebrity sports star who had invited Samuel today.

'He's a guest of mine,' the Harlequin celebrity addressed Shashi, without a hint of aggression in his manner, but firm of voice, as if telling him to back down.

'We'll see about that.' Shashi stepped away grimly, and almost ran towards RK's van.

'Hello Akrutiji,' the oily Samuel meanwhile had turned his attention to me. 'We meet again.'

'Yes, it's unexpected,' I agreed, as I stared at him, unsmiling.

'Why are you here?' Parvati spoke up, her tone curt. Her face was expressionless as she looked at Samuel.

'Hello, Mees Parvati,' Samuel turned his face to acknowledge her. 'Why can't I be?'

Parvati didn't answer; she simply waited, as if for him to continue.

'I came to meet my friend,' Samuel smirked at her, pointing to the sports star.

Then he noted how unsmiling Parvati's face was and her stony look. He decided to say more, perhaps in an effort to pique her interest.

'Alena and RK,' Samuel hissed, his face taking on a hard expression. 'And I heard Saddaq too, earlier ... all at one location! What could be sweeter? You know?'

There was nothing pleasant about the way he uttered those lines. But we now understood who his person on the inside here might have been. There was no junior spot boy as Samuel had led us to believe, when we met him. He had been cunning, leading us on, making us believe he was spilling vital news while actually playing us, imparting wrong information.

His mole on this closed movie set was the Harlequin celebrity sports star—it couldn't be clearer. The token guy on the inside, doing a song in this movie for laughs and a celebrity bonus. Possibly not taking anything or anyone too seriously while inviting friends and acquaintances over to see him perform on set.

That's why he had asked Jehaan over, no doubt, as a sports star inviting a senior sports journalist contact to a performance outside of his sport, perhaps in the hope of publicizing this special appearance.

A careless, if confident creature, this celebrity sports star, possibly never expecting that those he spoke to about this movie, like Samuel, might take some of his confidences very seriously indeed. With perhaps even more serious consequences.

'Have you visited here before?' Parvati asked Samuel pleasantly. But I knew she was listening to his answer very carefully.

'Wouldn't you like to know?' Samuel's face turned shrewd in his reply. 'How would it help you, though?'

'Did you meet Alena here earlier?' Parvati asked, ignoring his counter-question.

At her second question, Samuel's face turned dark—he looked as if he would like to strike Parvati.

'Don't talk to me about meeting my wife,' he rasped, his tone high-pitched. 'You do not get to decide when and if I should see her.'

'Relax,' the sports star, who was hanging a little away, so as not to appear intrusive, had stepped up once again, his eyes inquisitive. 'Relax, Samuel.'

'Why don't you carry on with your business,' the sports star turned, addressing Parvati now, with the high-handed loftiness of a minor celebrity. 'Me and my pal will carry on with ours ...'

Parvati opened her mouth to answer, her eyes glinting dangerously, though her manner was controlled and calm. But before she could say anything, a shrill scream rent the air.

'Help!' we heard. Then, even as we dashed instinctively towards the source of that shout, again, louder, a second time, the deeply panicked cry: *'Please help!'*

16

We were unprepared for what came next. Who, if anyone, is ever prepared for *murder*? But let me describe our initial discovery.

Following the source of that shout, we found ourselves in the greenery just a little behind the carnival set. It was a clever bit of outpost, a small hilly mound jutting out on the flat land. The victim was found behind its mass. Clever, because just a step this way or that, the victim or anyone there would be in plain sight of all on the carnival set. But behind it—everything stayed perfectly hidden. As we approached the lady who had continued to shout for help, all of us running hard, we saw the victim.

The lady who was shouting was a dancer from the song. She stood as if turned to stone, her Harlequin mask off, her face terrified. Next to her, a human body lay on its side, inert. It appeared collapsed at an odd angle, as if after a struggle. A red dupatta, wound closely, snaked around its neck. When I first took in the form, my heart almost stopped.

Shashi, who had dashed up at the sound of the shouting to join us without having reached RK's van, let out a convulsed sound, as if mortally wounded. He had to be steadied by Parvati's hand or he would have fallen right there.

'*Roop* ...?' Shashi whispered, almost inaudible, as he inched forward, afraid to confirm his desperate fear, we could see. The form was dressed in the costume RK had been wearing for his shot that afternoon—blue shirt and jeans.

Parvati and I, we were, for a moment, forced to confront that wild fear, the fear that the superstar who had beseeched us for help had been felled, at a faux carnival on his own movie set. But that day, we stood corrected.

'Oh, thank God, thank God,' Shashi cried brokenly, as he reached the body, his words incongruous, given that we were witnessing a death. But we knew why he was crying—his relief, despite appearances, at the fact that the victim on the floor was not his friend. For though it looked exactly like him from a distance, it was not RK who lay immobile on that ground that day.

'That's Mohan, Mr Kamal's stunt double,' the Harlequin sports star who had rushed to the spot with us spoke up, his tone disbelieving. 'He's been ... strangled?'

The production team had also run up moments after. They confirmed that the body on the ground was Mohan Tawade, the man who filled in for RK in dangerous action scenes. The red dupatta wound so tightly around his neck—that might indeed have been used to strangle him. Near him, his shades had fallen, the glass cracked in one eye.

'What were you doing here?' Parvati asked the dancer lady who was sobbing now, her panic at the discovery having resulted in a large audience from the set running over.

'I was going to the ladies' bathroom,' the woman choked out, between sobs. 'It's over there.'

She pointed to a small outhouse just a little after the hillock on the green. The only access from the place where the

Harlequins were rehearsing, to the restroom, or bathroom as she called it, was past that hillock outcrop.

'I saw the red dupatta trailing from behind that,' she sniffled, pointing to the hilly mound. 'So, I went to pick it up, thinking someone from costumes had dropped it and left it behind. Imagine my horror when I saw it was wrapped around Mohan's neck tight, and he wasn't moving or breathing!'

'What did you do then?' Parvati asked quietly.

'I bent down immediately, tried to unravel it from his neck. He wouldn't respond to my calling, and his body felt cold to touch. I knew something terrible had happened. I began shouting for help,' the lady replied tearfully.

As soon as we realized the body had not been RK's, Shashi had left the hillock, running to the vanity van so he may be near the superstar. He did not wait to hear the lady, his priority was only RK.

The police had been called. They would arrive in a while, given the set's out-of-the-way location. And a doctor, to confirm the death.

'Where's Samuel?' Parvati asked suddenly, as the lady paused for breath. We looked around. But apart from all those supposed to be on the set—production in-charges, dancers, various costume aides and the main crew—there was no sign of our unsavoury guest.

The celebrity sports star, still hanging around, shrugged when asked, this time by me. 'Where's your friend?' I quizzed him.

'I don't know,' was the answer—then he showed anger. 'There's a murder on the set and you're worried about my friend's whereabouts?'

Parvati nudged me to stop questioning him. There would be time enough for that later. And the police would soon be here, asking questions too.

'Let's find Mr Kamal,' she said.

We both walked the distance to his van, to find it surrounded by his security personnel. They may have been present earlier too, but we never noticed them, and he had never mentioned them. But they were here now, all around his van.

'Parvati and Akruti, Private Investigators. He's expecting us,' Parvati said firmly, when one of them barred the door to the van.

'Yes all right, let them through,' another said. Clearly, word had been left about our expected presence.

We stepped inside his van to a flurry of activity. RK was surrounded by the powers-that-be of the main crew, explaining what had happened outside.

Shashi stood a little bit away, watching hawk-like, to see if RK was being able to handle all that was coming at him by way of such forceful animation.

'He's already been through Mr Pickles' murder,' I said to Parvati. 'And now this? Not even a day later?'

'I know,' Parvati's eyes were serious as she observed RK's face take in all the information being discussed. 'It's a lot to handle. And all this, on top of the initial screaming at his home.'

'I want to speak to these people,' RK, wild-eyed, voiced suddenly to the cacophony around him, gesturing towards Parvati and I.

Shashi began escorting the body of crew members out of RK's van immediately. They knew better than to linger when the superstar had expressed a desire to be left alone with the investigators.

'Tell me,' said RK, not waiting for the door to close, even as the last crew member took his leave. 'What is to be done?' His voice seemed to crack, as if he was under tremendous pressure, now rendered almost unendurable.

'Samuel Rodrigues, Alena's husband was here,' I told him sombrely. Despite all that RK was going through, I believed it was important he knew this. 'And now he's disappeared. We don't know if he's visited the set before. We need to let the police know.'

'Roop, I thought it was *you* ...' Shashi choked out, interrupting the conversation flow, clearly having not had a moment to address RK privately earlier. '*I thought you were dead* ...'

'Mohan does resemble me,' RK said to Shashi, wearily. 'But he's *not* me.'

Then he looked up at Parvati, his eyes haunted. 'What do you make of this?' he asked.

Parvati turned to look straight at RK, so he would realize how serious she was.

'Mr Kamal,' she said, 'You have been hearing screams at home for close to a month. Your pet was murdered yesterday. Today a stuntman on your set was murdered, strangled in all probability. The one constant factor around which all these bizarre and terrifying occurrences revolve—*you*.'

'What are you implying?' RK leaned forward, his eyes locked on Parvati's.

But I already knew where she was going with this. The murdered man was not RK, as he had so obviously pointed out. But Mohan had most probably been strangled from behind, given his body's awkward angle. He was dressed in RK's clothes. I had seen broken glares lying next to his body. If he had been wearing them, his features would have appeared disguised to an outsider. He may not have been RK. But suppose the killer, not knowing otherwise, had strangled Mohan—*believing he was RK*?

17

The situation could not be hushed up, of course. The cat's murder and the stuntman's strangulation (the police confirmed it) almost immediately after, was what dominated the news in the city that week and the next. In the 1990s, the multiple news channels we have today did not exist as yet. But the print journalists were having a field day. And the afternoon tabloids were spicing up the story considerably.

A superstar's life in possible danger on a movie set—a ghostly movie at that. And two eerie murders … it was a made-for-print scandal, a story that no paper wanted to miss. And the publicity served to make our job more difficult because the attention affected RK terribly.

That day on the set, he had understood Parvati's point of view. He realized, as did Shashi, listening in, that the fatal strangulation which had taken his stunt double's life may well have been meant for him. He understood that Mr Pickles' heinous death and this murder might be related—and it could be to either do away with him or to get him to succumb to pressure.

But pressure for *what*? This was unclear to us all. RK was the common link, of that there was no doubt. Added to this, the bizarre screaming in his home, and we had a series of absolutely inexplicable occurrences with him at the epicentre and no clarity on why they happened, or if they might reoccur.

The only thing we were certain of now was that this investigation had gone way beyond what we had initially started with, which was really very little. Now, we were looking into ... *murder.*

The police had arrived later on set that day, led by the dour Addl CP Mhatre, and they had got to work straight away. Mohan's body had been taken for a post-mortem, while the rest of us on set were quizzed till late hours. But apart from confirming the strangulation, there was little to go on, even for them. No one had seen or heard anything before the body was discovered.

'This is no haunting,' Mhatre had stressed to RK, as he took his leave post questioning him on set. 'A murder is a real and present danger. Of *this* world alone.'

Mhatre's comments, indeed his show of sympathy towards the superstar's state of mind—the second time he had shown tacit support for RK, by stressing again that this was no haunting—was most out-of-character.

But it was clear that RK was in a fragile state of mind given all that had occurred. He would certainly need every reassurance he could get. Maybe the dour Mhatre, under that sullen exterior, hid an empathetic persona? He had picked up on RK's strange vulnerability, at odds with the power his superstardom conveyed, just as I had. And he had tried to offer succour in his own gruff way. There was little else he could do.

Because at this point, it was a puzzling, convoluted case. What was the motive for all that had happened? Did it involve some conspiracy by those around RK? Was Shashi involved?

Was Alena? Or Saddaq? Was it the RK fanboy Aman? Or then the unsavoury Samuel who had threatened revenge on RK in our presence, and been on the set the day of the murder, then disappeared? And most puzzlingly, *why?*

It was a confounding time, and Parvati and I, as investigators, were both worried and at a loss. No doubt that Addl CP Mhatre was in the same boat, with the press and RK's fans demanding answers when there seemed to be none.

Production on the movie had been halted, the set declared a crime scene and there was no apparent end in sight till the police conducted a thorough investigation into the stuntman's murder.

There were already rumours that this film was cursed, being a ghost movie in the first place. Romantic musicals were formulaic enough in the 1990s but the prominent supernatural thriller angle to this one had fed into the public imagination such that it took centre stage. Bollywood loved its superstitions and clung to them dearly, and these occurrences had upped the superstitious quotient to the max. It was a media circus, and everyone professionally dependant on the film was adversely affected by the hoopla.

RK was told to stay at home by his producers, keep a low profile till the furore died down. This made him even more restless and edgy than he had appeared earlier, because he was forced into being at the mercy of those unpredictable and nerve-wracking screams at home. Professionally, he was known to do just one movie at a time, giving his all to it, so there was no question of another film intervening as necessary distraction.

And because he had been advised to lay low, he could not travel to the hospital to meet Alena, who was slowly on the mend, ten days or so after her encounter with Saddaq. The good part about her being away from the set on the day the stuntman was murdered was that the press had no idea she was in hospital.

They hadn't singled out her absence on the set, nor pursued it as being out of the ordinary, given that all actors need not be on set all the time—they are mostly required only when their parts are being filmed. Regardless, her hospital admittance had not come out in the open, and the powers-that-be around the movie, and around Saddaq, wanted it kept that way.

'I cannot visit her,' RK confided brokenly to Parvati on one of his numerous phone calls to us, just after the stuntman's death. 'The press interest is too high, they might track me and find out about her being in hospital, which won't do at all. But I really need to know how she is—first hand, from someone I trust. I don't want to send Shashi, he doesn't like her. And Aman's leg is acting up, he's in pain he says. I've not seen him at all, he's either resting or sleeping. Do you think you can go see her for me? She really showed a lot of interest in the two of you—maybe you both could cheer her up?'

Parvati agreed to his request. We needed movement on this case and speaking to Alena would help us in this regard. The fact that RK had sent us might help lower her guard; maybe she would tell us things she would not normally have, in a more formal space.

Parvati and I travelled to meet Alena together.

'We didn't get to speak to Shashi again on set as we'd planned, before Mohan's body was found,' I told Parvati in the car on the way to Alena's hospital. 'But the entire case became even more sinister that day, so we need to look at it afresh now.'

'Agreed,' Parvati, who was driving, concurred. 'Death is always serious business. Your instinct was right. This case is most certainly about more than just screams ...'

'*Things are not always as they appear to be?*' I quoted her earlier phrase, the one fast becoming a hallmark for this entire case.

Parvati gave me an exasperated half-grin, then her expression turned contemplative. 'Shashi seemed genuinely relieved that the body was not Mr Kamal's. That kind of emotion cannot be faked, Aku.'

'Are you saying we don't look at him as a suspect?' I asked.

'No, I'm saying we need to keep that in mind about his character,' Parvati was being her maddeningly cryptic self, but there was no time to quiz her further—we had arrived.

The city hospital Alena was housed at was state-of-the-art, and her room swanky. She was on a private floor, as befits a star of her stature. When we walked into the room, the blinds were drawn tight. We could barely make out her diminutive form on the bed.

'Alena,' Parvati spoke hesitantly, having requested her aides and suchlike from her entourage to step outside for the duration of our visit. We weren't sure if the star was sleeping.

But Alena wasn't asleep, just very subdued. She winced when Parvati determinedly drew apart a bit of the blinds, allowing for some sunshine in the room, which smelt dark and medicinal, not exactly a recipe for positivity, to begin with.

'Why are you here?' she asked warily, squinting at us both, as her eyes adjusted to the sunlight. 'I'm not going to talk about Saddaq if that's what you're here for. I don't want to discuss what happened that day.'

'We're not here to talk about Saddaq,' I reassured her, as I handed her the roses we had picked up en route. 'These are from RK. He told us to deliver them personally.'

'He's such a romantic.' Her expression brightened dramatically as she reached for the flowers. 'Roop sends me a bouquet day and night, the hospital doesn't know where to keep them! I've sent so many to the children's wing, it makes them happy!'

I studied her delicate features. The bruises were healing, the purple welts around her face and throat fading, ten days or so into recovery. But it could've been vastly different if we hadn't got to her when we did.

'Alena,' Parvati said softly. 'You're looking better. Mr Kamal will be happy to know this, because he isn't doing so well ...'

We had thought we would need to nudge her into speaking, but she burst forth in tremulous sentences, as if she had needed to tell us. Her voice was hoarse from the injury to her throat, but the words still flowed.

'Samuel—you need to protect him from Samuel!' she said.

We already knew Samuel had no love lost for RK, we learnt it directly through him when we'd met. But Alena's anxiety-stricken state told us there might be more to it, information she might be privy to.

This was the opening we had needed, the possible lead we had come for. We were near her in a trice, bending low so we could hear her strangulated whispers.

'Why Samuel? What is he going to do?' Parvati asked, her gaze intent, fixed on Alena.

'I don't know.' Alena's eyes filled with tears, her expression crumpled. '*I don't know.*'

'Alena,' Parvati said firmly, sitting at the foot of her bed and taking Alena's hand in her own as she spoke. 'Alena, you need to help us with whatever you know. Mr Pickles is dead, and Mohan Tawade, Mr Kamal's stuntman as well. You knew them both, you are a part of Mr Kamal's work and his life. Both these incidents might seem unrelated, but it could be that they are not. Do you understand what I'm telling you?'

'You're saying Roop is involved, that there is someone after him.' Alena breathed slowly. She let her hand rest in Parvati's for a bit. Then she defensively pulled it away and sat up, her face set. 'I told you,' she forced out, her eyes obstinate. 'I don't know what Samuel will do.'

'How do you know he'll do something at all?' I asked her, curious now.

'He told me,' she said simply, her big dark eyes now on me. 'He visited.'

'He came *here*?' I was incredulous. 'Alena, he's spoken to the press once already, exposed your marriage through them first. What would stop him from going to them and telling them about you in hospital? About Saddaq beating you up, this fact which you're so anxious to hide for God knows what reason!'

Alena sat up straighter and her face became set into a stubborn mask. *How odd*, I thought, watching her. How a lovely face can transform in one second.

'He won't,' she said emphatically, even though her voice was hoarse. 'I know he won't.'

'Why do you say that, Alena?' Parvati addressed her, her gaze steady.

'*Because he told me so!*' Alena said, her voice trembling, unconvinced even though her expression didn't change.

'Alena,' said Parvati, gently, intently, as she faced the star squarely, 'Alena, are you *afraid* of Samuel Rodrigues?'

The set mask crumpled. Alena's eyes swam once more in tears. 'I don't know what to do,' she whispered. 'He came up, saying he was my husband, I was asleep, they allowed him in. He just won't stop stalking me. He says I *belong* to him. By law even. *He* must decide what is in my best interests. *He* needs to be the one in charge ...'

The hysteria rose in her voice, even though she could barely form the words.

'He says if I don't accept his terms—*he'll kill Roop* ...!'

18

Was Alena telling us the truth? Was she really as scared of her husband as she claimed to be, and scared of him doing something terrible to RK? Or was that display a marvellous piece of acting from India's leading acting talent? That was the debate on our minds when we left the hospital that night, after having spoken to Alena.

'Do you actually think she's frightened of him?' I asked Parvati in the car as we left the premises. 'Or do you think there's more to it?'

'More as in, is she in cahoots with her greedy husband and eyeing Mr Kamal's vast wealth?' Parvati looked at me for a moment before focusing once more on the road, as she drove.

'From Samuel, we know she's been giving him money when he asks,' she mused. 'Also pleading for a divorce at the same time. But always amicably, it seems—he didn't mention otherwise ...'

I nodded.

'Difficult to tell at this point,' Parvati mused. 'Her behaviour is confusing. Even the fact that she believes Samuel will not expose her hospital stay, despite having gone to the press to expose their marriage earlier. Perhaps she believes its worth his while to stay silent, so he can extract funds from her without conflict. Or then, of course, she is working alongside him. Regardless, whatever their equation, both Samuel and Alena could not have factored in the Saddaq beating for sure. Also, if she is in cahoots with Samuel, that performance she gave us today was an inspired piece of acting ...'

'So, it may well be that she is telling the truth?' I asked. Parvati didn't reply, so I didn't push the point.

'What do we tell RK?' I asked instead. My sympathy for the superstar was growing in leaps and bounds. This brawny, chiselled man, muscled and bulky, never appeared more unsettled and vulnerable to me than now. His world was coming apart. And he was unravelling with it.

It occurred to me how vastly the general perception of someone, even a superstar, differed from reality. RK appeared to be at the peak of his career, it was natural to assume he would be surrounded by fawning fans, movie moguls, directors and the like begging an audience for a film story narration or then just general lackeys running to fulfil his needs, even whilst not on set. The truth couldn't be more starkly different.

RK, famed for complete attention to just one project at a time, was living an isolated existence, at least at his home. There were no fans in his immediate surroundings, the security at his gate and Shashi's obsessive attention to RK's need for privacy took care of that. No family had visited him for a couple of years, by his own admission to Mhatre. And his schedules were so erratic, driven by his complete immersion in his movie projects, that he lived a spartan existence by choice.

Oddly enough, his present movie project too, was being shot on a closed set, no doubt mitigating the number of hangers-on, fans and assorted aides around him, at least whilst on the sets of this movie.

In fact, no lackeys and the like waited on him hand and foot at home either, we had witnessed this for ourselves at his mansion, when we visited. His house help actually appeared to be trained to be as unobtrusive as possible, even quartered in a separate section of Taqdeer altogether.

The ever-protective Shashi vetted his future film narrations, it seemed, and strove to make sure such distractions were few and far between, whilst in the middle of a big-budget filming. All this combined, and you had a superstar living in an ivory tower, only interacting with Shashi or a chosen few, like his fairly recent romantic interest, Alena, or then us, or then his adored pet earlier, or his houseguest sporadically, but otherwise, removed from larger company so as to focus completely on his craft.

Regardless of the eternal entourage—fans, hangers-on, his movie production juniors, aides etc.—that manifested around him professionally, whilst generally filming or travelling, his private life was spartan, shielded. To me, it seemed therefore quite evident that his minimal meaningful social interactions meant his psychological vulnerability lay utterly bare, ripe for any lurking evil to prey on. I snapped out of my thoughts, to hear Parvati answering my question.

'We tell him what Alena said, naturally,' Parvati replied. 'It's not like they don't talk on the phone, Aku. She might've already told him what transpired by now, for all you know!'

I nodded. The case was looking difficult and I couldn't get a fix on any one lead. So many suspects regarding the suspicious scream at his home—Shashi, Alena, Aman, Samuel, Saddaq—how to catch a break in solving this as it became deeper and more dangerous, with murder as the watchword now? Each time we spoke to someone, a new twist was thrown up.

'Don't despair,' Parvati caught my expression as we drove. 'Something will give. It often does. We have to be alert and see it for what it is, when it does.'

'And till then?' I asked, morose.

'We work for it!' Parvati said. 'Go over everything. Keep at it. Let's go back to where it all began. Let's visit Mr Kamal at his home again. We should be able to interview Aman there as well—I had requested it earlier.'

I looked at Parvati. Her doggedness was what kept my spirits up when cases hit a stalemate, and today was no different. What she suggested was the obvious thing to do, and the picture instantly cleared when she said it.

'Yes,' I told her, brightening up a little bit at the prospect of seeing Aman again. 'Let's go to RK's house.'

The next day found us at RK's home following our decision the previous night. He was housebound and restless, pacing like a caged animal when we met him. Again, as before, he was in his dressing gown, but thankfully there was no liquor in his hand this time.

'I'm not drinking,' he said moodily, the moment he set eyes on us, and noticed mine travelling to his empty hands. 'All this is beyond opiates. I need my head clear.'

This time as well as the last, RK was already in his study when we got there, unlike the first time we had met him, the time when we had been kept waiting for over an hour. I wondered if he'd taken to living in his study, which was easier to access than his bedroom, given the terrifying noises in his home. Also, the minibar was well stocked in the study. Today though, he seemed sober if terribly sad.

'I'm glad to see that,' Parvati addressed him sombrely. 'How are you doing?'

'What do you think?' he met her eye. RK had seen better days, that much was clear. Dark circles, red eyes and dishevelled appearance—his dressing-gowned look and rumpled hair completed the picture of sadness. But could we really expect more, given he'd lost his beloved pet, his paramour was in hospital, his movie at a standstill, his stunt-double murdered, his fans up in arms, and his home under attack by some supposed malevolent energy?

'I think you need to be cheered up,' a voice said from the far end. We turned to see Aman Azad's tall figure limping into the room. Despite the leg acting up as RK had mentioned to us earlier, Aman wore a welcoming smile on his face.

'It's nice to see you two again,' he said, nodding at us both before walking over to RK and giving him a firm, long hug. RK looked brighter for it, we saw that. Aman had a way of conveying optimism by sheer presence alone. I had noticed this when we met the first time. 'I was told you'd like to speak with me today.'

I wondered how much he knew of all that had been going on since we last saw him. We hadn't bumped into him again since the day we had been introduced—when the sad business of Mr Pickles' death transpired, RK had mentioned Aman being at his check-up, he had not arrived till after we'd left that night.

And clearly, looking at the way RK had hugged him now, as if greeting him after long, he and his houseguest weren't really meeting much, though living under the same roof.

'We came to see how Mr Kamal is holding up,' Parvati told Aman politely. 'And to ask if you could shed any light on these strange events.'

'Well, I came to see how he's holding up, myself.' Aman turned to her. 'I haven't really been around much. My leg took a turn for the worse—the weather sometimes does that, my bones hurt more when it rains—and I've been confined to bed rest, more or less, these past days.'

'Aman came in very late the day Mr Pickles was killed,' RK informed us moodily. 'He couldn't really sit with me, though he wanted to—he had to go up and rest, on doctor's orders. Even though I was so shattered that day, I didn't expect him to. I want him to get better, *that* is most important.'

RK's generosity shone through at this speech, it wasn't missed on anyone. Despite going through such a rough patch, he was looking out for his protégé of sorts, making sure he was okay.

'Maybe we can all feel better if I fix a good cup of coffee for everyone on this gloomy day,' Aman said, smiling at his mentor warmly after his declaration. 'I've become an expert at it. RK keeps some wonderful coffee from all over the world, and a brewing machine here!' He pointed to a little alcove in the massive study, a little ahead of the minibar. 'We can talk after.'

'This study is truly remarkable, it has everything including books!' I said, following Aman to the alcove. 'I'll help you fix the coffee.'

It would give me an opportunity to observe Aman in his comfort zone, maybe he would feel more at ease and reveal something we didn't know. Also, I quite enjoyed being around his magnetism.

In the alcove, which was so wide it was almost a private room, without a door of course, we found the ledge holding everything that coffee lovers would covet. Aman seemed familiar with the layout and he moved naturally around the place. I busied myself finding and counting the coffee cups.

'Have you made much headway?' Aman asked as he fiddled with the brewing machine. 'I heard about the death on RK's set, he mentioned an extra being killed. And right on the heels of his cat too. RK is beside himself.'

'We're trying,' I said, unwilling to admit the stalemate. 'It's early days, a work in progress.'

'What about the screams in this house?' Aman continued. 'Any clues?'

'Tell me,' I faced him, struck by a thought. Given he had spent so much time at home since his return from the Bali vacation, I wanted to see if he had experienced anything himself. 'Did you hear anything?'

Aman met my eyes, his striking light ones catching the meagre sunlight in the dim alcove. 'Since my return, I've been at the doctors or the physiotherapists, quite frankly,' he said. 'And asleep, on painkillers, whilst at home. It's also possible the soundproofing in the middle rooms downstairs might extend to where I sleep.'

Clearly, he was reluctant to say RK was the only one who'd heard the scream in this house. But the way he was putting it, he was saying it, without saying it.

You don't know we've heard it too, I thought to myself. You think your mentor is losing the plot.

'I know you've said your leg's been worse, you've been out of sorts, on painkillers,' I said to Aman. 'But do you have any idea of what's happening in RK's world right now? After the murders?'

'I know the movie is on standby,' Aman said to me, deftly pouring the coffee into the mugs as he spoke. 'After someone was found killed on the sets. I don't know names or dates, forgive me, I haven't been following the news or reading papers at all. I've been in so much pain, I've only been resting. All I know is RK is home after an extra was killed and his cat is also dead.'

His body gave an involuntary shudder as though overcome with emotion for RK's loss.

'Well, RK seems happier whenever you make an appearance,' I said, to uplift the strained ambience that had crept in now. 'And he's restless here. Maybe when you feel better, you can try and spend more time with him, now that he's free and at home?'

'Yes, I'll do that,' Aman said lightly, as he swung the cups onto a tray, a sudden movement despite his hurt leg, as if to shake the previous mood off. 'Whatever you say, lovely Ms Akruti!' He limped back into the study, holding the tray up high, as if showing such a flourish of goodwill would help dispel all the demons lurking in the aftermath of all that had happened.

As he passed me, I smiled at the compliment. But I was well aware that Aman Azad had avoided any kind of real or deep conversation with me. He had been charming—but elusive in an unobtrusive, subtle way.

Aman was an enigma of sorts, I decided. Suave in a city-slicker way, despite having lived in a small town. Charismatic, with an open ease of manner and knowing how to use that to his advantage. And yet, for all that appeal, somehow—*hidden*?

'I need to find out some more about you,' I said to myself as I followed him out to the waiting RK, who had been briefed on our Alena visit by Parvati, outside. 'Your presence and life here may seem an open book. But I need to see if there is anything you aren't telling us.'

19

'Do you think Aman is a strong possibility as a suspect?' I quizzed Parvati that evening, after our visit to RK's home. The day itself hadn't yielded much. RK was low and gloomy for the most part, Aman a tad reserved in our presence, though his casual charm was still on display throughout our visit.

'He is so guarded with us, despite his charm,' I added, to help Parvati get a better sense of what I was thinking.

'At this point, we cannot rule anyone out, as you already know, Aku.' Parvati had turned her clear brown eyes to me to emphasize the same.

'Yes, I do,' I said to her. 'I just have this feeling that we ought to know more about Aman. But we don't, or for that matter, can't, because he doesn't allow us in. Am I making any sense?'

We were sitting in our office, using the soft board up on the wall as a chart detailing our progress so far. But there were no obvious leads, or any one person who was perhaps more inclined to have had a stake in frightening RK, or in the murders that followed one after another.

'You are quite right to feel so, Aku,' Parvati mused. 'Aman lives with Mr Kamal. Yet, he is somehow absent in all that has happened so far. Which makes me wonder as well—is there something we're missing when it concerns him?'

'Or, when it concerns Alena,' I concurred. 'Post our visit, we still don't know if she's for real about loving RK or a brilliant actor in cahoots with her husband to scare our superstar!'

'When I told Mr Kamal what she said about Samuel threatening to kill him if she didn't accept his terms, he wasn't surprised,' Parvati said. 'He believes what Alena says, heart over mind.'

'So, what was his reaction? What did he propose Alena do?' I asked interestedly. 'Bend to Samuel's wiles? Hand over her finances and all monetary control to Samuel as he wishes?'

'I think you know the answer to that.' Parvati glanced at me, amused at my interest. 'I think Mr Kamal will brave out Samuel's threats, rather than let Alena go back to her husband.'

'I think there's a lot missing from backgrounds on each of our players, not just Aman or Alena,' Parvati continued, her tone now sombre. 'We know precious little about Saddaq especially. Nothing at all in fact, other than what's in the public domain. We still need to talk to him.'

As she spoke, I looked up from the newspaper that was lying on my desk, the one my eyes were idly skimming over.

'Parvati,' I said, equally sombrely. 'Look what's boxed into this column, in all the news about the murdered extra.'

The news items on RK's halted movie and the mysterious death had continued with monotonous regularity for the better part of the week in the print media. We had come to almost ignore such items, they were so lurid and tended so brazenly towards sensationalist viewpoints. But in doing so, today, we had almost missed a news item of rather startling relevance to our case.

'It says RK is in trouble because he may have tampered with heritage property,' I read. 'His home falls under heritage property guidelines, he cannot change the structure unless permissions are taken, which apparently he didn't do. Heritage conservationists are preparing to fight a case. And it says he might have paid the powers-that-be a tidy sum of money to look the other way whilst he was doing up his mansion a few months ago …'

'That's interesting,' Parvati said softly, taking the paper from me to skim over the item herself. 'It projects him as someone not entirely innocent …'

'How bizarre it would be if it were RK who was making all this business up, about the screaming at his home to divert the attention of the conservationists from the actual point of interest—his role in restructuring heritage property!' I voiced my thoughts immediately as they struck me.

'That *is* an idea.' Parvati looked at me appraisingly. 'It's happened before—the complainant, thinking himself ultra-clever, is actually the mastermind.'

'But,' she continued, her eyes narrowed in concentration. 'It doesn't explain how *we* heard the scream too, at his home that day. Unless there's an accomplice involved as well? Also, even if Mr Kamal is the greatest actor on the planet and managed to convince us that he is as disturbed as he appears to be when actually he is not—it doesn't explain why he kept the screams hushed up. If the motive was to get at the conservationists, he would've shouted the bizarre happenings at his home from the rooftops, a while ago.'

'Also,' I said, agreeing with Parvati. 'It doesn't explain *murder.*'

'Absolutely,' Parvati concurred. 'Even if the extra was dispensable to Mr Kamal, it would take a very stoic person to kill his own beloved pet to prove a point.'

'Or then, it would take a psycho,' I added. 'We all know the pressure under which Bollywood superstars operate. Maybe RK actually cracked, became—*not* normal?'

Parvati looked at me carefully. 'Do you believe Mr Kamal ought to be included in the roster of suspects in this case? Even whilst he is our client?'

'You told me yourself,' I said to her. 'We cannot rule anyone out. Therefore—*everyone's* a suspect in the murder investigation and the screaming for now. Including our client, the hugely successful and no doubt talented Mr Saurav Roop Kamal himself!'

As if on cue, Parvati's phone rang.

'It's Mr Kamal,' she said. 'He's asked us to come over. To discuss something important, he says.'

'But we've just returned from his place!' I said. 'What is so important that he cannot tell it to us on the phone?'

Parvati gave me one of her exasperating nods, the one which meant 'calm down.'

'When it's like this,' she said to me as we gathered our belongings, preparing once more to go to RK's mansion, 'we go where the action is. Who knows what knowledge it might lead to.'

And so, we did. We arrived at RK's place late. It was dark, the grounds were lit up, the gothic lamp posts built at even distances in the tall shrubbery shining their secrets. But the entire place still appeared shadowy—a heavy sort of feeling that didn't subside even when we approached the actual mansion.

'I find this house oppressive,' I said to Parvati as we made our way in. 'Even if the screaming part wasn't there.'

Parvati gave a little shrug, as if what I felt at this point was of little consequence.

'Concentrate,' she said to me, as we rang the doorbell. 'Not on how you feel, but on what *is*.'

Shashi opened the door.

'You weren't expecting to see me, I take it?' he remarked without his earlier irony when he saw our surprised expressions.

'Actually, Mr Kamal didn't tell us much,' Parvati said smoothly, gliding past him to the inevitable study, the room in which we always met the superstar.

'When will you learn,' Shashi continued, following her, as I fell in behind them both. 'Every career decision Roop takes is in consultation with me.'

'Career decision?' I echoed, as we stepped into the study. 'Since when do *we* become a part of that?'

'Roop has accepted an invite request sent sometime ago.' Shashi turned to face me. 'For a film awards show in a different city. And given all that has happened so far—he'd like you both to accompany him.'

20

'I would like it very much ...' RK began without preamble as soon as we entered his study, 'if you two would accompany me to Pune over the weekend.'

I looked at Parvati. Pune was a three-hour drive from Mumbai. Another city, but still close enough to Mumbai should we need to be back for any reason at all. It was not undoable.

'You need a holiday?' Parvati asked benignly, but I detected a glint in her eye. She already knew this was a career move, Shashi had voiced it seconds ago. But she was also tuning in to RK's mood, watching for a break, any sign that all was not well in his demeanour.

Notwithstanding the sadness that was only natural, given all that had occurred, RK however, didn't seem as if he was out of touch with reality. He wasn't drinking. He wasn't in his dressing gown, as he had been when we saw him that morning. He just seemed a man deeply unhappy. And if I were being completely honest—severely stressed.

'Not at all. A holiday is farthest from my mind at the moment. Alena and I had been invited, separately, as stars in our own right, for an awards show of a film magazine. They had booked tentative slots for this month earlier in the year. With Alena about to be released from hospital, I would prefer she take it easy. But work cannot wait. Given all that has occurred with the movie and with Alena—the producers feel its best, now, after our low-key phase, we put on a front as if we're in action once again. Let some normalcy be shown. So, I've confirmed my presence at the show, as has Alena. Maybe if we put up a front of normalcy, our movie will then be allowed to continue filming …'

'I see,' Parvati said. 'It makes sense for us to accompany you, as you've engaged us to solve this case. Moreover, these malefic incidents seem to be happening primarily around you. But I'd like to know *your* reasoning for asking us—what exactly do you have in mind? And have Alena's injuries healed enough for her to be doing this show?'

'You are going with me because I feel safer when you both are around,' RK said. 'You saved Alena when she was being beaten. You were the ones who arrived first when Mr Pickles was …' he trailed off, choked, then composed himself. 'You were on set, putting things in perspective for me, even when Mohan was found, so horribly strangled … You always know what to do.'

'Anyway,' he continued. 'I just feel that it's better if you two were with us. Besides, as you said, I'm the common link to all that's going wrong. You've accepted this case, I think it's important you come along. And yes, Alena will be fit enough to travel, she says. She hasn't healed completely, but well-applied make-up will take care of her appearance.'

He had answered Parvati's questions artfully enough, with the emotionality that by now we understood was characteristic RK. But the unease that emanated from him had intensified under her scrutiny, I could feel it.

'Are you two the only big stars being felicitated?' Parvati asked the question that was crucial at this juncture.

'No, that is not possible in an awards show of this stature. There will be many other stars, some big, some not so much.' RK had a wary look in his eyes as he said this, and I caught on immediately. So too, did Parvati, for her next question was in keeping with our surmise.

'Will Saddaq Haque be there?' she asked.

'I asked the organizers this,' Shashi entered the conversation, as we knew he would. He was the one taking care of these matters, after all. 'And they informed me he had been invited a long time ago, like Roop had. But, in light of what's happened with Alena, even if only you two were witnesses—I'm not sure he'll come,' he added.

'He might, though,' I spoke up. I somehow felt he would appear, because Alena was going to be there. Don't ask me why I felt so, I've always just had a hyperactive sixth sense. And being there, we could also use the opportunity to interview him for this case. And be present in case things got heated between all three of them.

Even if my gut proved wrong and Saddaq didn't show up, it might help to be around the two lovebirds. Because, apart from Saddaq, there was also Samuel Rodrigues gunning for RK. Supposing he turned up to make good his previous threat? Our presence would help defuse tensions, I felt.

'I wanted to discuss this with you both,' RK was saying, his eyes troubled. 'I've confirmed my presence, as has Alena. We really need to be visible now as I said, and this is the perfect opportunity. But do you think it would be safe, us going?'

'I don't think you have a choice,' Parvati said sombrely. 'You cannot spend the rest of your careers hiding. There is no movie being made at present—the set is sealed as a crime scene till the police are done. Meanwhile, your producers feel you ought to be visible.'

'So, you're okay with Roop going for this?' Shashi spoke up, his eyes concerned. I had been noticing for some time now how Shashi's attitude towards us was different. *He's significantly less hostile,* the thought came to me unbidden. We might have broken through his defences, somehow, in all that had transpired thus far. Or then his concern for his friend topped his distaste for us.

'I think they cannot spend the rest of their careers cowering from what they don't know,' Parvati addressed him. 'They need to do what's necessary.'

'Will you be able to come with us?' Shashi asked. There was no doubt he would be going along too. He always did.

A slight nod of acceptance from Parvati in my direction, and he had his answer.

'Yes,' I said, speaking for us both. 'We'll go with you.'

'That's good.' RK's voice held genuine happiness on hearing us accept. I looked at Shashi.

He seemed calm, pleased even when I accepted his offer. How odd, I thought. This was the man who couldn't stop being sarcastic every time he set eyes on us. What changed from then to now? How had he become almost tolerant in his interaction with us? Shashi's amiable behaviour was more than just acceptance of our presence as detectives on this case. It went deeper, as if he was attempting to be supportive of us now.

I stole a glance at Parvati, wondering if she too had noticed Shashi's turn of temperament.

But she was preoccupied, her eyes on RK as he spoke about the upcoming trip.

'It will be a change from all this business in Mumbai,' he was saying. 'A chance for us to regroup, recover, away from all the wrong publicity.'

'There will be publicity, Mr Kamal.' Parvati's words had a note of warning for him.

But he was looking upbeat after she gave his journey the all-clear. 'It won't be the sort we're experiencing now,' he said. 'It will be about awards, at least.'

The shrill ring of the study phone interrupted our dialogue. Shashi picked it up, being nearest to the machine.

'I see,' we heard him say. A split second later, he had put the receiver down and was hustling me and Parvati to the door. He knew RK had been ordered to stay indoors for now, even though that would change, come the weekend.

'What's the hurry,' I asked, almost annoyed. Here I had been thinking all was finally well between us, and now he was escorting us out? But it turned out Shashi's mind was on a different track altogether.

'We need to get to the hospital,' he said. 'Saddaq has been spotted trying to get to Alena's room.'

21

That phone call about Saddaq from one among Alena's entourage at the hospital was bad news indeed. No doubt Shashi had requested updates from her people, set up a net in the way connected filmis tend to, to keep him informed of Alena's progress. Or maybe it had been done at the request of RK. Whatever the background, it had translated into crucial information being imparted to us at the correct time.

We left RK's house immediately in a body, everyone except the superstar himself. He was the most panicked among us. And he had been warned about leaving his home.

'Please make sure she stays safe,' he pleaded, as we left. 'Don't let him get anywhere near her.'

This was turning out to be a long day. And an eventful one. In Mumbai traffic, especially in the late-hour going-home rush, getting to the hospital soon wasn't really on the table at all.

I do not want to bother with hospital names in this narrative—in any case, stars prefer the anonymity larger hospitals provide, and discretion from any investigators they engage. So, I'm leaving out such names and locations, even concrete dates, unless really relevant to this story. I had mentioned the hospital being state-of-the-art, with Alena being on a private floor, as a prominent celebrity. But that still did not prevent our nerves from being on edge all the way to the place.

Who knew how badly Saddaq was stoned now, if rumours on this habit of his were true. Or how much damage he might do if he got to her. Even Parvati's normal composure seemed a bit off. She was a champion of the underdog—I had seen this at our first case when she spoke up, more than once, for one of the reticent beauty contestants and stood up to a mean girl who used to repeatedly throw jibes. But there was a vast difference between confrontations with a bully our age and build, and a man perhaps twice our age and size, as was the case now. Regardless, I could see that she meant to try.

The car inched along. We had all piled into Shashi's vehicle, he had a driver and we figured we could run up immediately upon reaching the hospital instead of look for parking, as we would have had to, were one of us driving. Parvati's car had been left at RK's home. We would go back for it later.

Finally, we reached and all of us pushed our way into the elevators. It was crucial that we got to Alena as soon as possible. Visiting hours were probably long over, but men of Shashi's stature never let such things come in their way. We simply accompanied him as he strode purposefully towards her room once the elevator doors opened. Funny how he seemed to have disliked Alena, but knowing she was RK's lady love and unsafe now, he was doing everything possible to protect her.

'Shashi's commitment to RK appears utter,' I thought to myself as I followed him into Alena's room. 'Is it selfless, I wonder? Could he really be involved in scaring his best friend with all that awful screaming, despite all these appearances of loyalty? Or commit murder? With what motive in mind, though?'

When we entered Alena's room, an unlikely sight greeted us. We had already encountered various members of her personal team on the way in. A super successful star always boasts of an entourage—this was true even back in the day. The groupies came with the territory, Alena was no different—in fact, she was the norm, being ultra-successful at the time. But at present, these members had been asked to stand outside, a fact not lost on all three of us as we hurried to her room.

'Alena …?' Parvati was the first to speak as she stepped inside, hurrying up to the slight form who was sitting up on the huge hospital bed. Next to her, eclipsing her tiny build by his brawny form, loomed an all-too-familiar figure.

'Hello, Parvati. Good evening, lovely Akruti. Shashi, delighted as always,' Alena murmured, and I wasn't sure if she was being a bit rude in that effusive courtesy or that was her natural style of greeting, now that she appeared considerably better. It was now late evening, still, the blinds were semi-drawn, not fully shaded, as at our last visit, just the previous day. And her voice had lost its hoarse undertone.

'May I introduce you,' she continued with that exaggerated brightness of hers. 'This is Saddaq Haque.'

The bulky form had been sitting near her bed. Now he rose up, extending his hand formally. This was the unlikely sight we had witnessed upon entering the room. The tormentor and his prey sitting quietly, heads together, whispering intently to each other as we arrived. *What was going on?*

'Before you say anything, let him speak, please,' Alena commanded. She was almost fully recovered I realized, because of the strength in her voice and in her tone itself. It hadn't been so apparent when we had visited earlier, just the previous day. Just how deceptive was Alena, really? Or how good an actor?

We waited, regardless, in deference to the patient's wishes.

'I didn't come here to harm Alena,' Saddaq said to us, addressing Parvati because she was nearest to the bed and in his direct line of vision.

His expression was sheepish, a tad nervous, but he continued in the same vein.

'Um ... I know my actions were unforgivable ...' Apologizing was possibly rare in the life of this superstar, a healthy ego substituted for an overactive one, as with many celebrities. But he was trying valiantly to convey something. Then he did.

'But I want Alena to forgive me, I have been working on getting her to, all this while ...' His face appeared to finally melt into contriteness, that same expression I had witnessed in trailers of so many movies. Was it real, though, the remorse he was expressing?

'I got ahead of myself that day. I wasn't thinking straight,' he continued. 'I wouldn't ever want to hurt Alena. My jealousy, my emotions got the better of me. I acted out the turmoil I was feeling inside. I couldn't bear the thought of another man with her, even if only for a movie. I love her, you see ...'

'So at least you are admitting you were there on the set, that you did this,' Parvati said in a low tone, cutting Saddaq off from grovelling any further. 'That's why you're here.'

'I'm here because I felt I would die if I didn't see my love,' Saddaq said, melodramatically.

Saddaq's erratic behaviour and explosive temperament had a flip side, this absolute, explicit remorsefulness. It was a pattern we'd read about time and again, when doctors documented how certain abusive men operated.

Also, it explained in part, why their victims sometimes tended to tolerate their actions over very long periods of time—they believed these men every time they effusively apologized, when they promised not to repeat the violence again.

Something more, though, was emerging to both Parvati and me as Saddaq spoke. RK had told us Saddaq knew about how serious the romance was between him and Alena. But it was fast appearing that, in fact, *he didn't.*

I was looking at Saddaq's eyes, checking to see if his pupils appeared dilated. An addict is known by such signs, I knew. But the crafty actor whipped out his shades in the semi-dark room and put them on in front of us.

'Your friends are here,' he addressed Alena. 'I shall go now. But leave word I am to be allowed in, the next time. What a fuss was made today. I had to use all my influence to get in.'

He bent down to kiss her forehead, a gesture of love and leave-taking. But Parvati wasn't done.

'Why don't you sit down and talk to us,' she said, cleverly using the opportunity that had presented itself as an occasion to grill him on our case if possible.

'I came to talk to Alena,' Saddaq told Parvati. 'I think I've said what I needed to.'

'Your conduct left much to be desired,' Parvati pressed on. 'At least offer some explanation, speak to us as you would to a witness who saw what we saw that day.'

Canny Parvati had acted on his Achilles heel by underlining the very behaviour he was here to seek forgiveness for.

'I offered all explanations to Alena,' Saddaq said to Parvati. He remained standing though, as if waiting for her enquiries.

She did not hesitate.

'Do you know Samuel Rodrigues?' she asked.

'I do,' Saddaq's face showed no expression. He waited, as if for another question.

'What do you make of him?' Parvati tried to delve further by this innocuous enough query, get the uncooperative Saddaq to reveal *something*.

'Samuel Rodrigues is a little person in a little universe,' Saddaq said. 'He believes he can control Alena because of some long-ago legal document. But this is 1998. No one needs to stay on in a marriage if it is unhealthy.'

'But *you*,' Parvati persisted. 'Has he threatened you?'

'What does it matter?' Saddaq said. 'The important thing is—he cannot control me. Or Alena.'

'What about RK?' I voiced, bringing up the elephant in the room because no one else did. He was the reason we were on this case. We needed to learn if Saddaq had anything to do with the screaming and the murders surrounding RK.

'He has enough to worry about now, don't you think?' Saddaq said, purposely facing Shashi now. The dark glasses hid his eyes, but his tone was hard enough. 'What with his movie stalled and his stuntman murdered, not to mention that cat ... he needn't worry about Alena, he should concentrate on his own troubles.'

'What do you make of his troubles?' Parvati asked quietly. 'Have you visited the set earlier? Or his residence? Are you'll friends?'

'The set Alena, my girlfriend, has been filming at shouldn't be a closed set to me. But I visited only once, that unfortunate time as you know.' Saddaq paused for breath, then continued. 'As for visiting RK's home—I've been there several times, over many meals in the past. We were not enemies. I don't believe we are, even now. It's up to him, though.'

'What is?' Shashi, very quiet all this while, spoke for the first time.

'To mind his own business,' Saddaq retorted, now facing Shashi again. 'To keep his nose and self out of Alena's affairs. Once and for all.'

With that, as if having decided he'd been around long enough, Saddaq spun his heel, squeezed Alena's hand, nodded at me, and strode out of the room.

22

There was a silence in the aftermath of his departure, a strange sort of pause. We didn't quite know what to say, that interlude had been so very unexpected.

'Does Roop know you haven't told Saddaq?' Shashi was the first to break that unnatural calm, speaking up quietly, with a sort of contained emotion.

'Haven't told him what …?' Alena's voice had lost that exaggerated brightness of before. Had it been a performance, for Saddaq's sake? She now seemed withdrawn, curt even. It was clear she didn't think much of Shashi. We knew that the dislike was mutual in any case.

'… Know that you haven't told Saddaq that Roop thinks of you as his wife-to-be. Roop's love for you is very strong in Roop's mind, even though it's only a few months old. He's thinking marriage, for heaven's sake. And supposedly you feel the same for him, as you lead Roop to believe? Does Roop know you haven't actually spoken of how serious you both are about each other, to Saddaq?' There was a steely edge to his voice, as if he already knew the answers.

'I'm tired now,' Alena said petulantly, addressing Parvati who she thought of favourably, no doubt because it was Parvati who had rescued her from a vicious beating not so long ago. 'I want to rest.'

Without so much as a backward glance, Shashi turned and left the room, just as Saddaq had before him. We knew what he was asking her was important, because that cosy little scene between Alena and Saddaq in front of us had shown us a fondness we would not have believed if the beating of before had been our only benchmark.

'Alena, is what Shashi asked you true?' I could not help but redirect his question to her. It was important we understand how it was, that a man who had almost fatally injured this lady was now holding her hand and supposedly whispering sweet nothings, in the hospital bed *he had put her in*!

'Saddaq is a difficult man to convince.' Alena raised her comely eyes to me, clear as day. 'And he has a temper. You saw what happened when he got jealous on the set. That too, because I was in Roop's trailer with you guys before the song. I don't want to inflame him.'

'Are you saying that he doesn't know at all, how you feel about RK?' I asked, incredulous.

'Do you feel the same way about Mr Kamal, as he does about you, Alena?' Parvati spoke now, her tone extremely soft. 'Do you look at him as your future husband?'

A lot rested on Alena's revelation. If Saddaq did not know of the depth of RK's involvement with Alena before his breakdown on the set that day, we needed to discount him from our list of possible suspects regarding the screaming at RK's home. Why would he attempt to frighten RK if he didn't have a motive at all?

'Of course, I do think of Roop as my future husband, you know that!' Alena fixed her wide eyes on Parvati now. 'I'm just wary of inciting Saddaq's temper. He'll get to know eventually.'

'But why is RK under the impression that Saddaq knows about you two?' I probed, puzzled at her duality.

'He mentioned that Saddaq knew, and was unhappy over it, when we first asked him about you two. *He said you had told Saddaq ...*'

'I might have led RK to believe that I told Saddaq, when I didn't,' Alena admitted, showing no remorse in her expression. 'Not in so many words anyway. But male stars all have massive egos. And we were in the middle of a movie together. I had to keep RK happy ...'

'Besides,' she continued. 'Saddaq's character is such. If he was so upset just because he came to the sets and found me in RK's vanity van, imagine how upset he'd be if he knew what was really going on between us!'

'Those who want to know have a way of finding out, Alena,' Parvati said, still very soft. 'Despite your movie being a closed set.'

I knew she meant Samuel, because he had got the information quite smoothly, courtesy of his shady friendship with that Harlequin sports star. Samuel had lied to us saying he'd paid some junior spot boy to keep us from finding out his actual source, but I was sure that the method he had suggested would be effective enough too, should anyone else wish to try it.

'Yes,' Alena said. 'They could.' It was as if she too understood the unsaid regarding Samuel.

Still, hers was a cryptic answer, and she wouldn't qualify it further. Did it mean Saddaq knew of her liaison with RK early on, but went on to simply ignore it as a PR rumour, because she didn't tell him it was true? Or did it mean he really had no clue how serious it was?

Also, what did we know of their private conversations anyway? It could well be that Saddaq had confronted her about RK, and she had denied it utterly, such was her confessed fear of him. Most importantly, what was it that they were whispering about, with their heads so close, when we entered the room today? It couldn't all have had to do with his exaggerated apology—they had both looked too furtive for that, I reflected now.

'I want to rest,' she repeated, this time to us both, signalling an end to the evening, firmly, with no room to manoeuvre.

'We will be in touch, Alena.' Parvati's face was grave as she gave a last look to the star on the bed. 'Remember, *dishonesty doesn't pay in relationships in the long run*. For *anybody* ...'

Leaving a stricken Alena behind, we moved towards the elevator doors. A little way off, on a side bench, we found Shashi waiting for us. We must have both looked surprised at seeing that he had waited, because he mumbled out a curt explanation.

'It's started raining outside,' he said. 'And you came in my car. I didn't want to leave you stranded here without transport at an odd hour.'

'That is very nice of you.' Parvati's face hadn't lost its grave expression I noticed. 'We would've found a cab, but the fact that you waited is heartening.'

Parvati had retreated into her thoughts after this, but Shashi broke the spell once he was done calling for his car.

'No doubt it is difficult for Alena ...' he stated.

We both gawped at him. Was Shashi actually sympathizing with Alena? But he hadn't finished his sentence.

'... Being so adored. By three men, two of them superstars, no less.' He was being sarcastic, of course. As he choked out that last sentence, we realized how very angry he was. But, of course, he would be—Alena was playing a very dangerous double game, trying to show two men that she was exclusively in love with each of them. And one of these men happened to be Shashi's best pal.

'And we, mere mortals, not even worthy of a straight answer,' Shashi continued bitterly. He was referring to her shunning him earlier. But I had the answer he didn't get from her. In part, at least, because she was still talking in riddles to us too.

'We're going to Pune on Friday,' Shashi said with a sigh. 'Saddaq is expected, most probably.'

We looked at each other in silence.

But Shashi wasn't done. He spoke now with a deep foreboding, as if arising from the depths of his being, 'We are mere spectators. Roop, Alena and Saddaq in one room—how can each survive, with this level of emotion on display? Someone will pay a price. Let the curtain rise.'

23

After these fraught days, Pune would be a relief for RK, I thought to myself. And perhaps Shashi too, because whatever agonies RK appeared to be going through, it reflected equally on Shashi's face, such was his empathy with his superstar friend.

We were to leave on the morrow. The intervening days that week after our hospital visit had been low key, as we strove to get our affairs in order before the three-day absence from the city on the weekend.

The stars would reach Pune with their respective entourages, we knew. As for us, we were driving down in Parvati's car. She still had to collect it from RK's mansion, having left it there during our dash to the hospital, and being in no hurry to collect it after, as we had the use of my car as well. But hers was better suited for long journeys.

We were going to Pune with no great expectations, just trepidation as to the expected gathering there. There were many questions and no real answers in this case where everyone, including our client, seemed to be a suspect. My initial gut feeling, a sense that something ominous was hanging over this case, also persisted.

The premise itself was complex, luridly sensational in all aspects—typical Bollywood masala, in fact, involving glamour, sleaze, lucre, and the occult to boot. Mysterious screams in a superstar's heritage home. Not just a murdered cat, but a murdered extra on the sets of his film, the movie being ghostly, at that.

Of the two superstars in love with the same lady, one was on edge as manic screams resounded in his supposedly 'haunted' mansion, the other famously hot-headed, a rumoured drug-abuser.

The bizarre nature of this was worthy of a Bollywood blockbuster, surely! Add to it, more masala: the lady's wayward husband, threatening further mayhem. And they were all to converge in Pune that Friday? Recipe for disaster? Absolutely!

'I'm not looking forward to this weekend at all,' I told Parvati as we made our way by cab to collect her car from RK's that evening.

'We have to get through it,' Parvati said, equally grim, because she knew what a circus we had signed up for.

'We'll stop here,' she told the star-struck cabbie who had hoped to get right into RK's mansion and take a dekko.

But Parvati had stopped the cab at the outer gate, intending to walk the rest of the way, past the mansion's gardens, up the drive to where her car had been parked. The hangers-on, RK's assorted fan club and tourists at the gates, watched us as we drove up.

There was a path for walking up, used nowadays by the help, no doubt. We got off, and after going through the gate security were left on our own to stroll leisurely past the lovely green heritage garden that lined RK's massive mansion. The rains had made it even greener.

'It really is quite sensational as a property,' I told her, looking around us as we walked up.

The manicured lawns, the evenly spaced lamp posts up the drive, the massive shrubbery and tall palms on the outer edges, separating his world from the junta outside. It had an eerie beauty, mesmerizing if one thought about it. But eerie, certainly, for the sheer isolation of it. Upon closer look, the lamp posts revealed faces, grinning gargoyles that leered as one passed them. Lovely if one had a taste for Gothic architecture. Simply scary, especially at night, if one didn't!

'I wonder if he will be able to part with this,' I mused to Parvati as we walked. 'If Madame Alena marries him and gets her way. It does have a definite grandeur. I find it oppressive, but I suppose it could grow on one.'

'You keep saying you find it oppressive,' Parvati chided me gently. 'Have you thought, why exactly? Could it be because you sense something's off—or is it really these grounds, his opulent home, that give you that feeling?'

I was a little taken aback at her artless chiding. I didn't think she would mind me expressing how I felt about these grounds or his house. But I decided to think about it a little more. Was it because of that sense of unease I'd felt from the moment RK got in touch, that I reacted so each time we came here? Or did it have to do with the atmosphere of the place itself, a house that lent itself to the ghostly, whether or not you were a believer in the occult?

'There's my car,' Parvati pointed out, ending my introspective mood for now, as we neared the porch of the mansion.

We weren't really going to go inside today. We knew RK planned to leave earlier than us, be in Pune to rehearse for his special performance for the awards. He might have already left, for all we knew. We just needed to fetch Parvati's car and depart. But that was not how it happened.

As we walked up, nearing the car, the front door slammed. To our surprise, out came Alena. We were a short distance away and hidden from her by the shrubbery, as the drive curved ahead. Yet she was clearly visible to us.

She looked well enough, given all that she had endured, and the fact that she had been discharged from hospital only very recently. Cunningly applied make-up might have taken care of the rest. But she didn't look happy. In fact, she appeared downright furious.

'He can't talk to me like that,' she screamed, thinking no one was watching. She kicked a bush nearby furiously and pummelled fisted hands in the air, a gesture of great wrath.

'Who does he think he is? Telling me I'll never stay here? Telling *me* to go to hell?! We'll see about that!' she yelled to an invisible audience, then got into the car that had whizzed up with great haste. With a roar, it pulled away ahead of us as we turned the curve. But what we had witnessed remained with us in the atmosphere, as if a cloud, invisible but menacing.

'That was interesting,' Parvati spoke up. 'It seems Mr Kamal hasn't left yet ...'

'And from that display of temper, whatever happened inside has been quite unbecoming for the lovely Alena,' I added grimly. 'Looks like there's trouble in paradise ...'

24

The phone was ringing off the hook as we re-entered the office for a final check, post retrieving Parvati's car from RK's mansion. As we were leaving, I noticed the mansion's famed name, elegantly carved into a stone nameplate, high on the gate entrance, partially obscured by the security personnel.

Taqdeer, that legendary moniker, as famous as the superstar himself. Hindi word for fate or fortune, or then, destiny. *I hope you remain a part of RK's destiny, he loves you quite a bit*, I thought upon sighting it so elegantly scripted there. At present, its destiny wasn't too clear.

Not for this house, nor its owner, what with the screams and the murdered Mr Pickles and the threat of Alena's disenchantment with the place. It needed all the luck it could get, I thought wryly. For that matter, to solve this case, so did we.

Parvati dashed to pick up the receiver as we entered the office. It was late, our secretary had left. And we were due to leave too, for the early start to Pune the next day.

'Hope everything is well,' I overheard RK's baritone crackle, too loud over the long-distance line as he addressed Parvati. 'And I will be seeing you here tomorrow. Just called to check. The organizers want to speak with you, should I put them on?'

Parvati spoke to the organizers about our rooms—RK being a superstar had been allotted a five-star hotel for the stay, the same venue as the awards show itself, but we needed to be around him, despite the place being full. That was why the organizers were calling. Earlier, this had apparently been an issue, one we hadn't even been made fully aware of, but RK had used his considerable influence and got us accommodation not just in the same hotel, but on the same floor too. They were calling to appease us.

Parvati put down the receiver, having conveyed our gratitude, not even having known it had been an issue till now. Shashi must've known, told RK, who had sorted it out. All without our knowledge.

'That was nice of RK,' I said to Parvati, as we finally got done with all that we needed to take care of at the office, and made our way out. 'To have made sure we were staying nearby, in the same five-star.'

'Aku,' Parvati's eyes glittered, as they did when she had an epiphany. 'Did you not notice the obvious?'

'Meaning?' I said, puzzled. 'RK knew there was an issue, we didn't. He had invited us in the first place, so he sorted it out himself. Not top of his to-do list when he reached Pune, I'm sure, but a significant gesture, nonetheless … oh.'

I stopped short when the impact of my own reasoning finally hit me. We had arrived at the office maybe twenty minutes past fetching Parvati's car from Taqdeer. That means we had seen Alena screaming outside RK's door twenty minutes ago.

The drive to Pune is three hours on clear roads. There was no way RK could've made it to the city from his mansion in twenty minutes. Therefore, he must have stuck to his original plan, having left early and had been in Pune rehearsing all this while. The organizers in Pune were with him when he spoke to us a few minutes ago. In other words—*he was not the one Alena was screaming at when she left his house!*

'Who was she so angry with, do you think, Pari?' I quizzed Parvati, most curious at this unexpected turn of events. We had seen Alena absolutely furious. Not irritated, not mildly annoyed—simple and utterly manic in her anger, pummelling the air and kicking the bushes, a dramatic display of underlying temper that I doubt she would let us or anyone else witness, if she'd known we were around.

'I don't know,' Parvati's brow was furrowed as happened when she was disturbed. She looked grave.

'*Aku, whatever's coming up ... I don't like it. I don't like it at all.*'

I nodded, as chilled. The shape of ongoing things did not bode well for the future of this trip.

'RK may have had some of his entourage over at his home,' I offered by way of defusing the mood. 'Might be them? Or her own hangers-on? They might have displeased her?'

'Could they be authoritative enough to tell her she'd "never stay" at Mr Kamal's house?' Parvati mused, as she locked our office door for the weekend. 'Or to tell her to "go to hell"? I doubt it.'

Then she glanced at me. 'Think closer home.'

'You mean Shashi?' I said. Naturally, it could be Shashi. He was always lurking and we didn't know yet if he had accompanied RK to Pune, or would follow later, like us.

'It could just as well be Aman, though he told us he was confined to his room, on painkillers,' I added.

'There are others with access too.' Parvati met my eyes. 'Now that Alena has free reign on Mr Kamal's property. Even when he's not around.'

'Ohhhh,' the import of her words dawned on me. How stupid of me to think only of Aman or Shashi when we had two more players, both of whom were connected to Alena, *both of whom had threatened her as well*, and one had threatened RK himself, before. Both were 'closer home' in this case, as Parvati put it.

'You mean Samuel or Saddaq?' I said. 'Do you really think she'd allow any of them on RK's property when he wasn't around?'

'She allowed *both* of them into her room, didn't she?' Parvati said. 'Both of them had threatened her in different ways, one had battered her almost to within an inch of her life. Yet on different occasions, she granted access to both. Despite us cautioning her, despite her supposed fiancé, Mr Kamal's wishes. Who is to say she might not have allowed them access to Taqdeer, even in Mr Kamal's absence? Aku, Ms Alena has a mind of her own, over and above the demure act. My real fear is something else ...'

'What?' I asked, sceptical and worried now.

'That what we've been witness to, all the tender loving around Mr Kamal and her sweet frailty in the hospital bed, it's just a fraction of her real self. What we've seen of her around Mr Kamal, or other people, is what we see in the movies—an inspired performance. The actual Alena might just be the person we had conjectured about earlier. The one who married perhaps a like-minded, greedy, ne'er do well like Samuel. More specifically, *the one we witnessed when she didn't know we were watching*, the one outside Taqdeer today—*frustrated, arrogant, passionately angry ...*'

'... And scheming with either, or both, of her lovers for a share of RK's immense wealth!' I completed Parvati's sentence. 'Scheming, that includes this frightful screaming business ...'

'So, you don't think the grounds or the home are oppressive by themselves, any longer?' Parvati changed tack, lightening the mood, her eyes teasing.

But I couldn't shake off the awful foreboding. 'If indeed this home is haunted,' I said quietly, 'it is by an evil that walks alongside us. It is mocking us because we do not understand it yet. But, Pari, if we are to save RK—for this case, if anything, is about his sanity—we *must*.'

25

My foreboding was prescient, and the stakes higher than just RK's sanity. But when we left for Pune, we weren't to know that yet.

It was a fairly uneventful journey, delightful even, the rolling hillocks and flatlands in the three hours to Pune shining magical green, courtesy of the rains. Even the winding ghats on this trip did not bring on a spell of vertigo as I was prone to, whilst on them. It seemed as if nature was conspiring to make the journey to Pune uplifting, given what was to transpire when we finally reached.

We arrived at the venue to find it a buzz of activity. The hotel that was booked by the film magazine was going to host its awards show the next night in its banquet hall. Such events also took place at outdoor venues, but the rains at present could play spoilsport, the organizers knew. They preferred not taking chances.

'You're here,' RK called out upon sighting us from onstage as he practised for a dance sequence between awards. The hall was filled with his scattered aides, as also, various personnel from the magazine, the event production, the sound and lights teams, make-up … and cameramen rehearsing the shots they would take the next night.

His choreographer gestured for him to pay attention, but just before that, he shouted to us, 'There's a party tonight. My room! You *both* have to come!'

Such in-group celebrations were common on out-of-town tours, I knew, not just from my own experience travelling for large events as a supermodel in the past, but also from cine magazines and assorted gossip coverage. Why not, I thought. It would be a good chance to see Alena and RK together again, after all that had transpired. It would reveal if their private dynamics had altered. Parvati had similar thoughts I knew as she nodded her acceptance to me.

I held up my hand to RK in a gesture of a thumbs up, as confirmation about the plan at night.

But Parvati was concerned about something else. Or rather, someone.

'Where's Shashi?' she asked looking around at the buzz of the banquet hall. He didn't seem to be around. Normally, he would be hovering around his friend. His absence was puzzling us.

We had our answer though, as a helpful junior assigned from the film magazine, stepped up to reply to Parvati, having overheard her asking me.

'Are you looking for Mr Sunder?' she asked. 'He'll be here soon. The rains on the road held him up. He was at Mr Kamal's house almost all of yesterday, sorting out Mr Kamal's final costumes for the performance tomorrow. The clothes took time to be delivered. He had to wait for them to come from the designer, before he left for here. He likes to handle all aspects concerning Mr Kamal himself, you see ...'

Parvati thanked her and turned to me. Our eyes met in knowing. The magazine aide had let on a very important detail in her casual relay of information. Shashi had been held up at present, that was fine. But what concerned us was what she's said before that.

He had spent 'almost all' of the previous day at RK's house? Would this timeline include the part when Alena had visited Taqdeer? And if so, *was Shashi the person she had been so furious at*? What *was* this mischief brewing?

The magazine junior's presence was beneficial in any case. Parvati decided to quiz her about other pressing concerns.

'Will Saddaq Haque be here soon?' she asked, nonchalantly.

'Mr Haque is already here,' the magazine junior said to Parvati, her eyes lighting up in excitement. 'He's in his suite, waiting for his turn to practise his dance number for the show tomorrow.'

Parvati smiled at the girl, nodding for her to go ahead as she was summoned to attend to other matters.

Parvati then turned to me, but I pre-empted what she was going to say.

'He's here too,' I stated. 'So, almost every single player in this drama will be present tomorrow at this show … With the exception of Samuel?'

'You know, Pari,' I continued, a thought striking me as I was thinking of Saddaq.

'When we walked into that hospital room of Alena's … the way she and Saddaq were sitting together, it seemed almost as if they were plotting something …'

'That air of conspiracy around them?' Parvati arched her eyebrows. 'Hmm … yes, I picked up on it too. But I wonder if we are reading too much into a simple gesture of contriteness. Maybe he was just telling Alena how very sorry he was …'

'Or then he was plotting with her about something,' I said darkly, not really in the mood to let Saddaq off the hook so lightly. 'Did you notice how fast they drew apart as we entered? As if they had a guilty conscience about sharing something, and didn't want us to notice.'

'Alena is an enigma,' Parvati mused. 'I cannot make out if she is sincere at even one thing—does she really love Mr Kamal or is she stringing him along for his property? Does she really fear Samuel or is she playing a part to get us to think so, as she plots something sinister with him? Because, Aku, he is a sinister man ...'

'And finally, does she fear Saddaq's moods, as she explained to us that she did,' I continued Parvati's chain of thought. '*Or is she playing the biggest role of her life and stringing him along too ...*'

'The part of the abused girlfriend ...' Parvati's face was grim—I knew she was recalling how she had intervened that stormy night as Saddaq was pummelling Alena into the rain-soaked earth. 'The helpless victim who cannot stand up for herself ...'

'And yet we saw her in a state very far from helpless,' I remarked tartly, as Parvati snapped out of her reverie. 'We saw her so charged, so angry at Taqdeer ...'

'... That she came across as the aggressor,' Parvati completed my sentence. 'The question is—who was she so furious with? And why?'

26

'Aren't you a vision,' Parvati grinned as she entered my room that night. We were going to the get-together in RK's room in some time. There was no need to dress up, the magazine's big awards night was on the morrow.

But being a part of the glitz that day, with all the extraneous paraphernalia—the aides, the cameramen, the flashy stage costumes—had brought back my modelling days to me. I was nostalgic and had tapped into that feeling without reservation, even whilst getting ready for what was to be just a small, in-group party.

No wonder Parvati was grinning at my Seventies-channelling black jumpsuit with the flashy silver-sequined belt, my silver disco ball earrings, complete with the straight hair, bouffant held back in a rainbow-hued Pucci-style scarf.

'You really pulled out all the stops!' she said, laughing at me affectionately.

'No place more OTT than Bollywood,' I told her airily, not at all piqued at her humour. 'I'll be right at home!'

I knew I was looking more camp than classy, but I needed a little lightness to dispel the gloom, to set aside our apprehensions concerning the next night for a while.

Parvati was her elegant self, form-fitting dark jeans, a white woollen pullover and eye-catching gypsy earrings. She looked casually cool, classic Parvati. For a moment I wondered if I had overdone it, but when we entered RK's suite, I knew my dress code had been spot-on.

'Look who's joined the party!' Shashi Sunder, of all people, opened the door to RK's palatial suite when we rang. He was wearing a child's paper hat, pointy and with a streamer running down from the top, in multi-coloured hues. On a child it would have looked festive, on the sullen-at-most-times Shashi it served to look incongruous at best.

Down the side of the hat was emblazoned the film magazine's name and logo. Obviously borrowed from the loot kept aside for whatever party was planned after the awards function the next night, I thought. Shashi smiled at us. Which itself was unexpected.

'It's been a nightmare of a journey,' he said. 'Took me seven hours to get here in the rain and the traffic jams backing up the ghats today. I could use a drink—or several!' He sauntered off leaving us to take stock of the room.

Upon stepping further into the suite, we realized it had the air of a child's party more than an adult one. Streamers with the magazine name in tinsel, balloons floating around with the logo in black. Music playing without any playlist, based on the preference of the invitees present, who were DJing all at once and arguing too, it would seem. Bags of chips, assorted drinks, champagne and the like littered the centre table.

Several faces we half-recognized as part of RK's entourage back at the set, or Alena's at the hospital, or both. Numerous up-and-coming stars. All in various stages of glitter, all dressed or if we were to be honest, over-dressed, as if at a grand ball. There were masques and feathers and shawls and stoles aplenty. In all the dress-up, the cacophony in the room was utter and commendable.

'I thought this was going to be a *small* affair,' I mouthed at Parvati, rolling my eyes dramatically.

We saw Alena in the distance in a long white faux fur coat.

'*A faux fur coat*?' Parvati mock-groaned as she set eyes on her. 'Really? In this humidity?'

Alena was also wearing a hat, fashioned as a paper crown. She saw us enter and made her way over, carefully picking her route through the crowd, invitees sitting or kneeling or draped over the sofas, till she reached us. As she walked, we noticed her coat open to reveal a playsuit, a tight, sparkling bustier and short shorts over knee-high, black, buttoned boots. She had a staff in her hand that she waved gleefully at us as she approached.

'Compared to her, you're plain Jane,' Parvati whispered, sotto voce. 'Why couldn't you dress up a little, Aku? Be a little—y'know—*flamboyant*?'

I was already out of breath laughing at Alena's outfit, as at Parvati's mischievous comments, when we saw her. I had been as flamboyant as I dared, but even I couldn't ever hold a patch on Bollywood!

'Compliments of the magazine committee,' the object of our attention trilled when we were finally face to face. 'Isn't this sooo fun? They're hoping the knick-knacks and us, of course, will make it to the press tomorrow as pre-publicity for the event. There was a photo call earlier, but none of us turned up!' She giggled this last bit of information and batted her lashes. 'Do I remind you of the Queen of Hearts?' she asked, posing in a way that revealed the full extent of her assets. But down-to-earth Parvati was the wrong audience for such mystique.

'From *Alice in Wonderland*?' Parvati said, innocence personified, no trace of sarcasm evident in her voice, and I had to hide behind her to keep down the laughter that bubbled up when she said this. Whether or not Alena was channelling the crazy Queen from the beloved, iconic story, we certainly needed a white rabbit, pulled from a hat at least, if not a rabbit hole, to keep the sense of utter chaos, this feeling of an unholy current unravelling, at bay.

Alena's face up-close showed heavy make-up, no doubt covering the remnants of the bruises she's gotten from Saddaq's attack on her. She drifted off as we took in the room.

The thumping music was already grating on my nerves and we had only been here a short while. Normally not vocal except when sarcastic, I observed Shashi went quieter and quieter sipping his drink in the corner of the room, as the party wore on. The hat was tilting at an odd angle on his head, as if about to fall off.

'Wonder what's on his mind,' I said to myself.

'So, what do you think?' A voice we both knew spoke up right next to us and we turned simultaneously to see RK in front of us.

To our disappointment, he wasn't dressed up at all. Jeans and a dark navy shirt—not even a hat on his head.

'I couldn't,' he said quietly, noting the surprise in our glances. 'I'm not ready yet to celebrate anything. But the magazine insisted, my producers in Mumbai agreed, there was a press call to go though, so I put up with it, hosted it even. Besides, it's Alena's first party since that awful night on the set. Look how happy she is … I couldn't say no to *that*.'

Alena was twirling in the distance in her super high boots, her long fur coat swinging. Her face looked alive, sparkling. She saw us looking at her. And not missing a beat, she blew a kiss at RK.

'I have a surprise for her,' RK said fondly, completing the gesture with his own flying *bisou*. 'It's coming at the very end … She suspects, I think, that a surprise is coming, but doesn't know when …' Another guest, a familiar face, a star wandered up to greet RK. Distracted, he left us to say hello.

'Drink?' Someone asked, but neither Parvati nor I wanted one.

The bell to RK's suite rang again and again, and more people, all dressed to kill, waltzed in.

'Not sure we can get anything done in *this*,' I told Parvati, struggling to keep my voice over the music. We both noticed RK's nemesis Saddaq didn't seem to be around. It occurred to me that he may well have been invited as professional courtesy—most of Bollywood was a law unto itself, overlooking personal enmity in favour of business and keeping up appearances, especially where press might be present, no matter the seriousness or depth of grudges held.

Also, Tinseltown's code of in-group omertà, or silence in the presence of outsiders, Mafiosi style, never let up in such matters. What happened in Bollywood, stayed in Bollywood. It was why Alena's beating on the sets had been hushed up as if it had never happened, and it was why no police complaint had ever been filed. It was probably why Saddaq might just have been invited to this party despite its host wanting to have nothing to do with him. An awards event weekend hosted by a cine magazine meant the press were ever present. Faced with outsiders, especially the press, more often than not, Bollywood closed ranks, put on a show of unity, no matter inner rumblings. The question was—if an invite had indeed been extended, would Saddaq attend?

'Bollywood stars are known for late entries, or then making an entry,' I voiced, to Parvati, who appeared to have guessed my thoughts. 'The night is still young. Saddaq might as yet show up.'

'The evening is sure to get interesting, if he does,' Parvati remarked dryly. 'Given that Mr Kamal has planned this fond surprise for Alena, as he mentioned just now. And Saddaq didn't seem to know the depth of their liaison, as we realized at the hospital in Mumbai.'

There was some commotion at this point, the burgeoning crowd parting and regrouping, as a cake was wheeled in from the door. It came on a trolley and rested right in front of the twirling Alena.

'Oooo,' she said, her eyes lighting up. 'I love cake! This is my surprise, isn't it?' The cake was loud, and pink, and rather small, given the entire roomful of a crowd it was supposedly meant for.

There was an envelope, attached to the cake, but it seemed no one was paying much attention to its arrival, all intent on conversation and laughter. Since we had been observing Alena with RK, we continued to watch her, even as he moved away with his guests.

Alena reached for the envelope, as pink as the cake it came with. She opened it, read the note inside, taking her time, not just glancing through it. A puzzled, uncertain expression crossed her face.

She looked up, as if to determine where RK was. She noticed him in conversation with someone, noticed the effort involved to pick her way through the crowd to get his attention. Then, a shrug of a gesture, as if to say *what the heck, it's a cake, meant to be eaten*, and she was cutting it without further ado, without even inviting those around her to join in.

'Rather selfish of Milady,' I commented to Parvati as we watched her, transfixed. She was easy on the eyes, and this narcissistic, self-absorbed quality we were seeing, added to her aura. We could not look away, it was a movie playing out in front of us.

'Yes, she doesn't like to share,' Parvati agreed, watching her, equally mesmerized.

Alena cut a large piece. Then after a quick, almost furtive glance to see if anyone was watching, she popped the whole thing in her mouth. Not a dainty nibble either, given her delicate features, small size and regal costume. She ate it fast and furious, the whole chunk right down, a gulp and swallow, and then her chocolate-smudged hands, without a tissue available, disappeared into the coat.

'Would you believe, she's wiped her hands on the coat!' Parvati said, in an astounded voice.

'Yes, the lady's a tramp,' Shashi spoke up from behind us. We turned to find he had joined us from his corner of the room, his drink still in his hand. *Alena has a whole crew watching her*, I thought wryly, *she certainly owns the room today*.

I was to regret my uncharitable thoughts the very next instant. Alena dropped to the floor barely a few minutes after ingesting that cake, clutching her stomach, her mouth foaming.

'Catch her,' the person next to her said, even as she hit the floor with a thud. Luckily, it was densely carpeted, but even so, it was a hard knock.

'Is she having an epileptic fit?' someone else asked, in the general commotion immediately after.

'Give her air, give her space!' This from Parvati, who had dashed over alongside me as soon as we witnessed Alena hit the floor.

RK, having rushed over, turned distraught and hollow-eyed, cradling Alena's inert form as she lay, now unconscious. Shashi, witness to everything leading up to the fall, left immediately to call the hotel doctor for Alena. The lights were turned on, the music turned down. Everyone blinked at each other in the suddenly too-bright space.

Miraculously, Shashi returned with the hotel doctor, his efficient way with the powers-that-be amply evident at the appearance of a medicine man so quick, that too at this un-Godly hour.

'*Is she all right*? *Is she*?' RK choked out, hyperventilating in worry, as the man bent over Alena.

'Call the ambulance now,' the doctor responded curtly. '*This lady has been poisoned*.'

27

There could be no doubt about it. The danger that stalked RK at home had also followed him to Pune. And had struck him where it hurt most—at the lifeblood of his precious paramour. This was what both Parvati and I concurred on, as we went over the events of that Friday night, now from the vantage point of a good day and a half later.

The preceding hours had seen us relive the horror of Alena's beating at the hands of Saddaq Haque just a couple of weeks previously, as we rushed her by ambulance to one of Pune's premier hospitals, where she was treated for severe poisoning.

Because we had acted so quickly, she escaped with her life. The foaming from her mouth was due to the poison acting, not an epileptic fit, the doctors told us. But she would make a full recovery, they were confident.

Such an incident could not be kept out of the papers. The fallout was glaring and harsh. RK's producers had intended this trip to have given them a fresh start, a sidestepping from the series of misfortunes plaguing them.

Instead, it became a media circus once again, this time involving Alena and the unfortunate magazine awards show, which was obviously cancelled in the light of the sobering events.

The police had arrived that night itself—not Addl CP Mhatre, he couldn't be there so fast as this had happened in another city, not Mumbai. As was routine, everyone present had been questioned, their statements taken down, the room swept, the remnants of the cake sent for analysis. And we knew there was poison in that cake when the results came back.

It was now Sunday, the day we were to have headed back to Mumbai after the show. But we needed to get to the bottom of the entire poisoning situation, and the answers could only be found in Pune.

'What a strange way fate has of shifting the goalposts,' I remarked to Parvati as we proceeded to RK's suite. 'We were dreading most of the principal players in this drama—RK, Alena, Saddaq, even maybe Samuel—meeting in the same room at this awards show. And now, in the blink of an eye—the show has been cancelled ...'

'But under such horrifying circumstances,' Parvati said, her expression serious. 'We could well have had a third murder on our hands, had we not acted as fast as we did.'

'I know,' I agreed. It had been a miraculous escape for Alena, a second time in a short span. Both times, strangely, we had been around to come to her aid. This time, it had also been Shashi's influence and the actual availability of a hotel doctor which had allowed her survival.

But while she had been lucky, we were still clueless as to what had led to an act of such malevolence. And the glaring question—had the cake actually been meant for Alena, or did she just happen to become an unlucky pawn who had eaten a creation meant for RK?

Regardless of who it had been meant for, there could have been collateral damage, had others at the party ingested the cake. Despite its small size, whoever sent it had been ruthless enough to overlook this fact. It was simply luck that no one else had, given Alena's instant claiming of the cake. But had it really been meant for her?

My instincts had warned me about this case from the beginning, but even I could not have guessed that there would be two deaths in its unravelling and an attempt on a third life as we continued. *Things are not always as they appear to be*—Parvati's earlier words, suggesting layers to this case, rang truer now, than ever.

The man at the epicentre of all this, RK himself, hadn't shifted out of the hotel yet. The entire time before now, he had stayed with Alena in the hospital. But today, on the urging of his staff, he had decided to return to the hotel for a short rest. It would hardly be a rest, he knew this. We were waiting for him, counting on him being alone today, so we could have the opportunity to discuss and deconstruct the events that had caused such a furore in Pune.

He was still occupying the same suite as he had when the incident played out. The Pune police had already come around in his absence and examined the premises. It was our turn now. And unlike the police, we had actually been present on the scene of crime as it had unravelled.

'Did you notice, Aku, that there was a note,' Parvati mused, as we walked to RK's suite. 'We were all watching her—that in itself was fortunate, because we saw her fall and rushed to her without a moment's delay. But do you recall there was a note with the cake …?'

'Yes, I remember that,' I said, trying to comb my memory for all that had transpired that moment when Alena received the cake.

'Alena took the note—Pari, as I recall, she looked a bit … surprised when she read it?' I added.

'Yes, that's right, I remember that,' Parvati said. 'Then she looked around, as if for Mr Kamal, but then let it be when she saw how many people she'd have to go through to get to where he was …'

'And then she ate the cake,' I concluded the memory. 'But Pari—*what happened to the note*?'

Parvati looked at me, her eyes narrow, that look she got when on the track of something important.

'The police didn't mention finding the note—I had told them I saw her read it and checked with them again today. Alena is in recovery and hasn't been cleared to be questioned yet …'

'So apart from me and you, do you believe no one else saw her read the note?' I asked, dumbfounded.

'Me, you and Shashi,' Parvati corrected me. 'Remember he was alongside us, watching while she ate the cake. It's possible he was watching her when she received and read the note …'

We left the rest unspoken as we reached RK's door. But it lingered between us, the unsaid. Shashi may have been watching Alena for a long while, especially if he was our mischief-maker … *was he the one who not only watched Alena but also poisoned her?*

I recalled his aloofness, standing alone in the party, sipping his drink before he came over to join us. It could be that that was his nature—reserved, full of controlled angst. Or, it could be more … *him waiting to see his plan play out?*

RK opened the door on our knock. His entourage had been dismissed for now, it seemed, because there was no one around him in the room at least.

'Shashi's agreed to stay with Alena, because I've come back,' RK told us, his eyes bloodshot, possibly from lack of sleep and worry.

My eyes met Parvati's—*was leaving Shashi with Alena wise, given he was also a suspect for us*?

'I know what you're thinking,' RK was prattling on. 'That Shashi doesn't even like Alena, why would he stay with her? Thing is, he'd do it for me. *Shashi would do anything for me*.'

We didn't tell him that this very notion was what was worrying us in the first place. That Shashi would do anything for RK—*did it mean eliminating someone he didn't think much of, to begin with?*

'There's a nurse with her as well,' RK continued, allaying our fears temporarily. 'I've engaged her to be with Alena at all times. Alena woke up a few times, but was groggy and didn't recognize or engage with anyone. But the doctors said it's fine, to let her body rest and heal. The police haven't been allowed to talk to her yet.'

'I cannot risk Saddaq trying to reach her.' He looked at us both wearily. 'The hospital is a private space. I do not trust him being alone with her, with just hospital staff present. There's no telling what he'll do. That's why I had to ask Shashi, apart from the nurse.'

'Does Saddaq know she's in this hospital?' I asked, curious.

'Saddaq, like all top stars in Bollywood, would no doubt have found out,' RK said, grimly.

'I believe he's left for Mumbai,' Parvati interjected. 'The hotel staff informed me. The police mentioned it as well. He was pressured by his staff not to intervene, or draw publicity to himself. I think he understood, even if he might have wanted to go to Alena ...'

The police had obviously not considered or then already discounted him as a possible suspect if he had been allowed to leave Pune so soon. There was nothing connecting him to the mystery cake, and he hadn't been present at the party.

'Was Saddaq invited to the party at all, RK?' I asked, suddenly wanting to know this as fact, instead of simply surmising as we had done earlier.

'Not by me directly.' RK's voice remained grim. 'If I could help it, he would be nowhere near Alena. I hadn't factored him in when I considered hosting the party at the request of both the magazine and my producers. But he was notified by the magazine's event organizers. The magazine wanted some press for the awards if possible, even if informally, to appear out of the party. I wasn't happy about it, but it was business. In any case I was present, I would make sure that Alena stayed far away from him, if he attended. But wisely, he didn't.'

Whether Saddaq had decided to stay away completely, or simply make a late entry that night, we would never know. Till the time Alena was poisoned he hadn't arrived, and that was the reality, because that meant he wasn't on the scene of crime when it transpired, at all.

That Saddaq had an intimidatory role to play in Alena's life was, in any case, known to very few, given his earlier beating of her had been covered up so thoroughly. Also, having witnessed his recent contriteness and clear bond with Alena at the hospital, I was inclined to stop short at thinking of him as the person wanting to harm her. Perhaps Parvati felt the same.

If the poisoned cake had been meant for RK, not Alena, I could not see Saddaq as having sent it, either. His rage, as we had witnessed on set the day he beat Alena, seemed more impulse driven than planned, and sending a poisoned cake required meticulous planning. But at this point, who, if any, knew the real story? We could not actually discount any of the players quite yet.

'Mr Kamal, was the surprise you had planned for Alena, to be a cake?' Parvati, bringing the topic even more firmly back to that fateful night, asked RK gently. 'Remember you told us you had a surprise planned for her?'

'I did.' RK looked at Parvati, his eyes misting over. 'But I told you it had to come at the very end of the party. The party hadn't even picked up yet. It was a cake, yes. But not *that* one, not the one that arrived, it was too small. Mine was meant to be enjoyed by everyone—in fact, I was going to have someone pop out of it and sing for her ... she loves cake ...'

We looked at him in silence. Truth be told, we didn't quite know what to attribute the extravagance of a person popping out of a cake to—RK's generosity or his OTT Bollywood flair, further magnified by his besotted mind?

'As you know, that didn't happen,' he said ruefully, wiping his eyes.

'The cake that did come in was tested by the police. It *was* poisoned,' Parvati spoke up. 'In many ways, it was fortunate Alena behaved as covetously as she did ... her immediate succumbing to the poison had everyone panicking and no one else touched the cake.'

'Do the police know who sent it?' RK asked.

'Not yet, from our conversation earlier,' Parvati filled him in. 'It was sent over anonymously, apparently, to be delivered to RK's suite. The hotel staff forwarded it there, they did not have a reason not to. They knew of the party, they assumed it was meant for the guests. The police are trying to trace its bearers, with no luck so far. That night, when exactly did you see Alena, Mr Kamal? When did you rush to her?

'Not till she had already fallen,' RK met her eye. 'People started calling and screaming to help her, that's when I knew and rushed to her.'

'Did you happen to see a note?' I asked him carefully.

'What note?' he looked at me, curious. 'There was nothing in her hand, nothing on the floor.'

This stumped us. We had been watching Alena all through the time before she fell and after, knew no one could have gotten so close as to have picked up or pocketed that note without us knowing. Even if we thought the only other witness, Shashi, had somehow taken it, we knew it actually was not possible. He hadn't come close to Alena—when she fell, he had watched Parvati go to her, realized it was serious, and had gone to fetch the hotel doctor.

Parvati and I looked at each other in silence. We had seen the note. We had seen Alena read it, noticed her puzzled expression and then her eagerness to eat the cake. Yet, the police had found nothing in the room. There was no note in her hand, nothing on the floor. Finding the missive was vital, it would offer us a clue as to the sender of the cake, at least.

Which begged the question—*where was it*?

28

Staying back in Pune was futile after we had combed RK's room for the possibility of the note and found nothing. Besides, though I'm documenting only this case here, we had other cases to attend to in Mumbai—work beckoned.

For RK too, despite the situation being as grave as it was, the pace of work had picked up suddenly. Bollywood is nothing if not business. The stalled mega-budget ghost movie had been revived; its producers had decided to shoot its other scenes in alternative locations, while leaving the carnival set for the Mumbai police to deal with.

So RK, too, had to return to Mumbai. As time meant money, he had no choice in the matter. His producers were clear on this because the movie stalling earlier had meant considerable losses in the intervening time.

Alena could not be shifted back to Mumbai immediately. She was still weak, needed rest, and was forbidden to travel for another day or so, the doctors had indicated. It was decided that she would stay back in the Pune hospital with her entourage to help, if needed.

As Saddaq had left for Mumbai already, there was no threat of him trying to meet with her. This meant Shashi would accompany RK back to Mumbai instead of holding fort at Alena's room as he had been doing in RK's absence.

Security on her floor had been upped, a cautionary instruction issued stopping her husband from visiting her, though honestly, legally there may not have been grounds to detain him if he arrived and wanted to see her—they were married, and besides, she always allowed him access. Regardless, Alena was being taken care of to the best of RK's ability, without him being physically present himself.

It was time to leave Pune, and so we did, thanking the magazine organizers for the effort they put in, despite the way everything had turned out. En route to Mumbai, in Parvati's car, we had a chance to discuss the case thus far.

'Do you think someone from the magazine could have sent the poisoned cake?' I asked Parvati as we negotiated the lovely green roads back to the city of our birth. 'Because they'd sent all those props, streamers, balloons, and whatnot with their name emblazoned on them as propaganda for the press?'

'The police investigated that part,' said Parvati. She had been in constant touch with the Pune police and had been kept in the loop as far as we knew. Dealing with the authorities always came easier to Parvati, her father and brother both being in RAW. 'They are still on it, but I don't think anyone from the magazine did it, Aku. My guess is, it's linked to whatever or whoever is targeting Mr Kamal all this while.'

'You mean to say that this incident is not isolated, it's simply a continuation of what has been happening around RK—the screams, the cat murdered, the extra killed on set, and now an attack on RK's lady love as well …'

'Recall Aku, that the extra was dressed as Mr Kamal. It might well be that the killer believed the extra to *be* Mr Kamal.' Parvati's tone was sombre, even as her eyes were on the road.

'Using that logic,' I said carefully piecing the incidents together in my mind's eye, '... the screams were to scare him, initially. The cat was his, it was meant to warn him or further terrify him. Then the killing was to do away with him?'

Then clarity dawned as I reached the next step in the series of incidents.

'When that didn't succeed, when the killer realized the extra was gone, not RK—the cake was sent ...?' I added, trying to think clearly. '*Pari, do you believe the cake was meant for RK, not Alena, in the first place, as we'd been pondering in Pune*?'

Parvati's expression was grim.

'It might well be. Or it might not. Which is why finding that note is crucial. It might provide some answers,' she said.

'But in all this, I cannot understand the glaring issue,' I said to her. 'It is clear RK is being targeted. But for what reason? *What is the motive*?'

'And if the motive involves doing away with Mr Kamal, would Shashi, so loyal to Mr Kamal, really be involved? *Are we on the right track including him as a suspect*?' Parvati murmured softly.

'Finding motive will give us the real picture,' Parvati continued. 'Getting to it is vital, because it will link everything. But motive, really, *is* what had been eluding us all this while. All these incidents are connected ... but *how?* And—*why*?'

'Do you think Alena is connected in more than just the poisoning?' I asked. 'For instance—who did she lose her temper with, that day at RK's home?'

'She has fallen into "victim" mode in this entire saga effectively, courting our sympathy, first with Saddaq's aggression on set, then with the poisoning. But, Aku, are we missing something? Is she really a victim, or is it an act? Has she been hatching a plan with Samuel to get to Mr Kamal's finances, or just playing with his emotions somehow, with Saddaq on standby?' Parvati thought aloud. 'And if she is involved, how on earth did she get herself poisoned to within an inch of awful consequences?'

'Then, of course, there is Shashi—ever present, a sullen influence, though always efficient,' I added. 'But how can we exclude him without a good reason? He could've been at Taqdeer, the unseen person we saw Alena getting furious at. Recall how that magazine junior said that he spent "almost all day" waiting for RK's costumes that day …'

'And then, there also lurk the shadow players—Saddaq, Mr Kamal's rival in the movie business and in love,' Parvati continued. 'Who was invited to the party but never attended, wasn't present. The mysterious Aman, who lives in Mr Kamal's house, yet, like Saddaq's absence at the party, never really seems to be around at the mansion. And Samuel—the ne'er do well, who wants a big piece of Alena's finances. And full control of her …'

'It's a dangerous sort of cobweb,' I mused. 'So many players, and a connect we can't seem to get to …'

'A connect that began superficially enough, with some scary screaming at Mr Kamal's home,' Parvati added.

'And then translated into *murder*,' I finished her thought.

'We will need to do more legwork,' Parvati said determinedly. 'If we are to arrive anywhere at all. We must be alert, Aku. Alert before the killer gets another opportunity to strike again.'

29

We were back in Mumbai. And a day post our return, we headed to another location of the sets of RK's movie, which had commenced once more.

'What are we hoping to find here?' I asked Parvati speculatively, en route, once again.

To me, this particular set visit didn't really seem to amount to much. As it was a different set to the one the extra was found murdered on, there was no point in searching the location for clues that might have been missed. The carnival scene with Alena and the Harlequins was not being revisited either, so we could not hope to meet even that shady sports star celebrity friend of Samuel's who was doing a guest appearance for that particular song.

As Alena herself was still in hospital in Pune as far as we knew, I doubted we would see the likes of Saddaq, or for that matter, Samuel nosing around at this location. I, therefore, did not get why we were visiting RK's set that day at all.

'We're hoping to *listen*,' Parvati said enigmatically.

'*Listen?*' I asked, incredulous. 'To whom?'

'To anyone who might want to talk, to tell us what they might not have, earlier,' Parvati explained, patiently. 'Recall there was panic and confusion when the extra, the stuntman Mohan Tawade, was strangled. No one from the movie really had a chance to speak *to us* properly, the set was taken over by the police soon after.'

'So, we're here to see if they can offer some clues,' I said, still doubtful how this would help our case, if the police had already interviewed them and found nothing of significance.

'We're here to *listen*,' Parvati repeated. 'When at a stalemate—the only thing left to do is to push harder and hope something opens up. So, we wait and we keep our eyes and ears open, and we make ourselves available to anyone who might want to talk about Mohan, about his connect to Mr Kamal, about Alena …'

'… Or Saddaq, or Samuel,' I completed the sentence for her. Parvati's course of action was actually the most sensible thing to do, I realized. Because if we were getting nothing from the source, RK, or from the suspects, having spoken to all of them by now—best go around them and seek information *about* them. If we dug hard and long, who knew what skeletons might tumble out, eventually?

'So, we just hang around all day?' I asked. The prospect seemed both boring and thankless at this point, or maybe this case was getting to me more than I admitted.

'Pretty much,' Parvati smiled at me and got out of the car. We'd reached our destination.

As detectives engaged by RK, it made sense to be around him, given that our main premise pointed to him being the primary target for increasingly serious malevolence. However, RK had upped his own security considerably. Our sticking to him was not really necessary for his protection, we all knew this. This visit was purely for Parvati's proposed plan of action. To *listen*, be open, allow for information to come in from sources apart from the key players.

The location this time was made to resemble a home. One room of a home, actually, the room where RK's scenes were being shot.

As this was a ghost movie in the romantic-thriller genre, there were several extra hands working to put together the machinery for the eerie background noises that RK would then be filmed responding to.

How very ironic, I thought. This is art imitating life. Because, in RK's actual house there were several eerie screams, what brought the case to us, in the first place. And RK had already become a nervous wreck responding to those when he engaged our services!

RK was getting make-up done at present we were told, which suited us because today we were here to mingle among the others on set. We said we were in no hurry to meet him immediately; we would still be around when he was done.

Leaving Parvati to make nice with other supporting actors gathering slowly, I wandered in and out of the make-believe room, weaving my way to get a sense of the rest of the huge set.

'I don't know how much we will get, out of this visit,' I said to myself. 'Might as well enjoy being on a film set. Channel where I might have ended up, had I not taken up detective work …'

'Akrutiji … Akrutiji,' a voice called out from behind a huge wood panel, interrupting my introspective mood.

Idly curious, I made my way past a heavy curtain attached to a screen, to get to the panel where the voice was originating from.

I found myself face to face with an unfamiliar person. An extra, hoping to say hi to me, no doubt—as I had mentioned before, I was used to this kind of attention, having been a top model just a few years ago.

'Akrutiji, it is so nice to meet you in person,' the man in front of me said, extending his own hand, to grasp mine before I could actually offer a handshake.

I shook his not-too-clean fingers and began to turn to make my way back to the room where the rest were gathered in. But he continued to speak.

'I have been a fan of yours for so long,' he said to me, in Hindi. 'Then I heard you gave up modelling. I didn't realize you were a part of this movie …'

'I'm not actually a part of this movie,' I replied to him in Hindi as politely as I could, smiling simultaneously, to thank him for being a fan, before preparing to make an exit. 'I'm here to help someone.'

'RK, is it?' the man asked eagerly, his face expectant. Something about his expression made me delay my departure.

'Why would you pick RK over the others here?' I asked him curiously. 'Because of what's being written in the papers?'

'No, because he's been on my mind a lot. He's a good man, I've heard. A friend from my village used to correspond with him regularly,' the man said. 'For a very long time, in fact. Over years and years. Our village knew RK to be a nice man, but he used to have problems in his career. My friend was always supportive and encouraging of him. Of course, afterwards, he became a superstar. I thought of him now and mentioned it to you because I felt, maybe he has career problems again, in all that has happened recently? I wish him well because of that old connect. Our village is very far, but still it was like RK was one of our own, because of the letters he used to send Aman …'

I started at the familiar name from this dishevelled-looking person. I leaned closer to take a proper look at the man.

He wore a nondescript shirt over brown pants. A youngish if careworn face, and eyes that looked weary as if from some great strain or turmoil. Not shifty, simply tired, I noted. So, I made a bigger effort at being approachable now.

Of course, I couldn't quite fit this man in, as being friends with the charming, dimpled, well-turned-out Aman we all knew. But I had to make sure.

'Aman?' I asked softly, hoping that serendipity might have put me in a position of learning something finally, about RK's reserved houseguest. 'Was your friend's name Aman Azad?'

'Yes,' he replied, but did not smile. 'He came to meet RK around seven months ago. After so many years of writing to him, he wanted to meet him in person, take his blessings ...'

'I see,' I said. 'And that does not make you happy?'

He looked at me strangely, as if I was someone slow-witted.

'It makes me very happy,' he said. 'It made us all very happy ...'

I still did not understand why he was looking so strained, his words and his expression at such odds with each other.

'I haven't introduced myself,' he said simply. 'Akrutiji, my name is Amrut. Amrut Tawade.'

I grasped the last name and suddenly the dots connected.

'I came from the village three days ago,' the man called Amrut said, his voice thick with emotion. 'To collect my brother after the police finished their post-mortem. *I'm Mohan Tawade's brother*.'

30

No wonder Amrut Tawade wasn't concerned about Aman's fortunes at present. He was here under very difficult circumstances, of an entirely sobering nature. I scolded myself mentally for not recognizing the signs earlier—the weary eyes, the strained face, the halting voice—the man was not jealous of Aman from his village for having sought to meet his idol. He was not going to be telling me something salacious about Aman Azad at all. He was simply grieving for his murdered brother.

'I'm so very sorry for what happened,' I said to Amrut. 'You came only now for the last rites?'

'They had trouble contacting us,' Amrut said, his face working to contain his sorrow. 'Then I had to put together the money for the journey ...'

'And now?' I asked, feeling worse and worse. Sometimes, the tremendous disconnect between the poverty-stricken areas in rural India and its big brazen cities hit very close to home.

'I've cremated him without my family,' Amrut said his voice shaky. 'There was no money to take him back home like that. And it had been too many days. I cannot go back either, I have no money. The set-in-charges, one of the junior ones who knew Mohan, worked something out for me on this film.

I cannot take his place, I'm no stuntman. But I can work as an extra hand in any capacity they need. So, I'm here on this set since yesterday, trying to earn enough to go back home.'

His words shook me up. That he had to scramble to get enough money to come to Mumbai to collect his brother's body was bad enough. But that he couldn't pay his way to return with it was just too saddening a scenario to stomach. Now he was stuck here, having cremated his brother, working, ironically enough, on the same movie as his slain sibling, till he managed to find enough funds to return.

'Surely there must be a way?' I said. 'Have you asked your friend Aman to help?'

'I have not, and I won't,' Amrut shook his head decisively. 'I do not want to beg. He came here on his own steam. He got lucky to have met RK. I don't want to intrude on his good fortune by worrying him for funds. Actually, I didn't even know how he had fared till Mohan wrote to me around a month before his passing. I didn't know till then that Aman had actually met RK even. Good for him. Though what his fiancée back home must be thinking, I don't know. He has stayed for so long, and I don't know if he told her he met his idol.'

'Why, didn't he come to seek RK's blessings in order to act in the movies?' I asked, puzzled by Amrut's last sentence.

'To act in films?' It was Amrut who looked puzzled now. 'Aman didn't come here to seek RK's blessings in order to act. He came here to seek his blessings in order to get married.'

'Have *you* met Aman since you arrived?' I asked, feeling a little befuddled by his revelation. The lure of Tinseltown was immense, I knew this, and Aman's would not be the first story of a villager abandoning family duties back home to pursue the arc lights.

But I still felt it might have been hard on the lady he had left behind. Especially if he continued to use his considerable charm with the ladies in Mumbai, as he had with Parvati and me, earlier on. In fact, he certainly seemed to have brushed off any rough edges from his hometown, appearing suave and polished when we met him—at first impressions, seeming not at all like a villager, but a city-slickened Bollywood hopeful, I recalled.

'No, I just arrived three days ago,' Amrut answered. 'Aman doesn't know I'm here. We are too proud to ask for favours from people like ourselves. We can work for what we need.'

'Did Aman know Mohan was here?' I asked, curious about this unexpected connect. 'Did Mohan write to you that he'd actually met with Aman, or just that he'd heard via some filmi set gossip, that Aman had finally met his idol RK?'

It was dawning on me, that if Mohan and Aman were from the same village and knew each other, Aman didn't appear to have known of Mohan's murder when we'd last met. Aman had mentioned not following the news, not knowing the dead extra's name … what a shock it would be for him when he found out, if indeed this was the case. I concentrated on Amrut's words.

'Does it matter?' Amrut said listlessly, as if that was something of little importance now. 'Mohan's gone now …'

'Hey there—you're needed.' A junior production hand appeared in the far distance and waved impatiently to Amrut, no doubt to help with some props he was balancing in his arms.

Amrut folded his palms together as if in namaste, a farewell to me, and shuffled off to do the task assigned.

I moved disheartened and thoughtful back towards the room where I'd left Parvati. The timelines coincided I thought—Aman left his village seven months ago, got into a bad accident. Took him maybe a month, to not just get back to some sort of mobility but to break through RK's security circle and meet with his idol finally, to secure an invite, and then begin to stay at Taqdeer, six months ago.

But Aman had apparently changed track post his accident—decided he wanted to enter films without telling his fiancée back home from the looks of it. Was that because of the accident and his close brush with mortality? Did he not tell her so as to hold on to some shred of dignity, like Amrut had when I saw him earlier, till he could make something of himself, after his injury?

Had he assumed, with the patient forbearance of the very poor, that his fiancée would overcome any worry she might feel at his continuing absence till he chose to make his turn of fortune known? He had certainly worked hard on himself, managed to change from the kind of gauche villager I saw in Amrut, to the suave man we had met, in such a short span ...

I needed to speak with Parvati on this. I was also feeling weighed down by the depth of poor Amrut's misery, given his poverty and his pride, refusing to ask for much-needed help when he clearly required it.

I saw her at a distance speaking to a few production types, no doubt gathering any information we might get to shed light on our case.

But meeting Amrut had deflated my spirits—I wasn't sure I could help her by speaking to others at this point. So, I sidled up to her side and just quietly listened to her conversation with the production people.

'He was not inclined to make friends easily,' one of them was saying. I realized as I stood there that they were speaking of Mohan Tawade. 'He kept to himself.'

'But he was a good stuntman,' another addressed Parvati. 'Sure of himself and confident.'

'Yes, even the difficult action shots he managed with ease,' the earlier guy corroborated. 'There was no visible nervousness at all. In fact, he was so competent we felt he would rise fast in the stunt scenario. He was quick and efficient.'

'Rise fast?' Parvati questioned. 'Was he new to the profession?'

'He was,' another in the cluster of movie professionals surrounding her said. 'In fact, I think this may have been his first or second movie. He got lucky, he was taken on because of his strong resemblance to RK. He imitated RK's mannerisms quite comfortably ...'

'But none of us knew him apart from work,' said someone at the back. 'He was rather a sullen type.'

'He was?' Parvati frowned in concentration.

'Sullen or shy, we couldn't quite make out,' said another. 'But who has the time to find out? This profession is such, we are thrown together for a short time. We do our jobs and move to the next film. Those who are friendly make the most of it, they network. The rest ...' He shrugged his shoulders.

'One or two of us did get a slightly shady vibe from him,' a third addressed Parvati.

'How do you mean?' She turned to him, interested.

'Concerning someone's money that went missing on set. I think he was involved, got found out and then pulled up for it. It made him even more sullen or bitter. I don't want to make a big deal of it,' the man said to her. 'I do not want to speak ill of the dead. Besides, we are needed on set now,' he added brusquely.

'Thank you for your time,' Parvati said to them, sighting me finally as they moved off in a body.

'Aku, where have you been?' she said, then not waiting for me to answer, hastened on, 'I was searching all over for you. Get your handbag, we're leaving.'

'Why?' I asked, a bit unnerved at her haste after the seemingly leisurely interview of before. 'What's happened?'

'It's Alena,' Parvati replied. 'She sent word via Mr Kamal's private phoneline, it was conveyed to me by someone from his entourage fifteen minutes ago. But I couldn't locate you so I made use of the time by speaking to the production people. She's properly awake. And asking for us.'

31

Finally, we might actually get some answers, I thought to myself. Madame Sleeping Beauty had awakened. And miraculously—we were being summoned to her bedside, instead of having to fight for a chance to ask questions of her caretakers and entourage!

'Are we returning to Pune?' I asked Parvati on the way back from the sets. Because of our hurried departure, we had not managed to meet RK, but that was fine, given time was of the essence now. Who knew which person the mystery killer would target next?

'No, she has been brought down to Mumbai,' Parvati said. 'She came in today, we're going directly to her at the same hospital she was at, earlier.'

'Did you get much done on set?' I asked her.

'Yes, I believe we have some sort of character sketch of the murdered extra—you listened in to most of it. Mohan was sullen, shady even apparently? But not enough to go on, there was nothing more of significance,' Parvati replied. 'What were you up to?'

I turned troubled eyes on her as she drove.

'I met the murdered extra's brother,' I said to her. 'His name is Amrut.'

'That's interesting,' Parvati said. 'He worked with his brother here? What did the brother tell you?'

'No, Amrut came three days ago from the village,' I said listlessly. 'He didn't have money to come here to collect Mohan's body before then ...'

'Did he tell you about Mohan? Any clue as to what might have triggered the strangulation? Any connect to Mr Kamal, apart from the obvious, that Mohan was his stunt double?' Parvati asked, her voice showing her deep interest. 'We've found out Mohan was competent workwise, new to the job, kept to himself and was pulled up for a shady dealing. And bore a strong resemblance to Mr Kamal, of course. So did his brother elaborate?'

'No,' I said. 'I was too shocked at the circumstances he was operating in, to ask much about his brother's character. But Pari—there is a long-time, indirect connect to RK, I discovered it by accident, as he was speaking ...' I was hastening to explain about Aman and Amrut, but at that moment, it was not to be.

Parvati was distracted by an errant motorcyclist on the road. She swerved to avoid him and the conversation stopped. There was no mishap. The motorcyclist veered off, waving an apology.

To a suspicious reader, this motorcyclist's sudden appearance might seem yet another effort at a random attack in this odd case, this time targeting us. But I'm happy to say that it wasn't.

Near-mishaps were part and parcel of driving on overcrowded city roads, with everyone squeezing through congestion to get ahead. Regardless, they still managed to unnerve one when they happened. And today, already under pressure from this never-ending case, we had been unnerved too. We weren't hurt though, just a bit shaken.

We were close to the hospital by this point, so I left the telling of the rest of my conversation with Amrut for later. Our minds were on Alena, and reaching her as fast as possible. Speaking to her was crucial now. She would impart clarity on what the note on the cake had said.

That would give us some clue as to the identity of who might have sent it, because neither we nor the police, so far, had any leads. And maybe her testimony would offer a possible link as to the other strange events preceding the poisoned cake.

'There's more on Mr Kamal in the tabloid press today.' Parvati's voice was grim as we reached the elevators to the hospital. 'Did you read it?'

'About him engineering false data on his home to keep the heritage activists at bay?' I responded as we both stepped into the lift together. 'Yes, I read it.'

'And paying off people in the civic body to make sure no further trouble was created,' Parvati said soberly. 'Wonder where they got all that information from …'

I shook my head to indicate my befuddlement as we reached Alena's floor. 'This case keeps getting murkier and murkier,' I said in despair, as we made our way towards Alena's room.

En route, we bumped into Shashi of all the people, returning from the room as we were on our way in.

'Are you both going to meet Her Highness?' he asked, nodding in greeting. 'Well, you can't. At least, not right now. The doctors are finishing up some tests, we've all been ordered out.'

We saw her entourage filing out from inside the room and realized he was right.

'RK's shooting at present, so he's sent you, naturally,' I said, as light dawned as to Shashi's presence on the floor.

'Yes, I was here helping with the paperwork when she came in,' Shashi concurred. 'As you know, Roop has only to ask, and I will comply ...'

'How is she?' Parvati cut straight to the chase. 'Is she coherent enough to answer questions?'

'She was asleep earlier, but she's awake now, groggy,' Shashi said. 'But she says there's something very important you both need to know. She wanted to meet you immediately, as she arrived, so I telephoned Roop on the set. Then she slept again, tired from the journey, and has woken up only now.'

'Yes, we got the message, left as soon as we could,' Parvati said. 'Thank you for that.'

'No problem,' Shashi said. 'I tried asking her about the note we all saw that night ...'

'You did?' Parvati's eyes narrowed as she looked straight into Shashi's eyes.

We hadn't discussed with Shashi about Alena reading the note that night, nor the fact that it had gone missing in Pune. The question on both our minds now, I knew: Did Shashi ask Alena only about the note's contents or was his intent far darker, as he fished to find out: *where had Alena kept that missing, incriminating note?*

'Don't look at me like that, I'm not dumb,' Shashi addressed Parvati. 'I realized that the note was missing when the police failed to mention its presence back in Pune. And she wasn't awake there, so I knew it could not have been discussed. You both didn't mention finding it to Roop either, but you asked him about it—yes, he tells me *everything*—so I knew it had not been found by you either. I had watched her with you two, as she read it that fateful night. I knew it was important …'

'What did Alena say?' Parvati asked him quietly. She knew this was the most important point, over and above all of Shashi's long explanations.

'She didn't.' Shashi met her eyes, his own clear and unclouded. 'She says she doesn't remember receiving a note. Or the cake either. All that happened immediately preceding her poisoning is a blank. *The doctors call it short-term memory loss …*'

32

Parvati and I digested Shashi's news in silence. He had just told us Alena had no memory of the note she had read only moments before she ingested the cake it came with—the cake that poisoned her, luckily not fatally because we had been so quick to react. The vital clue we had been counting on, therefore, was still missing.

Shashi was as yet on our list of suspects. He could be lying to us, sure, but there were too many witnesses around for him to be making this piece of information up. We could check its veracity anyway, when we were finally allowed to meet Alena or also, with her doctors. He knew this and possibly wouldn't be so stupid even if he was guilty. In this case, though, both of us believed he was telling us the truth. *How had an important note vanished so, into thin air?*

'Addl CP Mhatre was here too, earlier,' Shashi was saying. 'He feels that all these happenings around Roop are linked. The cat's death, the extra's strangling and the attempt on Alena. But Alena was asleep, and the doctors encouraged him to come by later—they didn't want to wake her. He wasn't happy, but he complied …'

There was a sudden interruption as one of Alena's entourage came up to where we were standing.

'The front desk at the hospital is asking for you,' the person said. 'They sent a message to be conveyed to you, RK has called—he wants one of you on the line.'

We knew that it would be some time before Alena's tests were completed. The doctors had just gone in as we had stepped onto her floor from the lift.

'Go,' Shashi said. 'Speak with Roop. I'll come and fetch you if she gets free of the doctors sooner than you finish with him.'

We left him standing there amidst her entourage and made our way back downstairs, to the front reception desk of the huge hospital.

An excited-looking receptionist handed us the phone. She had recognized me as a former supermodel, it would seem. 'It's RK,' she tittered. I smiled at her politely, noting her thrill at talking to the superstar. Whatever troubles RK was currently going through, evidently, his fan following was still intact.

Parvati took the receiver. She believed this call to be on account of RK's extreme concern, wanting to know about Alena and how she was doing after her transfer from Pune to Mumbai. He must've been calling from the private line set up in his trailer. We had left his set without saying goodbye earlier, as he had been getting ready for his shot.

But RK wasn't calling to *ask* us anything. He was calling to *tell* us something vital.

I heard Parvati's excitement as she spoke to him, but her tone was muted, muffled on purpose so as not to be overheard by the overexcited hospital staff waiting around us.

'Yes,' she said finally, before saying her goodbyes. 'I'll be here waiting ...'

As she kept the receiver down, Parvati's eyes shone, that brightness I'd come to recognize when on the track of something important.

'What did RK want?' I asked curiously, impatiently I should add, because her expression too, held that deep-seated excitement.

'Mr Kamal said he'll be coming to see Alena here as soon as his shift on the set is done, whenever that is,' she said to me. 'Come, we have business at the gate.' She tugged at me to follow her, and I did.

'What are we doing here?' I asked, now even more impatient because of her evasiveness.

'Waiting,' said the incorrigible Parvati.

She was exasperating me by withholding the information RK had shared; she knew it was getting on my nerves, but she wouldn't come to the point any faster.

'Waiting for *whom*?' I asked, now almost cheesed off.

But I already had my reply. Walking towards us swinging her huge work briefcase which no doubt also housed her laptop, was the very last person I'd expected to see.

'Tarini,' I called out, more in recognition than in greeting. 'From *Cine So Fine* magazine ...'

'I knew you'd know her,' Parvati said, satisfaction writ large on her features, as the journalist who had broken the story on Alena and Samuel Rodrigues's marriage walked up to us, waving to me in greeting. 'Because I don't know what she looks like. Mr Kamal sent her here ...'

'RK requested I give you this,' she said, removing a pink envelope, strangely familiar, from her briefcase. 'We spoke to him because Alena is well—indisposed.'

Her magazine was the one whose awards show had been cancelled in Pune, and Alena had been poisoned whilst in attendance for the same. The fact had served to make Tarini seem more contrite than eager as she handed over the note to me.

'The dry-cleaners found it,' she went on. 'Stuffed in one of the deep pockets of the faux fur coat Alena was wearing. The coat was a prop, meant as propaganda for our awards night. Alena was wearing it quite happily at the party the night before, we thought there would be pictures taken. The magazine name is embossed at the back of the coat. But then …'

Tarini stopped short at the memory of what had actually happened at the party. Then, as if dismissing the thought, she continued, 'Alena's staff returned the coat to the magazine after what happened. And we sent it for dry-cleaning in Pune itself.'

'The coat was removed from her person in the room when she fell, to give her air. I don't think the police realized she was wearing it, else it would've been evidence,' I said under my breath. I knew Parvati had already figured this out too. Clearly, neither Alena's staff nor the magazine staff had really given much thought to it, else the coat, housing this missive, would not be finding its way to us, but to the Pune police.

'So, while the coat was being cleaned, they found the envelope,' Tarini went on. 'And they called us. We called the Pune hospital to reach Alena, but they wouldn't allow contact or divulge if she was still there. The hospital, in fact, called RK, because Alena's hospital bills in Pune were paid for by him, apparently because she was poisoned at his party. RK was shooting, said to drop it off to you here. Anyway, thought this might be of sentimental value to her?'

I took the note, nodded to Tarini who gave us both a business-like smile. RK had as yet, and miraculously, managed to keep his romance with Alena under wraps from the press—paying her hospital bills because he was hosting the party at which she was poisoned? Interesting excuse, I thought to myself. But more importantly now—we had the missing note! Though, no doubt, the entire magazine had already read the contents of the envelope.

'Any news on our patient?' Tarini asked, as matter of course, her journalist training already telling her we would never be the ones to share any news with her or her gossip publication. 'We heard she'd been shifted here from Pune? Is that true? Is that why RK said you'd be found here?'

'I'm sure you'll get to know.' I smiled at her, and she took the hint without offence. I'd always been nice to journalists in my modelling heyday and they all remembered it. Professional courtesy went both ways, even all this while later.

'Speedy recovery to Alena from all of us at *Cine So Fine*,' Tarini mouthed briskly, already pushing away from us, leaving as rapidly as she'd arrived. She'd probably get to work on the story of Alena being back in Mumbai as soon as she got clear of us!

I clutched the note, hardly daring to believe it was now with us. This pink envelope was familiar and precious. It was the reason RK had directed Tarini to us immediately upon hearing from her. He had, perhaps, guessed it might be important.

But he had no real idea of how important it was. This ordinary pink envelope housed the very missive we had so intently been in search of all this while—*it housed the note Alena had read before eating the poisoned cake.*

33

'So, what are you waiting for?' Parvati's voice was brisk as she threw a meaningful glance at the pink envelope in my hand, then at me. 'Open it.'

With clammy fingers, I opened the envelope. Inside, there was the note that we, at a distance, had seen Alena read, its pink paler than the envelope it arrived in. In a bold scrawl, penned with a black marker and written across the length of the note, the message: *To dear Alena, from your ardent admirer.*

A seemingly innocuous message, innocent enough to allow this note to be handed over to us, by the magazine personnel who retrieved it from the dry-cleaners in another city. They possibly believed some fan of hers might have given her some gift, and she liked the note so saved it in her coat for later.

They didn't know the back story, had not witnessed the note arriving with the poisoned cake. Being unaware of the sequence of events, they had not realized it was important evidence. And they did not know the significance of these apparently innocuous words in the larger picture at all.

'Aku,' Parvati's voice had that low, silky tone that meant she was deeply invested in what she was revealing. 'Aku—the note is innocent enough. Unfortunately, it does not reveal the sender's name or identity, as we'd hoped. *But do you understand the importance of the clue it just gave us?*'

I nodded. I realized exactly what the note was telling us—only, it didn't make any sense.

'It's telling us the cake was meant for Alena, and only Alena,' I said, rather unsettled in this discovery. 'It's addressed directly to her, it doesn't mention RK at all—*so it had nothing to do with what's happening to him … ?*'

'Exactly. Which doesn't fit in with our theory of all these terrible events happening to target Mr Kamal alone.' Parvati's eyes became narrower, as if she was thinking hard. 'We need to review our work. Approach it from the angle just revealed to us …'

'Which is?' I asked, flummoxed.

'Let's go back a bit,' Parvati said. 'It's the night of the party. The cake is wheeled in, pink, perfect, if too small for a gathering of this size. Alena thinks the cake that has arrived has been ordered by Mr Kamal. She had been expecting a surprise, and possibly figured it might be a cake, knowing Mr Kamal loves to gift her traditional, feminine things …'

'Yes, recall the flowers RK kept filling her room with, when Saddaq had beaten her up,' I broke in.

'Exactly,' Parvati repeated. 'So, the cake arrives, and Alena makes a beeline for it. She opens the envelope, believing it …'

'Believing it to be full of profound endearments from her lover, RK,' I cut in once more, excited, as I worked out what happened that night.

'But she only sees *this*,' Parvati completes the thought for me. 'A one-line missive, curt and to the point, if flattering. Not professing any kind of bounty or words of love from Mr Kamal …'

'So, she is puzzled,' I continue. 'Hurt even? She looks around for RK, wanting, perhaps *needing* an explanation for this rather short and impersonal note, given their torrid affair. She still believes the cake is from him, and that this is a game she must play. Recall, the party is in RK's suite, anyone other than RK sending Alena a surprise would've sent it to *her* room, not his. She is still fairly certain this cake is his gift to her. And she expects something more, something she has to *find* ...'

'True,' Parvati's expression is thoughtful. 'She sees him across the room, a long way off, surrounded by people eager to talk to him. She doesn't feel up to crossing over all the way in that jamboree in those high boots and coat, so she shrugs, as if to say what the heck ...'

'She'll eat the cake anyway!' I add to Parvati's imagined reconstruction.

'Yes,' Parvati says. 'She possibly thought so. But recall, Aku, how she ate the cake ...'

'Furtively and quickly, she didn't want to share,' I said.

'Which is contrary to all the airs and graces she normally puts on,' Parvati reflected. 'Think for a minute—could her behaviour in gulping down such a large piece in such haste and possibly going for more, had the inevitable not happened, be because ...'

'She was expecting to find a ring or some such hidden inside,' I guessed. 'The note was curt, she might've thought, after the initial shock of reading it, that it was to befuddle her or throw her off. It might well be a game, the real prize was the one she had to find. *She believed the actual prize lay within the cake!* She wanted to reach it, and in the party mood she was in, didn't care for propriety, didn't offer *her* cake to anyone ...'

Parvati nodded in agreement. 'I believe this is what might have happened,' she said simply. 'And while her behaviour seemed most graceless to the three of us watching—Shashi, you and me—she was simply hastening to her objective. She believed, I think, that there might be a prize, possibly an engagement ring along with a more explicit note, buried in the cake. Hence her tearing hurry to get to it …'

'Such that she grabbed a piece, wanting to keep the cake and the game all to herself, then wiping her chocolate-covered hands on the faux fur coat,' I recalled, shuddering at the distasteful image of her dirty manners then.

'Ah, but held in her hands all along was the envelope with the note,' reflected Parvati.

'And while wiping her chocolate-soiled hands on the coat, she also managed to slip in the note in the coat pocket for later,' I said. 'Possibly intending to ask or tease RK about it, after the party …'

'Only she never got to doing that, or even checking the rest of the cake for her expectant surprise, because she was poisoned in that first bite alone.' Parvati's expression now turned grim.

'And the note lay in that coat, unnoticed and undiscovered till the dry-cleaners in Pune found it,' I added, quietly.

'But now it is here.' Parvati turned to me, determination glinting in her eyes. 'And we must follow the path it leads us to …'

'Which is?' I repeated my earlier question, the one I had asked before we began the reconstruction of that night in Pune when Alena was poisoned.

'We must broaden the picture, look at everything the other way round,' Parvati said. '*As if not just Mr Kamal, but Alena too, were in danger …*'

34

There was nothing left to do but head up to Alena's room, now that we had arrived at this new way of looking at the case post our reconstruction of events that fateful night in Pune.

Someone wanted to kill Alena or RK or both. That person was ruthless enough to have sent a poisoned cake to a party, uncaring of how many would actually ingest it, on its way to its intended victim. The question remained even if this person learnt of the party and its guest list, information available easily enough at the awards show dance rehearsals, or even through the magazine's event organizers, how could this person be sure that the cake would indeed be consumed by Alena?

Had this person been present then, in the room that night, watching to make sure Alena ate the cake? Was the killer in our midst, even now unnoticed? The thought was not comforting.

It was on my mind that only three from all our key players had been in attendance that night at the party—RK, Shashi and Alena herself. Of the three, I could hardly suppose that Alena, having fortuitously escaped death and lying near-immobile on a hospital bed, would have actually dared to risk her own life in such a terrifying manner. This case was becoming more baffling by the day, and as dangerous. I was troubled. Present matters, however, needed my attention.

Shashi hadn't come down to call us, which meant the doctors were still in Alena's room.

'You know, Aku, Shashi mentioned Alena had something important to tell us.' Parvati's expression was intent as we waited for the hospital elevators once more.

'He mentioned that she didn't remember eating the cake or the note ... so it couldn't be connected to her memory that night,' I said.

'Yes,' Parvati agreed. 'And yet she said it was important she speak with us.'

'The word Shashi used was "*very*" important. What could it possibly be?' I mused. 'That she was so insistent on it, even as she came back to awareness?'

'Also, don't forget she is recovering—her short-term memory might return sooner than we suppose ...' Parvati said.

'Let's hope it does. We could use a break in this case,' I finished.

I spoke too soon. We stepped into the elevator together, and ran smack bang into Samuel Rodrigues, already in the lift, also heading to the same floor.

'Hullo,' he nodded as the doors shut. We were disturbed, but we didn't dare show it. What was Samuel doing here? Who had told him Alena was back in Mumbai? And would he actually be allowed to meet her?

The ride up took place in silence—there were too many people in the elevator to warrant a conversation. But I knew Parvati was uneasy, just as I was.

There was another shock as we stepped onto the floor. Because pacing the corridor at one end was the brawny Saddaq Haque, his entourage watching him anxiously, a respectful distance away.

Shashi came up to us, wringing his hands in anxiety.

'Saddaq arrived a while ago, just as you both left the floor to attend to Roop's call,' he confided. 'He got to know about Alena's hospital transfer to Mumbai. He barrelled his way in, and nobody could stop him. But he has to wait till the doctors finish like the rest of us. Is *he* here too ...?'

The last line was because Shashi had just caught sight of Samuel, who had been lurking in the curve of the passageway after stepping out of the elevator. Now he sidled up to us, his gait cocky and confident, even though his expression was sombre.

'My poor wife,' he said as he came up to us. 'Who could have possibly done this?'

'How did you know she was here?' Parvati's voice, icy, yet polite, addressed him directly.

'I have my network,' Samuel said, looking at her without enthusiasm. 'I couldn't be with her in Pune, but I knew she'd have to be transferred here soon enough.'

'Were you in Pune for the awards?' I couldn't help asking, my curiosity was so high.

'How does it matter?' Samuel said. His expression was still sombre, as if he was truly put out over Alena's poisoning. 'But to answer your question—no, I wasn't. I was going to be at the awards on the day itself, I would've driven down to Pune in the early hours of the morning. But I got to know of the events of the party and Alena's poisoning a few hours after it happened, again through my network. I knew the show would be cancelled the next morning, and I was right.'

We waited expectantly as he stopped for breath, then continued, as if wanting to share.

'There was no point in going to Pune then, not unless I was sure I would be able to meet Alena,' Samuel continued.

'But she was unconscious, under very tight security and the police were around. I didn't want to complicate my position by insisting on seeing her. She was in good hands. I could wait. So, I did. And the moment I heard she was being shifted to Mumbai, I cleared my schedule. And now here I am. Can the room really fit so many visitors?'

Before anyone could reply to his unexpected question at the end of his monologue, the elevator doors slid open once more, and stepping out, to our surprise, and increasing dismay, full entourage in tow, was—RK.

We had spoken with him a little more than an hour ago, RK had said he would come by after his shift—what had changed so suddenly that he had to rush here? Now, worryingly, there were two superstars on the same floor, both on edge and anxious about their indisposed lady love. Her as-yet-legally wed husband, so far a shady presence, also waiting to see her. A packed floor, courtesy of various entourages, in a hospital, which by rule necessitated silence. And yet, emotions were at a high, ready to explode if instigated. It was a full-scale disaster waiting to happen.

'Oh my God, oh my God,' Shashi muttered, in near-panic as he wrung his hands and hastened towards his friend, telling us under his breath as he left: 'Please handle Saddaq. Roop is my responsibility.'

It was Parvati who moved first. Samuel had stepped back into the corridor at the curve of the passageway leading from the elevator to Alena's room. True to his shifty nature, he had no intention of coming into conflict with both heroes on opposite ends of the floor over his wife. But we knew he was fully invested in his golden goose of a life partner, he would not leave till he saw her.

Parvati approached Saddaq with typical coolness, her characteristic level-headedness evident in her expression.

No matter how she felt about him beating Alena earlier, today she was here as a mediator in case things got ugly and her body language conveyed that from the onset.

But she need not have worried. Saddaq stepped up as she approached, his expression subdued, his hands folded, in a typical, if filmi, namaste.

'Parvatiji,' he said. 'I'm not here to cause trouble. But I must see her. See for myself if she's all right. If she had died, I would not be able to …'

He left the last bit of his melodramatic sentence unsaid. Parvati observed him carefully, as did I, but today there seemed no trace of the supposed drug use in his eyes or manner.

'There are a lot of people waiting.' Parvati's voice was pleasant. 'You will have to wait your turn to go inside her room.'

But his docility surprised us on that.

'We can all go in together,' he said, his voice eager, vibrating with sincerity. 'I will not give anyone cause for complaint. This is a hospital, *Alena almost died*. You will have no trouble from me, I promise.'

Parvati looked at me, and I knew from her eyes that she was convinced. But our concern now lay elsewhere. *How would RK behave, seeing his rival here? And worse, seeing Samuel?*

We weren't in the mood for small talk and neither was Saddaq. Once we got his assurance that there would be no trouble from him tonight, we were content to leave him to his devices till the doctors allowed us in. In the meanwhile, we headed to RK's corner of the floor.

As we walked the length of the floor to the other side, I was surprised to note a familiar figure amongst the entourage milling around RK. He was trying to get closer to RK, pointing out his limp to those gathered, so that they would allow him the necessary space to get closer to the superstar.

'Pari,' I said, the surprise evident in my voice. 'Aman has come too.'

'I noticed,' Parvati said, a slightly different note in her tone, even as she doubled her pace to stride briskly up to RK and Shashi, conversing in low voices a little away from the crowd of his aides. I followed her to them. We could always catch up with Aman later—RK was first priority.

'Mr Kamal,' Parvati said as she reached RK. 'Did the shoot get over early?'

When we had left the set that afternoon, we had been informed that to overcome all the earlier delays, now that the film was rolling again, today's shoot was slotted as a day and night one. Which meant that RK would've been required to work continuously from the afternoon going into the night, depending on his takes.

He had told us as much when we spoke with him from the hospital later, saying he would come by after his shift got over, whenever that would be. So, how then, had he managed to convince his producers and directors to let him go, and arrive here to be at Alena's bedside so soon?

'No, it was slotted to be a night shoot too,' replied RK, to Parvati's query. We saw upon coming closer that he looked visibly shaken, drawn and tremendously on edge.

He met Parvati's eyes wearily as he delivered the next shocker.

'There was a mishap. A heavy set collapsed on an extra. He was in a critical condition, and had to be rushed to hospital,' RK told us quietly, then in a broken voice, 'I think this movie is jinxed. I think I am jinxed!'

35

Quick as lightning, Parvati had moved to stand beside RK. Her hand went to his shoulder, she squeezed it, a strong gesture of supplication and support. Parvati could always be counted on, to read a heavy or tense situation correctly and act quickly to defuse it.

'You are not jinxed in any way, Mr Kamal,' she said, clear and confident in her tone. 'You need to believe in yourself more. Accidents happen, they cannot be predicted. You know that.'

Shashi drew me aside as Parvati continued speaking reassuringly to RK who appeared to be listening intently to her words.

'This was no accident,' he said sombrely. 'The production crew have only just informed me, via the usual network I have in place. The heavy scenery set was deliberately pushed, so as to fall. Roop doesn't know, and I don't want to tell him yet in his current, anxious state. The set wasn't supposed to be there, it was wheeled in, and then deliberately let loose, shoved forcefully enough to crash down. It is too sturdy to fall on its own, without effort ...'

'Are you serious?' I asked him, horrified. 'Was RK supposed to be shooting around it at the time?'

What I left unsaid was—*Was it meant for RK, this 'accident'?* Did it mean that this was an attempt on RK's life, one that we could not have stopped, because we hadn't been around on the set then?

'No,' Shashi looked a trifle confused. 'It wasn't supposed to be Roop's shot. He was nowhere near the place. It was a random shot, of a person looking at some scenery. And they called in the extra to stand there for the long-distance shot. Then, this second scenery set was wheeled in behind him, though it did not catch anyone's attention. Only when it was pushed upon him, obviously by a person or persons unseen, they realized the calamity. That set is very sturdy, cannot just fall on someone unless effort is made to topple it. So, they realized it was deliberate, but didn't know who did it. It happened in seconds.'

I breathed a sigh of relief. Even if it was some sort of attempt at sabotaging this movie, for reasons unclear, at least it wasn't deliberately meant to target RK this time.

'The police haven't been notified, my network told me,' Shashi continued. 'The production unit covered it up by saying it was accidental. They want no more stalling of this film.'

I heard Shashi's disturbing last sentence in silence, as we turned to rejoin Parvati and RK, the latter looking visibly calmer after listening to Parvati's words of succour.

'I'm glad you're with me on this,' he was saying to Parvati as we approached. 'You too, Akruti. This run of bad luck is enough to get all of us superstitious. But it was an accident as you say. I should count my blessings. Others apart from me are also suffering. That poor extra, he too has had a terrible innings of late. First his brother gets strangled on set, then he gets so grievously hurt ...'

'What did you say?' I couldn't wait for him to complete his sentence. I almost shrieked, 'Who was the extra?'

'Amrut Tawade,' Shashi spoke quietly from behind me, in my ear, making me jump, I was so rattled. 'Mohan Tawade's brother.'

I could not contain my shock and I let out an involuntary cry of dread, '*Oh no!*'

Parvati looking disturbed, turned towards me, seeing my reaction. She left RK's side and came over to me rapidly, a frown furrowing her brow.

'What is this, Aku?' she asked in a low voice. 'You're supposed to help me keep the peace with Mr Kamal, not get him jumpy all over again. I know it's terrible news, but it was an accident.'

'But I just spoke to Amrut this afternoon,' I bleated, in real distress. The memory of that poor man who I had spoken to was being conjured up in my mind's eye, his predicament and his sincerity haunting me now.

Parvati's brow cleared, as if in understanding.

'I realize it's quite a shock,' she said soothingly. 'As you'd had an interaction with him just today. But accidents cannot be foretold. Now I need you to focus on our business.'

I realized Parvati didn't know this attempt on Amrut's life was no accident. She hadn't been there when Shashi spoke to me. I opened my mouth to inform her. But RK's expression, as he stood right in front of me, stopped me cold. Parvati couldn't see it, she was facing me with her back to him at present.

'What's *he* doing here?' RK asked, as if setting eyes on Saddaq on the floor for the first time, across the length of the corridor. His voice rose in anger, then, unable to control his fury, his words, so loud they resonated in that silent space, 'GET OUT! GET OUT NOW!'

Things were unravelling before our eyes, just as we had earlier dreaded. It was up to us to stop the momentum.

'Mr Kamal, you need to control yourself.' Parvati was back by RK's side, speaking in soothing tones, hushing his fury. 'This is a place of healing.'

I watched as she brought RK's anger under control, no doubt telling him about Saddaq's assurance that he would be no trouble at all. I knew she would try her utmost to extract a similar assurance from RK. Already jittery about the mishap on his set, and unrestricted by the caution required of a business commitment or press around, RK was showing his true feelings towards Saddaq. Even so, he needed to subdue himself.

It was necessary, I thought dully. Especially if all of us were invited by the doctors to go into Alena's room together. Everyone needed to be controlled and calm. In the meanwhile, I was still reeling over the attack on Amrut Tawade.

How very strange, I thought to myself. Why on earth would anyone want to target the poor brother of Mohan? He had only arrived in the city three days ago. And his circumstances were pathetic, he was working to pay the way for his return home.

'Akruti,' a familiar voice was calling. I looked up to see Aman detach himself from RK's entourage and make as if to come over. I watched as he limped up to me, eagerness writ large on his face.

'We meet in sad circumstances,' he said as he came close. 'It's too bad what happened to Alena.'

'It is,' I agreed, not really in a mood to talk. To save myself the effort of speech, I thought it better he talked. So, I asked, 'How is it you're here today?'

'RK needed me,' he said simply. 'Though my injury is acting up—I was limping here, you saw it.'

'I did,' I agreed absentmindedly, my attention still on poor Amrut.

'But when RK needs something, I'm always there,' Aman dimpled at me, his charm evident as ever. 'Also, he's always thinking about me ...'

'As in?' I asked absently, still.

'You'd think with all that's going on in his life right now, he'd have forgotten about my ambition of acting.' Aman dimpled. 'But he's always been so thoughtful. Let me move away from the grimness around us for a bit. Look, he got hold of the contact sheets and prints of my first photoshoot. The photographer sent them to him on set, he had someone from his entourage bring them along here, to show me ...'

The incongruity of Aman's vanity, given our surroundings in a sombre hospital environment, did not escape me. But this was Bollywood. 'Business, above all', this mantra came first.

I looked over the sheets and the bunch of pictures he produced, without really concentrating. A movement caught my eye, perhaps the door to Alena's room swinging a little. So, I hastily returned them all.

'You can keep some if you wish,' Aman dimpled at me, waving a close-up of his in my face. 'Maybe you can show them to your own contacts in showbiz too? You used to be a beauty queen, so you must have had film offers ...'

'Sure,' I told him absentmindedly, taking the one proffered picture and putting it in my handbag.

'His ego is a tad too much,' I thought to myself. It reminded me of some of the male models in my modelling days, the ones who checked their hair in elevator mirrors before stepping out.

RK certainly had a terribly vain houseguest, but I wasn't so sure if he could be a killer with this kind of concentration, solely and utterly on himself.

'What do you think of these photographs?' Aman was asking, his gaze intent.

I was to respond, but the door to Alena's room finally opened, suspending all conversation on the floor.

'She will see visitors now,' announced a white-clad nurse. And despite the misgivings among those collected outside her door, the entire gathering surged forward in a body.

36

'Six people maximum in the room please,' the nurse said crisply as she realized how big the crowd surging to see Alena was, various entourages included.

RK and Saddaq, as superstars, got right of way, as did Parvati and I because she had asked to see us specifically. Shashi would come too, as RK's inner circle. Before anyone else could volunteer as a sixth in the first group, Samuel Rodrigues had squeezed to the front of the gathering and wormed his way in.

'I'm the husband,' he said to the surprised nurse, elbowing the rest aside so there was no doubt as to his position.

'That makes six,' the nurse acquiesced, stepping back to let us enter. 'Everyone else to go in only once this lot has finished, please.'

'This would be the last place I would expect to see all our players in this case coalesce at,' I whispered to Parvati as we entered.

'Yes, I know,' Parvati shot back under her breath. 'Almost everyone connected is here.'

She said 'almost' because we both knew Aman had been left outside, but there was no choice in the matter, especially with Samuel asserting his legally married card. Aman would get to see her in the next lot of visitors, alongside her eager and waiting entourage.

Alena was lying on a huge bed, as before, in a room almost identical to her last one. She had an IV tube attached and seemed exceedingly pale. Dark circles lined her eyes, though her earlier bruises at Saddaq's hands had faded now. She certainly looked as if she'd been through a terrible time. Her eyes were closed when we entered.

'She's very tired,' the nurse told us. 'The doctors ran several tests and she was exhausted halfway through. Ideally, she should be left alone. But since you have been waiting for so long outside, I thought you should at least take a quick glimpse of her ...'

The well-meaning nurse was being kind, but encountering Alena in this state did not help any of us. We needed to know why she had been asking so insistently for us. And RK just needed to interact with her, we guessed, for peace of mind. Shashi, ever loyal to RK, had come as his aide and buddy, no doubt. As for Saddaq—who knew what he was really here for. Likewise, Samuel.

'When will she wake up?' I asked the nurse.

'It will be a while, perhaps,' the nurse said to me, her eyes flickering in recognition of my face. Possibly she had recognized me as the model I used to be.

'She had tubes down her throat all this while, she was being fed intravenously. They have been removed for now, but the result has been a very sore throat—she could barely speak to the doctors, and I think it's worse now. Even if she does wake up, I doubt she will be able to talk to you,' the nurse let on.

This wasn't the news we had been hoping to receive. If Alena couldn't talk when, or if, she woke up, how would we be able to find out what she wanted to tell us?

'Alena,' RK had taken her hand, and held it to his lips in anguish. 'Oh Alena …'

Not to be outdone, Saddaq went to the other side of the bed and held her other hand. He didn't say anything, though. He had promised not to cause trouble and he was being true to his word for now.

Samuel was watching this with ferret eyes, his manner displeased, to say the least. But he was also perhaps intimidated by the superstars in the room and their all-powerful aura. Whatever the case, he didn't go to the bed, he simply watched from alongside our remaining trio. He had no words at present to offer Alena either—his play was an unpleasant quietude.

An awkward silence descended. Opposing forces in a complicated and increasingly dangerous saga had converged together, in a hospital room, of all places. Any one of those gathered could be our perpetrator, someone who wished to harm Alena in a decisive way. And the lady who might hold at least some clues to that—unable to provide them at present. You could have cut the tension with a knife.

Thankfully, as a relief from this peculiar, jarring tableau, and possibly because the superstars present were massaging her hands, Alena stirred. She moaned softly. Her eyelids fluttered open.

She focused slowly, first on RK at one side of her, then on Saddaq on the other.

'Alena?' RK began, tentatively.

The lady's eyes were glazed, she was evidently deeply exhausted. She didn't reply, simply gazed at the two men, first one then the other.

Feeling left out, no doubt, Samuel stepped forward to say something. But sensing him move, Saddaq rose, his expression like thunder. Samuel stepped back, unwilling to take on the bigger built man at this point.

The sudden movement by the two men had caught Alena's eyes—she lifted them to take in the others in the room.

Her gaze travelled dully, first to Samuel, who she didn't react to, then to Shashi, who elicited a similar blankness, then finally to Parvati and I. Upon sighting us, she blinked, as if suddenly made aware that we too were in the room.

Then her face turned animated, she moved her head almost frantically, as if she needed to speak. She lifted her hand after untwining it from RK's, to beckon us close to the bed.

Parvati and I both stepped up, Parvati leaning very close to Alena so she could catch the words the bedridden star could barely force out. Whispered words, broken and raspy. Because her throat had become so sore from the tubes, she had lost her voice.

From the barely formed sentences, only some words were clear to us both. The rest was just breath, sour from the drugs she had been given. Yet, there was no mistaking the urgency in the words we could make out clearly.

'*Help,*' we heard Alena say. '*Save me …*'

37

Try as she might, Alena couldn't force out anything else. It was a shock and caused considerable anxiety to those of us watching to see her neck strain as she tried to tell Parvati and me something unintelligible. Her eyes were teary, the muscles and cords around her throat stood out from the effort of it, but no voice came through.

'Save you from *whom*, Alena?' Parvati coaxed, her voice urgent. '*Who is it?*'

There was no sound from Alena, just a very disturbed, if feeble, movement of her hands, as if asking for something.

The nurse had noticed Alena's immense agitation.

'Everybody out!' she said in a no-nonsense voice. 'This patient has had quite enough for today.'

'Please,' Parvati stepped up, drew the nurse aside as she moved to shepherd us out of the room. '*Please.* It's important ...'

She bent her head low and spoke to the nurse, I could not make out what was being said.

But a while later, the nurse appeared to have been appeased, to have fallen in with what Parvati was requesting.

'I will do it myself,' she said to her, even as she stepped up to once again instruct us to leave, this time her manner so firm that we all had to heed it.

Saddaq and RK left Alena's bedside reluctantly, both promising to return as soon as they could. The rest of us, including Samuel, were herded out without individual goodbyes—the nurse had had enough of seeing Alena tiring so, in her efforts to communicate.

As we arrived outside the room, we saw RK turn to speak to the nurse. Standing behind him was Aman, who had been waiting for RK outside all this while. He was dimpling at the nurse, his charm on full wattage to help RK, no doubt.

'Wonder what RK's requesting of the nurse,' I mused as I noticed them, but was also distracted by what was playing on my mind.

'Parvati,' I said, 'What did you tell the nurse?'

Parvati had stepped away to use the public phone booth at the corner of the corridor, no doubt a quick but necessary call to our office to catch up on our other cases. But she had heard my question as she hastened to re-join me.

'I explained to the nurse what had happened as quickly as I could,' Parvati said. 'I told her we really needed to know what Alena was so keen to tell us. Alena had asked to see us despite not remembering eating the cake, so it could be a memory from that day or a little earlier. But it was extremely important because her expression and manner conveyed it, as did her words. The nurse was close by, she heard her words too. Alena asked us to "save" her ... but from what?'

'But what can the nurse do?' I asked, sceptical.

'The nurse knows that it's a grave situation,' Parvati looked at me meaningfully. 'She offered to help.'

'How?' I asked curiously. 'How can the nurse help?'

'*By using a piece of paper and getting Alena to write down what she wants to convey to us*,' Parvati told me, her eyes glittering. 'I think Alena too was trying to ask for this earlier, from her agitated movements ...'

It was simple and ingenious; I wished we could have put it in action whilst in the room itself. But the nurse was adamant to shoo us out, believing her patient was being overexerted, so I guessed this way was better than nothing at all.

'Excellent, Pari,' I told her, glad Parvati had managed to convince the nurse to do this for us. It would help us figure out our next steps.

But what Parvati said next, chilled me to my bones.

'It's quite possible Aku,' Parvati leaned close to me as she spoke, '*that the murderer was in the room, among us today.* Hence also, Alena's extreme agitation—*it could be that she wanted protection from that person ...*'

I looked at her in horror, then gazed around us.

No more people were being allowed into Alena's room at present. Yet the various entourages refused to leave, preferring to hang around the floor in bunches of twos and threes, waiting for their respective stars to act first.

RK was deep in conversation with Shashi on one side, and seemed in no hurry to depart. Likewise, Saddaq was once more on the other side of the floor, speaking to his aides without showing haste either. Samuel was nowhere to be seen, but I doubted he would've left yet.

Any one of these could be our suspect. And we didn't know who, as yet.

'Did you realize, she didn't say anything to either RK or Saddaq,' I mused. 'Even though clearly very fearful after her initial grogginess, she didn't request help from either of them ...'

'Could be that she didn't want to appear to favour any one of the two superstars,' Parvati said. 'Whatever their personal equations, she was being cautious, even in such a drowsy state, because of her profession. Remember both are extremely powerful, Bollywood is a male-dominated industry …'

'*Or then she was afraid of them*—one or both,' I conjectured. 'So, she told a neutral party—us …'

We were both deeply troubled. Alena's words haunted us. We needed the nurse to come through with her mission.

I decided to bring Parvati up to speed about Amrut as we waited for the nurse to return with her missive.

'Pari, I need to tell you about Mohan Tawade's brother,' I began, as we started walking the floor's length to pass time.

'Go on,' Parvati said, her attention fully on me. She had seen how upset I was earlier when I got the news of Amrut being in a critical condition.

First, I shared Shashi's news—Amrut's critical condition was not an accident, it was deliberate; the set had been pushed on top of him.

Parvati's expression turned horrified, then grave. 'How obtuse of me,' she said. 'It should have struck me when Mr Kamal mentioned that it was Mohan Tawade's brother who was hurt. Random happenings in this case are not at all random, or even accidental. I was so busy firefighting to keep the peace between our superstars and keep up Mr Kamal's morale that I missed the connect. I'm so glad *you* didn't, Aku …'

I told Parvati how Amrut had called out to me on set earlier, and our ensuing chat. I outlined the tragedy he faced, of having to cremate his brother in Mumbai because he didn't have funds to take the body back to the village with him. I also told her about how he was working, strangely enough, on the sets of the same film as the murdered Mohan, so he could pay his way back home.

'Pari, remember I told you there was an indirect connect to RK, while we were in the car?' I continued. 'Amrut said he was from the same village as Aman, RK's houseguest.'

Parvati stopped short at my words, her attention laser-like on me.

'So Amrut Tawade knows Aman?' Parvati's eyes had narrowed. 'Which means Mohan Tawade knew Aman too …'

'Yes, apparently,' I concurred. 'All from the same village. Amrut said Mohan had written to him a month or so ago, about Aman finally meeting his idol RK …'

Parvati's face turned thoughtful.

'Aku,' she asked slowly. 'Were they in touch? How did Mohan know Aman had found Mr Kamal in Mumbai? Did they correspond? Or was it just because of some filmi gossip on the grapevine that he knew about Aman meeting Mr Kamal merely as an outsider would? Aman met and began living with Mr Kamal six months ago, remember? But Mohan wrote to Amrut just a month ago. So, he got to know or decided to tell his brother, only recently—but *how* did he get to know?'

'That part is unclear, Pari,' I said carefully searching my memory to recall all that Amrut and I had spoken about.

'Amrut was happy for Aman's success,' I continued. 'But he came across as a proud man. He didn't want to try and reach out to Aman for any help, financial or otherwise, in cremating Mohan or returning to his village.'

'Also, whether Mohan and Aman actually corresponded didn't seem to matter to Amrut when I met him, now that Mohan is dead.' I looked at Parvati carefully. 'But it matters, doesn't it? In this bizarre case?'

'Yes. In a case so baffling,' Parvati spoke decisively. 'Every *little* thing matters.'

'I'm not even sure if Aman knows that Mohan was the extra who was strangled,' I said, recalling suddenly again how Aman said he didn't read the papers, nor did he recall names.

'Are you both talking of that same extra?' Samuel had appeared from nowhere and had sidled up to us, his oiliness evident as he drew near. 'The one who was nearly killed on set today?'

Parvati turned to him and waited, her face showing nothing at all. We had been talking of Mohan, not Amrut, but silence was the best way forward at this point. We hadn't known Samuel had been around—we both wondered how much he might have overheard.

'Oh, I know a lot about the goings-on while that movie is being filmed,' Samuel leered at Parvati. 'Don't look at me so blankly. Just because I'm not a superstar doesn't mean I don't have connections everywhere who tell me things. You know?'

His tone fell several notches lower and he drew close to us then.

'I could tell you things …' he muttered, his face weasel-like in its craftiness. 'For example, I know that the extra who was attacked—yes, I know he was attacked, it was no accident—well, *what if I told you he's here …*?'

Parvati and I digested this news in silence, as Samuel continued, unable to stop the boastful flow of information he had garnered. 'He was brought to *this* hospital. RK insisted on a good hospital, because he is also a stakeholder in the film and it happened on the film sets. So, if anyone wanted to know where that extra was … *he's here …*'

38

There was a sudden crash of thunder, a sound so loud we heard it through the hospital's partially open window as we walked the corridor. The skies had opened up outside the building in keeping with the current mood—everything, including nature, was gathering to a heightened intensity. Even the rain, which poured in great sheets signalling a storm up ahead, conveyed a palpable sense of urgency.

Parvati and I, we had casually moved away from the stealthy Samuel, but what he had shared stayed right with us, pricking at our sense of thoroughness in solving this case. Samuel's boast of knowing every filmi detail had opened up an avenue for us, one we needed to tap immediately. RK's famed generosity meant the critically injured extra was *here*, in this very place, private and state-of-the-art.

'We need to see Amrut Tawade,' Parvati voiced what was already in my head. 'As in—*right now*.'

So we moved towards the ICU unit, where critical patients were brought in.

'Pari, we won't be able to see him if he's being kept here,' I told Parvati. ICU rules were consistent; one could hardly bribe one's way in, in these units.

Parvati had cornered a male attendant—the kind that helped push stretchers and wheelchairs around—on his way to the elevator and had struck up a conversation.

She returned presently, wearing a look of determination.

'He's been shifted to a private room used for critical patients who are in semi-recovery—Mr Kamal's influence,' she said. 'Let's go.'

We found the room, the floor and number of which Parvati had used her charm to wheedle out of the male attendant. Visiting hours were long over, the floor appeared deserted.

But we decided to emulate Shashi's aura of entitlement instead of waiting for permissions. Time was of the essence in any case, before another disaster occurred. So, we confidently strode into the room together.

There was a single male attendant sitting in a chair, who looked up, startled, as we entered. But before he could say anything, I stepped up. His gaze rested on me, and as I had gambled, the familiar flicker of recognition crossed his face. He stood up smartly, hands folded in namaste.

Naturally, he assumed we were connected to the filmi folk, having recognized me as a former model, and took it for granted that we had access denied to others—as most of the fraternity tend to get. We did nothing to change his impression, in fact, I nodded curtly, and told him to wait outside the room. He obliged in a hurry.

We walked up to the bed where Amrut lay, deep in drugged sleep, his head bandaged as also his right arm, which was in a cast and sling. The rest of him was under a heavy blanket, so we couldn't make out how much more of his body was injured after the set fell on him.

It pained me to see him so, the healthy man I had spoken to just this morning. Obviously, there was no family around—we knew he had been working hard to collect enough money to return to his family back home in his village.

I checked my watch. It was now nearing 9 p.m.—it had been a packed, eventful day, too cluttered for my liking, but what was to be done? It was unbecoming enough of us to trespass into a private room; what I was about to do next was even more questionable, but I had to do it, for the sake of clarity.

I glanced at Parvati for courage and she inclined her head firmly, as if in affirmation. I reached out and touched Amrut's shoulder gently.

'Amrut,' I whispered. 'Wake up. Wake up, we need to speak with you …'

After what seemed like ages, but what must have been only a minute or so, Amrut stirred, awakened by my relentless prodding. He appeared disoriented at first when his eyes opened. Then as he stared at me, trying to place my face, recognition dawned.

'Akrutiji,' he rasped out.

'Save your energy,' I said to him. 'Don't speak, unless to answer me. I know you got hurt—someone pushed the set on you. Do you know who it was? Did you see him?'

Amrut shook his head as much as he could under all the bandages.

'Amrut,' Parvati's voice was firm, she got straight to the point without introducing herself. 'Amrut, how did your brother Mohan know Aman had found RK in Mumbai?'

Despite the urgency of the moment, I noted how Parvati, who addressed RK as "Mr Kamal" in typical formality more often than not, kept to the colloquial "RK" this time, so small-town Amrut in his drowsy state would grasp the familiar abbreviation in her question faster.

'Mohan was in touch with Aman,' rasped out Amrut, in Hindi. 'He wrote letters to me. Over and over, about Aman. Especially when …'

'… When?' I asked urgently. I could hear noises outside the room, loud voices, as if arguing. A second later the door handle turned, and a nurse stepped inside.

'What are you two doing here? This is an ICU recovery room. You're not allowed at this time,' her tone was heated in righteousness. Behind her, the male attendant wrung his hands in distress at being upbraided.

'*Amrut*,' I pleaded as the nurse, her back rigid in disapproval, caught hold of my arm sharply, pulling me out behind Parvati, who was being led out by her other hand.

'In Bali,' Amrut rasped as I was being pulled away, my eyes on him still. '*When he was so happy about being sent to Bali ...*'

Something clicked in my head. I met Parvati's eyes in panic. Then in a sudden flash, I remembered the picture in my handbag. *The one I had taken from Aman*. I rummaged with my free hand, dropping some of my bag's contents on the floor as the nurse towed us to the door. My fingers closed on it, and I held it up as we reached the door, turning backwards towards Amrut even as the nurse pulled hard.

'Aman?' I asked frantically, pointing to the photo as the nurse practically heaved me to the exit, now bubbling self-righteous anger at my disobedience.

'*Is this Aman?*' I didn't care for my fallen things, only Amrut's answer. I could register that he was peering at the picture from that distance.

The nurse shoved me viciously outside, as too Parvati. The door slammed shut behind us both. But it was a swinging door. The hinges allowed a tiny swing backwards, as if in rebound. The door swung back, revealing Amrut for a nano-second and in that fraction, before it shut completely, I glimpsed Amrut's gesture, the action far away, but definite.

He was shaking his head, his eyes certain, if puzzled.

No.

39

It was making no sense, yet I had a terrible sense of foreboding as I watched the door to Amrut's room close firmly this time on our faces. I turned to Parvati, reacting to a sense of as-yet-unclear urgency within me.

'Did you see Amrut?' I asked her, my voice panicky. 'Did you see him, through the swinging door when I asked if the man in the photo was Aman?'

Parvati was briskly steering us to the elevators, her pace so fast it was almost a run.

'I saw,' she said shortly, not stopping to breathe. '*He said "no".*'

We were at the elevators now. She hustled us both in, pressing the button for Alena's floor determinedly.

'We have no time to lose,' she said shortly. Her hurried behaviour was echoing the screaming panic within me, but I hadn't really got clarity as to what we would be doing in Alena's room. We had been told to go out just half an hour or so ago, by the irate nurse on her floor.

'Why are we going to Alena's room?' I asked as the lift ascended.

'More than her room—the floor she's on,' Parvati answered curtly, checking her watch in impatience, before meeting my panicked gaze. 'Aman's there.'

I understood. Parvati needed to speak with Aman, we would then get an answer to the questions swirling in both our heads since our interview with the grievously injured Amrut. It would all be tackled in a civilized and mature way, unlike all the madness unfolding around us so far.

But, of course, that perfect situation was only my imagination.

When we reached the floor, Aman was nowhere to be seen. In fact, now, nearing almost 9.30 p.m., the floor appeared absolutely deserted.

'We haven't been away that long,' I spoke up, exasperated. 'Where did everyone go to?'

'Best case situation—they may have all finally gone home,' Parvati said, looking up and down the length of the hallway. 'But how quickly could they have left? So many of them?'

'Unless they were told to leave,' I added. 'Because they were so many, they might have been making a bit of noise?'

'They had been present for the entire length of time Alena has been here so far,' Parvati was thinking aloud. 'And not asked to leave before. No, it's possible they realized they wouldn't be meeting Alena today and left of their own accord, each entourage following their respective star …'

'And Samuel?' I said. 'What of Samuel?'

'Not sure,' Parvati mused. 'He was lurking around us just a while ago, wasn't he …?'

'There's a nurse's station,' I said, spying one at a distance, at the extreme side of the entire wing. 'Let's walk there to make enquiries.'

In the absence of anyone on this section of the wing, it seemed the most logical thing to do, so we headed that way. But despite the floor being clear, I couldn't shake that sense of intense foreboding within me. Thunder crashed outside the bay window that we passed as we walked, increasing my inner panic.

So many questions.

'Pari, something doesn't seem right,' I told her. 'The floor seems too quiet.'

'It's a hospital, it needs quiet.' Parvati looked at me, but her eyes told me she felt the same way I did.

'What Amrut said makes no sense. *Any of it,*' I continued.

'When did Mohan go to Bali? Was it with Aman? How could that be? Why did Aman not mention it before?' I was charting the questions we needed answers to.

'You haven't mentioned the two key questions,' Parvati said as we increased our pace to the nurses' station. 'Why did Aman not mention *knowing Mohan* to any of us before?'

'Maybe because it didn't really come up before Mohan's death? Though after Mohan had been killed, I had asked Aman if he had knowledge of what was going on with RK, since they apparently lived as strangers despite being in the same house,' I mused, troubled. 'He spoke of knowing that "someone" had died on RK's set, that he was in too much pain because of his leg to delve deeper, he claimed he didn't read newspapers. But Pari, could he really have been so removed from what was happening around his host? The papers had Mohan's pictures all over—*strangled* ...'

'Which leads us to the most troubling question in this case so far,' Parvati said stopping short, we had reached our destination. 'If Amrut didn't recognize his fellowman from the village as Aman—*who really is this Aman*?'

Before I could add anything to Parvati's terribly disturbing query, a nurse stepped up. I recognized her as the one in Alena's room, the one who had shooed us out less than an hour ago.

'I have your paper,' she addressed Parvati as she slipped something into Parvati's hand.

'Mr RK was concerned, as you were, since he also heard what Miss Alena had said to you,' the nurse was mouthing, as Parvati unfolded the paper bearing Alena's writing.

'So, he requested that I let his man stay outside Miss Alena's room for the night. Her night nurse would also be with her, inside, of course. Only one more person is allowed besides the patient at night in the room. Even if this man were outside, I thought this was against hospital rules, but Mr RK, he had all necessary permissions granted.'

The nurse was speaking, but I couldn't register her words. I was busy trying to decipher Alena's scrawl on the paper Parvati had been handed, its contents difficult to read, letters appearing reversed to me at this point, as I was standing opposite Parvati.

Parvati though, was present as never before. 'The man,' she asked urgently, as she looked at the note and handed it to me. 'Who was the man to be left outside Alena's room? What was his name?'

'There's no one there right now,' I added, recalling the deserted floor and the room we passed, as I glanced at the note. The letters swam before my eyes, the screaming panic within rose to a cresting roar in my ears as I heard the nurse tell Parvati, 'I didn't catch his name, but he was limping. The man with the limp.'

But she was addressing thin air, I was already running, running like the wind beside Parvati, to get to Alena's room, the paper she'd handed me crumpled, fallen to the floor in our mad haste. The words on it bore witness to our terrified dash. '*Aman*', the note said. '*Save me from Aman.*'

40

It seemed we flew past the length of the too-quiet floor, so fast did we run and then burst into Alena's room together. But we need not have hurried so. The tableau we were hoping to derail had already been put into motion. And it had been put together so ingeniously, we could do nothing to stop it.

We entered to find a deathly quiet room. The night nurse left in charge of Alena was nowhere to be seen. Not a person from Alena's entourage either, though I doubted they would have hung around her at night—also, it was against hospital rules, as the nurse had just told us.

The man called Aman was seated next to Alena's apparently sleeping figure, reading a book by the light of the night lamp. The entire tableau seemed so still, it appeared somewhat unreal.

He looked up as we entered, his manner casual, welcoming. *He doesn't know we've found out he's not Aman,* I thought. *He's acting.*

'I thought you might still be in the hospital,' he addressed me, easy, dimpling as he spoke. 'The rest have left. I was told to stay on by RK for the night, just in case of more drama, or if she needed anything. My leg was hurting, but RK's been called back on set, and Shashi too—they resumed the night shoot for the movie, it's on a tight budget given all the trouble, so they had to go. I couldn't say no to RK, obviously, no matter my leg!'

'I thought Mr Kamal mentioned he might ask you to wait outside?' Parvati, lightning quick on the uptake, spoke up, equally casual as we deliberately slowed our pace stepping further inside.

'Yes, but I convinced the night nurse to take some rest,' Aman grinned, flashing his charm and his dimples at Parvati. 'Alena won't need much looking after, she's on strong meds anyway. She'll possibly sleep through the night. The nurse wouldn't leave at first, but I managed. No one needs to know, and I'm trusted by Alena's significant other, RK, so it would be fine even if the hospital found out, which they won't. The nurse left, and I came into the room. Told her I was Alena's brother, in fact. Now, you ladies ought to go home as well. Get some rest. It's been a long day for all of us. But you two need it more than anyone else—you have to solve this case!'

'I saw your pictures.' Parvati was playing for time, time to be continually in the room. 'The contact sheets and prints, professionally shot.'

How to get Aman to speak, tell us what we needed and move him away without harming the vulnerable patient next to him?

Aman looked confused, then his brow cleared.

'The pictures were sent to RK on set. Did he show you the pictures there?' he asked Parvati, then turned to me. 'How come you didn't see them, then?'

'We were not together,' I said smoothly. 'In fact, I met someone on the set …' I was leading into disclosing my meeting with Amrut, his fellow villager, but Aman didn't allow it.

He put his book on the table alongside the bed and stood up with difficulty, leaning heavily on his left leg, his right leg held straight out, as if it was causing him pain.

'You can tell me about your set visit another time,' he said pointedly to me. 'It's better if Alena doesn't hear voices as she rests.'

Then he turned to Parvati, flashing his disarming smile at her. 'And you can tell me what you think of the pictures at length, later. I would love to know the opinion of a non-industrywalli. Tonight, it's very late, both of you must be tired. You should go home now.'

Parvati met my eyes. This was the second time we were being asked to leave the room. And this time there was no subtlety in the message. *Why did Aman want us out? Would he actually dare harm Alena in a huge hospital like this one, as Alena had feared he would?*

Aman eased forward, his limp perceptible as he moved towards the door. He opened it, as if being a gentleman came naturally.

'Ladies, may I show you out,' he said. His words were polite, his manner though extremely firm.

Parvati had been watching him with narrowed eyes, but as he moved, her face became set. She had noticed something that convinced her of her next course of action.

'Aman, we're tired as you said, but we needed to hear a few things from you,' Parvati said pleasantly, almost lazily, her voice silky, that special voice she used when she was on the track of something important. 'Once we have those sorted, we can rest tonight—won't you oblige? Alena seems too deep in sleep to be disturbed by our talk, she is on strong meds as you mentioned ...'

Aman looked uncertainly at her, then me. He hesitated.

'I was telling you,' I took over then. 'How I met someone on set today ...'

Aman waited for me to finish. He said nothing but his manner was impatient.

'His name was Amrut,' I said, looking straight into Aman's eyes. 'He said he knows you.'

Aman didn't miss a beat. 'Amrut? I don't know any Amrut.' His expression was one of patience, as if when dealing with a difficult child.

'Amrut—from your village?' I continued softly.

Aman looked perplexed, then his expression cleared.

'Yes, of course, Amrut Tawade,' he said. 'I didn't know he was in the city. I haven't seen him in, maybe, seven months? I last saw him when I left the village to come and try to meet RK. How is he?'

The question came spontaneously, as if from someone as interested as an acquaintance should be. All very natural-seeming and correct. But Parvati was having none of it.

'You knew his brother Mohan?' she said, still pleasant in her manner.

'No, I can't say that I did.' Aman looked genuinely perplexed. 'At least, not well. I knew who he was, when we were in the village, of course—it's so small, one knows everyone. But that was a long time ago. My life here is so different now.'

'Amrut mentioned Mohan—who worked in Mumbai—wrote to him about you. In fact, he said Mohan wrote to him regularly with news about you. Mohan told him how you found Mr Kamal as you had set out to do. How could he have known, if you claim you never met him here?' Parvati had changed tack abruptly. Her voice rang out, precise and clear in the noiseless hospital room, though she hadn't raised it at all.

'The story of me travelling from my village and then meeting my idol RK in Mumbai is not a secret.' Aman's charming, casual demeanour had vanished; his face took on a mask-like appearance, utterly blank. 'Mohan could have heard about it or read it in a filmi magazine. He need not have met me here to know that …'

There was a stirring from the bed. Alena came out of her inert state, no doubt roused by our voices. Her eyelids fluttered open—she awoke, groggily. Her gaze steadied, then settled, first on me, then Parvati. Comprehension dawned. She made as if to beckon us closer, then her eyes fixated on Aman.

Quick as lightning, her face changed. Even in her drowsy, just-awakened state, she went into absolute panic mode at the sight of him. As she couldn't scream, she began to thrash in her bed, dry-retching in order to get words out from a throat that failed her.

Parvati rushed to her side, but the man we called Aman was quicker. He had reached her before either of us could, his limp unnoticeable in the swiftness of his move. Then, holding onto her throat, he lifted her high, almost clean off the bed, tubes and all.

'You are *such an inconvenience*,' he mouthed, his voice low, guttural as he began deliberately strangling the still-thrashing Alena. Her dilated eyes went wide in terror and the effort to breathe. In front of our horrified eyes, RK's suave, in-control house guest had turned into an out-of-control monster.

Parvati and I, we had moved when Aman did, reached him as he began his throttling of Alena. Now we clawed at him to release her, desperate and persistent in our attempts, but the man possessed incredible strength. He was holding Alena up with one hand, and fending us both off with the other.

In an impatient move, he smacked Parvati, closer to him than I was, and sent her reeling backwards to the foot of the large bed.

'I don't want to hurt you, Akruti,' he said to me, as I stepped back from him, diverted momentarily by my concern for Parvati. 'Stay away and let me finish this.'

Parvati had taken a bad fall, landing at the edge of the bed. She sat herself up, a deep red welt already forming on her cheek, from where Aman had smacked her across the face.

Slowly, she inched to the other side of Alena's bed, the place where the bedside table and the night lamp stood.

'That's right,' Aman said, distracted by her movement and loosening his grip on Alena's throat a little, as he addressed Parvati. 'Move away from me. Do not come close. I can hurt you worse than I have …'

Parvati stayed silent, her eyes told me not to do more. I stood close enough to Aman to breathe the stale stench of his sweat, to take in the medicinal smell emanating from Alena. But I did not attempt to claw at his grip on Alena again.

Parvati had reached the chair on the other side of the bed, the one Aman was sitting on earlier. She lowered herself in it slowly, as if bruised badly from her smack. We both watched her in silence.

'You want to kill Alena?' she asked Aman simply, as if having a casual conversation, when finally seated.

'*She has been a huge inconvenience*,' Aman told Parvati, his grip around Alena's neck still loose.

'Why don't you put her down as we discuss this,' Parvati said, in the same tone as before.

Aman blinked for a nanosecond, as if thinking, then released the loudly gasping Alena, his face blank as before.

'Sure,' he said. 'A slight delay wouldn't affect my plans.'

Alena, released by Aman, hit the bed hard, spluttering and choking, gasping for air as she tried to crawl away from his bulk. Her eyes were tearful, but she couldn't move much nor speak. She whimpered as she drew the bed covers over herself, shrinking as far away from her attacker as she could, still sprawled on the bed.

'It isn't personal,' Aman spoke to the cowering form on the bed before him. '*But you are not really someone I see in RK's life in the long term*.'

'What did she do?' I asked, deciding to join Parvati in keeping my tone neutral, even conversational.

'What didn't she do?' Aman rolled his eyes. 'She came into RK's life like a whirlwind. I spent a lifetime building my equation with him, then finally managed to meet him. He gave me shelter, a roof over my head, and promised to fulfil my dream of acting in Bollywood. Getting all that to happen was in itself a miracle. And then *she* appears—to spoil it all!'

'That too, out of the blue,' he went on, now looking at Parvati. 'One meeting with her and it led to *such* an effect on RK. She wasn't just a fling, I could see that. It changed everything in the space of a few odd weeks. Just like that, my carefully constructed bid at a heart's desire career, aided by RK, was falling apart? I couldn't have that!'

'*So, you hatched a plan to do away with her*?' Parvati guessed.

'Not at first,' Aman's voice was detached, as impersonal as he had promised Alena when he let go of her throat. 'She's the reason behind all that screaming that RK has been hearing lately. I thought I could scare him into seeing her true colours as an unsympathetic lover or get him fearful enough to turn to me as a trusted confidant, who would then advise him to leave her for her cold-heartedness. But neither happened. Later, when I realized how deeply she had entrenched herself into his life, there was no other way out. I knew she had to go. Because if she hadn't come into his life and become such a fixture—none of this would've happened. My charmed life would still be on track, living in RK's home, and with his help, becoming a mega movie star.'

It wasn't RK who was being targeted by something malevolent as we'd initially believed, I thought to myself. The objective had been to obtain RK's full attention, to scare him into complying, but not harm him. It was the person we'd later hit upon—*the paramour Alena—who had been the intended victim*.

'Alena said she wanted us to save her from you,' I spoke over him. 'She told us this from her hospital bed today, so she must've been pretty spooked. But she had lost her short-term memory ... so it was from before that cake poisoning incident that she remembered something.'

Aman looked at me in chagrin, as if I was causing him some mild pain. 'Akruti, I wish you both had left the hospital earlier in the evening. Or even when I requested you to, a short time ago. Now I've been forced to include you and *her* (he nodded in Parvati's direction) in my elimination plan. And I really didn't want to do that. *But I do so hate being inconvenienced.*'

Neither Parvati nor I showed our feelings when he said this, but a slow dread had crept up on me at his words. Even together we had been no match for Aman's strength and build as he had squeezed Alena's throat, wiry though he appeared to be. How could we save Alena, or ourselves, from him when he decided on the time for our 'elimination' today?

A whine came from the direction of the bed. Alena, visibly shaking, cowered even further in terror, as she heard his words.

As I watched her tremble, I got a sudden flash of another time, in direct contrast to now, a time when she had been strong, scornful, very angry. And then the epiphany hit me.

'*It was you!*' I said. 'The person she was fighting with, at RK's home, before leaving for Pune. We first thought it was RK. Then, when we realized he was already in Pune, we believed it to be Shashi. We had even considered Samuel. But it was none of them. It was YOU!'

'It was,' Aman turned to me, his blank expression replaced by those disarming dimples as he smiled. How had I ever believed him to be attractive? He was dangerous, extremely so, and relentless in his utter, single-minded pursuit of his objective.

'I was at RK's home when she arrived that afternoon, and she didn't like how comfortable I seemed at Taqdeer, even without RK there. Shashi had been in and out of Taqdeer almost all day, waiting for RK's costume to arrive for the Pune awards, but he wasn't there when she arrived. Anyway, she took offence at my presence and how "at home" I was making myself. She told me I'm a guest, ought to behave as one, and that it would be *her* home soon. I told her I couldn't see that ever happening, that she would never stay there. We exchanged a few harsh words. Then I told her to go to hell. She really lost her temper.'

'Did you do more than just tell her?' Parvati asked Aman quietly.

'I may have held her by the throat—nothing too serious,' Aman retorted. 'She couldn't breathe.'

'*Hence her fearing for her safety*,' I said slowly. 'Especially now, as she is laid up and cannot defend herself or seek help by speaking. This is what she was trying to tell us, what she remembered—you strangling her at Taqdeer. Why did she not tell RK about this when it first happened?'

'Maybe she meant to, later on in Pune,' Parvati spoke up. 'There was so much going on. She was in such a rage outside Taqdeer, she possibly didn't take Aman as seriously as she took herself. Mr Kamal and she travelled separately to Pune, remember. And then, in Pune, post hectic rehearsal schedules, the very next night, she got poisoned …'

'When I saw how she was hell-bent on getting rid of me from RK's house—*I decided she had to die*,' Aman said. 'Before then, I simply viewed her as a lesser inconvenience, to be cajoled or frightened or eased out of RK's life. But she was proving to be bigger trouble than I had expected. I knew after that day that she wouldn't leave him either easily or quietly. So, I decided I would help her leave our lives. Permanently.'

We listened in absolute silence as Aman continued.

'I knew RK was planning that cake surprise for Alena at the Pune party. I had eavesdropped on his phone calls for a long time without him ever knowing. Taqdeer, his heritage house, is built that way—you can listen in to conversations from another room if you know where to stand, even though many of the lower rooms are soundproofed. The voice carries clearly, almost like an echo system in an ancient amphitheatre. He used to talk to Alena in the hospital, recuperating from that beating. They were both excited to go to Pune, some excitement after their movie stalled. And RK had dropped enough hints for Alena to believe he was sending her a surprise cake with a message. She was expecting it. The party was the perfect time, the obvious time for a cake surprise. After Alena's tirade against me, I thought—why not use that? *The anonymity that a large gathering would offer …* If executed right, Alena would not notice it was not RK's cake that she was receiving, but *my* special gift to her. I had addressed my note to her, but had requested delivery of the cake to RK's suite. I knew the party would be hosted there by him. I also bargained on the fact that the hotel would indeed send the cake to RK's suite, as all the stars were gathered there for the party, they wouldn't read more into it. And if she ate all of the, umm, *special* cake *I sent* …'

'You didn't bargain for her peculiar magnetism, such that all three of us—Parvati, Shashi and I—would be watching her at the exact moment she ingested *your* surprise *poisoned* offering,' I spoke up.

Here was the answer to our earlier conjecture, I thought, as to how sure the killer was, that Alena would indeed eat the cake meant to kill her. *He was absolutely sure, because he had overheard RK speaking to Alena about his plans for the party.* Aman did not need to be physically present in the room to ensure Alena's consumption of RK's surprise offering. He knew Alena would not leave a cake uneaten that she believed held the possibility of a special gift from her generous lover buried within. Regardless of who else also ate it, and perhaps got poisoned, she most certainly would. Aman had thought this plan foolproof, and his instincts had been right. Only—even though she'd eaten it as he'd planned—Alena hadn't died.

'Well, the plan might still have worked. She just didn't eat enough of the cake I sent.' Aman smiled at me ruefully, as if discussing a minor mishap, not an attempted murder.

'But who is the "I", Aman?' Parvati spoke softly. 'You mentioned you "spent a lifetime" "building an equation" with Mr Kamal. But you couldn't have. *Because you are not the Aman Azad from Amrut Tawade's village, the one who wrote letters to Saurav Roop Kamal for over a decade, the one who travelled to Mumbai to meet him, are you*?'

Aman stopped short, turned and took a long hard look at Parvati. Then he did something unexpected. He laughed, his dimples alight once more. *Such wasted beauty*, I thought. *Evil comes in very pleasant packaging sometimes.*

'Right on,' he said. 'Full marks for uncovering each hidden layer. I'm no villager. I'm a Mumbai boy, born and brought up in Bandra. The real Aman never made it a few weeks past the accident, seven months ago. I was broke, in a public hospital, recovering from a bad attack of dengue, when he was brought in. We shared a public ward together with others. He told me the whole sorry story, about his letters and communication with RK. How he was travelling here, to seek RK's blessings. For his marriage, mind you, not to join films. How RK had written to him for so long, *but had never even seen a photograph of his* ... And then, a couple of weeks later—he died.'

'Wasn't that convenient,' Parvati persisted, her face neutral.

'I thought—here's a plan made to be brought to life,' Aman concurred. 'Why should I not try to take his place? *Become* Aman? RK's generosity is legendary. I gambled on the belief that he would react to me as he did, upon hearing Aman's story. And it worked—he took me in, without reservation. He didn't know how Aman looked at all. *And one person can look so like another, given the right tools.* Thing is—I really do want to be an actor. You already know how good I am ...'

This much, at least, was too true. The false Aman had taken on the real one's persona with such searing conviction, everybody had been fooled.

'The real Aman, though, had come to seek RK's blessings so he could marry,' I said tartly.

'Either way, blessings are blessings,' Aman dimpled. 'To marry or to act ...'

'What is your actual name?' I asked curiously. I couldn't get over the out-and-out opportunist in him, his single-minded intent, a cunning risk-taker who had gambled on such huge stakes and had actually made life work his way for a while.

No wonder I had subconsciously, without realizing it, sensed a city-slickness in him, in his suave manner, when we had interacted at RK's home. He was no village boy, Mumbai born and bred, ruthlessly chasing his shot at becoming a silver-screen God. That is, till Alena's entry spoiled his happy ending-to-be.

'Does it matter?' Aman said. 'I'm Aman now. He looked enough like me in height and build. It was a failsafe plan. And it began to work like a charm.'

'The real Aman only knew Hindi, didn't he?' Parvati spoke up. 'He wrote to Mr Kamal in Hindi …'

'I convinced RK I learnt English at a missionary school in my village shortly before I travelled to meet him. He bought it,' Aman confessed, glee in his voice. '*The devil is in the details. And I covered every one …*'

'But then Mohan came into the picture?' Parvati interrupted.

'He saw me on the set of RK's previous movie, the only day when I visited RK there, post a doctor's appointment. Such a freak sighting,' Aman's face turned dark at the recounting, but I was only thinking of how a single, even chance encounter can either uplift or destroy lives. A single encounter with Alena had changed RK's attitude to matrimony. But a chance encounter with Mohan had led Aman to his undoing.

'Mohan was there as an extra hire,' Aman was saying. 'He wasn't really even in the business yet. What are the odds of that ever happening on the one day I visited RK on set? But it did, to my bad luck. Mohan had known the real Aman and was aghast when he made enquiries as to the story behind my familiar-sounding name. Because he knew I wasn't the Aman he had known in the village ...'

His words reminded me of what Parvati had spoken of a few days ago. '*Things are not always as they appear to be*.' We had been talking about Shashi then, but the veracity of those words was a constant throughout the entire case. One never could know what went on with people, what lay beneath the surface ...

'Mohan blackmailed you?' I couldn't contain myself. This case had twists and turns that were truly unexpected. No wonder my initial feeling of foreboding when it was being offered to us.

'Not at first,' Aman said. 'He got in touch to just express utter surprise at my presence, because I was not the real Aman Azad. But I told him I'd make it worth his while if we acted together, told no one. He had really wanted to be a stuntman. And RK was smitten by me, enough to give him a chance ...'

'So, *you* got him the movie, his first real gig as a stuntman,' I said.

'More gigs would follow if he held his tongue, he knew this. But how could I ever know that he'd write to his brother after a while, about meeting me?' Aman said. 'Why he did that I really am at a loss to say. I wasn't the real Aman, the one from his village—so why write to his brother about the fake Aman? Especially when I had warned him and it benefitted him to stay silent? And so late in the day, much after when we first met and he agreed to keep silent.'

'It is possible Mohan's conscience pricked him as time went by,' I interjected.

'Mohan didn't seem much of a "conscience prickling" kinda guy.' Aman looked a trifle amused at my words. 'Even if he wanted to cover all bases, *it was really an inconvenient thing to do …*'

'You did not know he had written to his brother till Amrut arrived in the city after his death, did you?' I interrupted.

'True, I did not know,' Aman said. 'I had needed Mohan to help me urgently, because Alena had happened to RK, a couple of months or so into my stay at his home. And he was threatening to marry her, spoiling everything we had planned for my career.'

'You needed to scare her away at the time?' Parvati said. 'Or rather—scare Mr Kamal into submission?'

'Yes …' Aman concurred. 'Initially, as I mentioned, there was no plan to kill Alena. I just wanted RK scared. Terrified enough to turn to me in great need, the only person living with him in his "haunted" home, one who believed in him. I would save him from this supposed entity, and as I bonded closely with him, I would eliminate Alena from his mind as well. Also, she was such a shallow creature, I felt she might reveal her true nature to RK herself, by not coming to his aid when he needed her. So, I came up with the whistle idea …'

'*The scream!*' I guessed suddenly. 'It was a whistle?'

'A pretty heavy-duty one,' Aman chuckled. 'You know those soundless dog whistles at different frequencies? This one was a bit like that, only it had a sound, a scary one. It was eerie, I couldn't get over it. And so perfect for what I needed to get done. I told you about the layout of RK's heritage house, Taqdeer—it's pretty wild. I could blow my whistle at one end and it would echo somewhere else, even with some of the in-between rooms being soundproofed. I had mapped the sound echoes throughout the house anyway—I had so much free time while RK was away shooting.'

I recalled my unbearable panic at hearing the scream at RK's and was struck by blinding anger. I had actually dared imagine a haunting instead of this demonic person's mischief!

'I wanted to make sure RK was properly scared. I wanted to do it when he was alone, so others would think he was imagining things. Of course, the fact that he began hearing the screams at Taqdeer the same night he did the Ouija board at the office to prep for his movie was pure coincidence, but what timing—I couldn't have planned it better, myself! Mind you, he is not easy to scare. It took a while.' Aman sounded almost rueful confessing this.

'But there was one time we heard it too …' Parvati said.

'That wasn't meant to happen,' Aman said jovially. 'I thought he was alone, he hadn't told anyone he would be inviting you home. The help, whom I normally grilled over such home invitations, didn't know either. Even so, you came and left quickly. So, I decided to stick to the plan, go ahead and scare him. How would I have ever imagined that you would return immediately? He explained later, Akruti, that you'd forgotten your sunglasses and both of you had come back to retrieve them. *That* was unfortunate timing. And here I was, bumping into both of you at Taqdeer, as I returned from Bali …'

'It wasn't you who travelled to Bali,' Parvati's tone was so low it was a whisper. '*It was Mohan*. You never travelled together. He went instead of you, *as you*, so all suspicion would be directed away from you. That was why you said earlier that you "needed Mohan's help urgently". Bali was your alibi. *He impersonated you for three weeks in Bali, the entire length of time of the supposed screaming "hauntings" in Mr Kamal's home …*'

'Right, again!' Aman was as yet jovial as he listened to us piece together the past few weeks' happenings. 'I managed to stay hidden in one of the unused rooms here, at Taqdeer, for that time. The help slacks in cleaning the unused sections, obviously, which worked out for me. No one ever guessed, not even when I called the help on the home number they normally answer, to ask about RK's visitors, that I was calling not from Bali, but from *within* the premises, in fact, from the unused phone line in the room. It's such a huge property—quite marvellous for such things, really.'

'I checked when we took on this case. Travel details said Aman Azad travelled, so Mohan obviously assumed your identity,' Parvati said, gravely. I knew she was making a mental note to never be fooled like this again, in future cases.

'Mumbai has a few enterprising networks that operate useful side businesses, like forging passports and travel documents for the right amount of cash.' Aman chuckled in the face of her gravitas. 'Mohan knew someone, got it done. RK saw to it that I was never short of funding, supposedly for my doctors' bills. And also, for this trip he was treating me to. So, it was surprisingly easy to pull off ...'

'Mohan would have had to tell Amrut he met Aman here eventually,' Parvati continued putting together pieces of the puzzle. 'In order to explain how it was that he had enough funding to go suddenly on an international vacation, a trip like Bali, so soon into a job. But he had told his brother about meeting you a little before that trip, anyway.'

I understood now, that regardless of whether Alena happened to RK or not, Aman's relentless single-mindedness in the pursuit of his movie career had already made him dangerous.

Alena's 'elimination' was only the tail end of a devious plan to gain complete control of RK. The plan had been set in motion much earlier and involved conspiring with the shifty villager Mohan Tawade, when Alena had entered the picture.

In fact, Aman's over-reaching ambition had set him on the path to becoming treacherous well before RK's home 'hauntings' had begun. He had already chosen the wrong path when he gambled with fortune, taking up a dead stranger's identity and impersonating him for months to weasel his way into an acting career via RK's goodwill.

He had even made sure to ingratiate himself with RK's house help, no doubt, by coming across as someone who cared deeply for RK. Which is why they did not think Aman's repeated enquiries about RK's visitors were out of place, even when he called whilst supposedly on vacation in Bali. For this reason, possibly, they had not thought his frequent enquiries merited a mention to us or the police while being questioned.

Alena had simply come into RK's life at the wrong time, a time when the superstar was being relentlessly puppeteered by Aman into establishing his movie career. And so, she became 'an inconvenience', to be done away with. As no doubt, had Mohan, at some point.

'Despite Mohan's help for the Bali trip, you had to kill him?' I asked, mincing no words. 'Later?'

'I did, because Mohan got greedy,' Aman's joviality faded. 'Asking for a whole lot of money. And appearing nervous after RK's cat died and all that press attention came into play. I had no choice but to strangle him at an opportune time on his own set.'

'The cat,' I turned wistful at the mention of poor Mr Pickles.

'He never liked you, did he?' Parvati spoke up.

Aman turned to her, his expression calm.

'No,' he said, evenly. 'So that creature needed to go. It was never in the same room with me when RK was around, so RK never actually realized how much that cat disliked me. It would always hiss and screech when I was around.'

'Animals sense danger to their own,' Parvati remarked, neutrally.

'They also sense bad people,' I said, under my breath so Aman won't hear. I recalled how Aman had shuddered when I had mentioned the cat's death to him at Taqdeer. I had believed at the time that he was upset over RK's loss. Now I knew he hated the cat, just as the pet hated him.

'Even the day we first saw you,' Parvati mused, 'The cat had already left the room. So, we didn't realize how much Mr Pickles disliked you. We thought Shashi was the only one he was picky about …'

'I wasn't going to kill it so soon, but it went for me when I was preparing to whistle the scream that day,' Aman was saying. 'Perhaps it sensed my whistle was behind those noises? Anyway, it surprised me, appearing like that, claws and teeth bared. I would've preferred strangling it, but I had to slash at it with the kitchen knife, the only thing handy as it attacked me. Then I had to carry that dead, bleeding thing and lay it outside the study door. Then blow the whistle for RK to find it …'

'Where's the knife?' I asked conversationally.

'At the bottom of the ocean, Marine Drive is perfect to get rid of such things,' Aman gloated. 'I got rid of it and arrived late back at the house, claiming being delayed at a long doctor's appointment as you know …'

'And the soundless bell around Mr Pickles' neck?' I asked.

Aman looked at me with indulgence.

'You liked it too, beautiful Akruti? I have it with me. As a souvenir. So pretty, to wear around the neck, later ...'

'So, Mr Pickles was killed by you, and Mohan too, because both got in your way. And you wanted Alena dead when RK wouldn't give her up. But why the attempt on Amrut?' Parvati spoke up. She knew I couldn't bear to hear more about Mr Pickles. 'Why mess with him now, when he had only come to collect his brother's remains? It was you who did that, wasn't it?'

'You've figured that out, haven't you? He got in touch with me,' Aman said, his manner detached as he spoke. 'As you already know, I found out Mohan had written to Amrut about meeting me only when Amrut got in touch with me after he reached Mumbai. He couldn't come meet me, RK's home being the fortress it is, but he called me. No doubt Mohan had even shared the phone number that RK allowed me, when he wrote him. Amrut needed money. He told me he hadn't wanted to call, but he knew Mohan and I were friends, and he really needed to return to his village. I doubt he realized properly that my voice wasn't the real Aman's, he was so caught up in his own misery. I told him I had a cold, so my voice wasn't as it should be. Anyway, I knew it wasn't good for me, this connect to Mohan when I had covered all my tracks. *Amrut seemed another inconvenience, like Alena was.* So, I found out where he worked, went to the set and hung around, then snuck up on him. I couldn't strangle him as I wanted to, there were too many witnesses around. So, I settled for toppling the scenery set on him. But it went wrong, like with Alena's cake in Pune. He didn't die.'

Was it introspection on his monetary practicalities, after my conversation with him on the movie set, that had led

Amrut to call Aman for financial help, despite his earlier reluctance? I shuddered, thinking what a near brush with death he'd had, on account of that one call. I was thankful he survived it. There were more questions to be cleared up by Aman, so I couldn't dwell on poor Amrut's close shave at present.

'Were you in Pune?' I asked, curious as to how Aman had managed to send the poisoned cake across all the way from Mumbai.

'Let a little mystery remain.' Aman turned to me. 'Why ask? It didn't happen the way I wanted it to.'

'Not everything does,' Parvati said simply. No sooner were the words out of her mouth, than the room door burst open and to my utter, incredulous surprise and, not to mention, relief, Addl CP Mhatre and his crack team of policemen tumbled inside rapidly.

Aman's downfall unravelled with incredible speed, in stark contrast to how long his sinister plottings had held us all mystified. Within seconds, the police had surrounded him. Aman first snarled in anger at his masterplan being thwarted so utterly, then put up a struggle at length when he was led out of the room. In fact, it all happened so fast I was almost breathless watching it in motion.

Would he have managed to make an escape without being caught had the police not arrived when they did? Would he have managed to add us all to his body count, his 'eliminations', before that, given our unexpected appearance in Alena's room was not part of his plan? Could he have indeed managed a smooth get-away, considering that as a seasoned risk-taker, his modus operandi included seizing chances and using them, as he had done all along, including the unexpected attack on

Amrut on set, his last brazen gamble before his failed attempt on Alena and his capture?

But it's useless to conjecture on what-ifs; our current rescue had played out conveniently and effectively, to my eternal relief. It was frightening how Aman's eternal-seeming cool composure had disintegrated into absolute animalistic chaos by the time the police dragged him out of Alena's room.

In fact, it seemed almost fantastic, looking at the sequence of events as a whole, that what began for him as an impersonation to fulfil a deep-seated career craving had led to an actual taking of lives down the line. The descent from crossing a moral line to complete unravelling had been utter and soul-destroying. All to satisfy a ruthless hunger, an over-reaching ambition to become a Bollywood star. The path to fame could be difficult, but also, as in Aman's case, extremely dangerous to self and others, if hubris and ambition like his ran unchecked.

'Not an easy person to deal with,' were Mhatre's only words to us, before exiting the room with his prisoner duly subdued and in handcuffs, post a terrific struggle. I was getting used to Mhatre's tart one-liners before making an exit, always spouting a pertinent thought, like some villain, or then, a wise man, in a play. But I was also mystified by what Parvati had managed—I was sure she had a hand behind Mhatre's surprise entry into that room.

'*How did you pull that off?*' I asked Parvati, wanting clarity on the speedy arrival of the police in this seemingly impossible situation.

'The bell here,' Parvati said. 'Aman may have had his whistle to frighten RK, as also his souvenir from Mr Pickles' collar, but Alena had a silent bell right here to help her, should she need it. You ring it to ask for assistance or warn the nurses of emergencies in this hospital—it rings only at their end. When I sat down to speak, I never stopped pressing it. Why do you think I chose this spot to sit, near her head, within reach of the button, so cleverly installed at her bedside table it appears disguised to those unaware of it? The bell was ringing for a while. Mhatre's cue to enter was when it stopped.'

I couldn't stop gazing at Parvati in admiration. She had been smacked hard by Aman, right across the face too, and appeared to succumb to his superior physical strength. But who could forget that this was Parvati, champion of the underdog, the one person in the world who would never tolerate a show of power over a (supposed!) weaker being. Of course, she had an ace up her sleeve—she was sitting in that chair to beat out a war cry and summon help, not because she was beaten!

'How did you know to alert Mhatre in the first place?' I asked, mystified at her ingenuity.

Parvati's eyes twinkled, she smiled one of her rare smiles. 'What was it Aman said to us? *The devil is in the details.* We were beauty contestants and models first, remember, Aku, before we became investigators? On the catwalk, the way we walked defined our career path. Don't tell me you didn't notice Aman limped on the wrong foot when we saw him earlier in the corridor. *I noticed.* I even said so, *but you never realized what I meant.* Mr Kamal had mentioned his left foot as being the one injured, but Aman was limping today all evening on his right. *It was his walk that gave him away*!'

41

Of course, the Mumbai police force's dear, saturnine Addl CP Mhatre and his band of merry men dominated the media the next few days for having successfully solved the mystery behind the strange events that shrouded the shooting of RK's ghostly new movie.

Bollywood was exultant with press quotes, now that business could continue as usual, without sets having to be dismantled and shoots being halted. And yes, RK's producers were also glad for the publicity, since it had concluded well—any creepy legend surrounding a haunted house movie is welcome, after all!

How exactly, though, had Parvati managed to pull off Aman's lightning-fast capture? I learnt later, the details of her meticulous plan.

Parvati had noticed Aman's limp when we saw him first, on the floor waiting to meet Alena. He was making RK's entourage step aside, using his limp as the reason to give him right of way to get closer to RK.

Quick to pick up oddities, she had made a mental note of the incongruity—he was limping on the wrong foot! In fact, the way she had told me that she 'noticed' Aman as we crossed the floor ought to have alerted me. There was a difference in her tone that I heard but did not follow up on or ask her about. I had simply assumed she meant Aman's presence on the floor, not the intricacies of his walk!

Then her instincts really began buzzing when Alena had whispered 'Save me' in her room. Acting purely on a hunch, Parvati had immediately got a message through to Addl CP Mhatre and his team to be on alert. *This was the phone call she had made from the public booth at the hospital after we were hustled out of Alena's room*—the one I had assumed was a quick call to our office to check up on other cases.

So, in fact, Parvati had alerted the police *way before* we had even gone down to meet Amrut on his floor that night at the hospital. She had noticed RK outside Alena's room, whispering to the nurse, just as I had. Aman was standing with him there, not budging. She had guessed with typical Parvati-esque prescience, that if her suspicions of Aman proved correct, he might find a chance to worm his way into Alena's room, then try and attack her.

And so, without concrete proof yet, but her every instinct buzzing a warning, she had confided to Mhatre her suspicions of Aman. He had listened, apparently, and then taken a decision.

It is possible Mhatre took his decision to go along with Parvati's plan as a simple precautionary measure. But I believe he was beginning to realize, as I already did, that Parvati had a nose for picking up the correct scent, and it might be worth his while to back her up.

Whatever Mhatre's thought process, Parvati now had an ally in the Mumbai police. Her hunch, of course, was proven correct almost immediately after she had alerted Mhatre—first in Amrut's room, when he couldn't recognize Aman's photo, and then in the note the nurse procured from Alena, where she wrote Aman's name as the person she needed to be saved from.

There was no further contact with Mhatre, though. In that earlier call, Parvati had already outlined her plan of a safety net signal, a way out, should things turn scary in Alena's room—the signalling via the silent bell, complete with the exact cue for when Mhatre should burst in! Because, unbeknownst to me, Parvati fully intended to be alongside Alena that night. Just in case Aman succeeded in working his way into Alena's room, Parvati was not going to have Alena sleep alone, regardless of the night nurse!

Mind you, as much as Aman proved to be a risk-taker, so too did Parvati. She had no way then, of knowing for sure that we ever would have need of this signal she had dreamt up for Mhatre's entry. But as in our earlier cases, she acted on her inner voice, and, as usual, it didn't let us down.

Later, when her hunch played out and we both were actually confronted with Aman's presence in Alena's room, she was in two minds about how exactly to get him to reveal himself, without inciting danger to anyone. Then, noticing him limping to the door, yet again on the wrong foot, as he made to ask us to leave, convinced her to speak up immediately. Her instinct had warned her this might be his end game, there was no other way but to call him out.

With an opponent as single-minded, as ruthless as Aman, there was considerable danger—even this plan was a risk, but it worked without a hitch. I was relieved at her foresight, even as I marvelled at the simplicity of the bell plan—no doubt she had picked up a few mean tricks from the men in her RAW family! *Things are not what they appear to be …*

Here I was thinking Parvati was hurt badly, being smacked hard by Aman, vulnerable and defenceless as she sat on that chair. All the while, she was actually the hunter, not the prey. As usual!

I was glad too, for the presence of the redoubtable Addl CP Mhatre and his Mumbai police team—despite his dour demeanour and his taciturn nature, Mhatre had come through for us, been there solidly when we needed him yet again, post our first case.

'I've no doubt that I'll be seeing you again,' Mhatre had remarked cryptically, even after all the formalities of Aman's arrest were done. Clearly, he expected to be handling other cases alongside us in the future.

If I allowed myself to get past his saturnine nature, I might even grow to enjoy having him around on another case, I thought. Or then, recalling the ironic expression in his eyes when he first saw me at Taqdeer after Mr Pickles was killed—maybe not!

Our client, RK, Bollywood superstar, called us the very next day post Aman's arrest, sounding rather thrown by the turn of events.

'Please come over,' he pleaded. 'Aman's arrested, Alena's in hospital and Shashi's ill in bed, running high fever. I have no one to talk to …'

Again, I was struck by the man's peculiar vulnerability, a trait common to many at the very top, I believed, isolated and cocooned as they seem, in their ivory towers of stupendous success.

'And we thought RK might just be our suspect,' I told Parvati as we headed to his home in her car.

'Why not?' she said to me. 'He was under suspicion at the time for concocting sympathetic attention in regards to his heritage property.'

'You know that turned out to be a fabrication,' I said to her.

Mhatre's team, while grilling Samuel Rodrigues as a suspect in Mohan's strangling had uncovered his bluster about harming RK and Saddaq for being friendly with Alena for what it was—just bluster.

They had also uncovered his unsavoury tactics of befriending gossip magazines with a view to plant malicious stories about those he had an axe to grind with. This included RK and Saddaq, both. So the stories eventually picked up by soft supplements of mainstream papers, on RK especially, were Samuel's doing and untrue, even as they continued to run unchecked long after he had been warned. We had come to know this only now, after Aman had been arrested.

'We hadn't any idea at the time …' Parvati said. 'Everyone's a suspect …'

'Yes, yes, till proven innocent,' I completed her sentence, playfully knocking her shoulder.

'Though in this case, I think we have a new mantra,' she said, smiling at me, before her eyes turned serious. '*Evil often hides in plain sight*.'

I sighed at her words, recognizing their veracity. I had actually been rather taken by the charming, dimpled Aman Azad, not really giving his easy casualness the distance it deserved, allowing myself to be played, initially at least.

'I know, Pari,' I said ruefully. 'We suspected everyone, but perhaps went easy initially on the one who we, or rather I, was most comfortable with. A momentary lapse of judgement on my part at the beginning, but it won't reoccur!'

'I didn't mean you.' Parvati looked at me, her bright eyes taking in my contrite face. 'I meant Mr Kamal. He was going utterly crazy over the supposed ghostly screaming in his home, and all the while it was his one house guest, the person he had taken in, offered food, shelter, all manner of comfort to, who was gunning for his sanity … *and his paramour.*'

'True,' I mused, disturbed at the word picture she painted. From the start, the ominousness of this case had unsettled me. Later, following Parvati's advice and focusing my feelings on the mansion grounds, I had sensed evil around the house.

Perhaps subconsciously I had picked up on Aman's evil—he was a house guest after all. Whatever it was, my gut feeling had been right, there was more to this case than the screams that it began with, and I was glad we had decided to take it on then.

'I also have a mantra for you,' I told Parvati. '*Things are not always as they appear to be* …'

'Yes, true,' Parvati laughed at my bringing up of her own words at the start of this case. 'That mantra, actually, sums up this case entirely. Nothing was what it seemed when we took up the case, not the hauntings, not Alena, nor Aman!'

'Not you, either,' I teased, recalling how she'd turned the tables on Aman in Alena's room.

'Mr Kamal, though, was consistent all through,' Parvati mused. 'He wasn't imagining those screams …'

'Poor RK seems even more vulnerable now,' I voiced what was going through my mind.

'Stop feeling sorry for him,' Parvati said gently. 'He has so much many don't. By the way, I have to make one stop before we get to Mr Kamal's.'

We pulled up in front of a city hotel. Waiting in the driveway was a familiar person, one I had not seen since our case at the beauty pageant. Parvati was already out of the car, greeting her adored sibling enthusiastically.

'Brij,' I acknowledged his kiss with a wide smile as I stepped out to say hello too. Now, unlike Aman's, these dimples I could admire without my conscience pricking me about their owner's credibility, any day! Parvati's brother, pretty high up in India's RAW hierarchy, had obviously flown into the city on one of his clandestine operations, and had taken time out to meet us for a nanosecond.

'I hear there's one more success to your roster. I come bearing gifts,' he said mischievously handing over a basket to me.

'When I knew Brij was coming to the city, I asked him to help transport *that*,' Parvati smiled. 'So, your wonderful, fragile superstar is not so lonely anymore …'

I looked down into the basket. Lying nestled in a blanket's fold was a beautiful black Labrador puppy.

'No one can replace Mr Pickles.' Parvati's eyes were knowing, as mine turned a trifle moist at Parvati's generosity and wisdom. 'But why not give Mr Kamal someone to help share that big home? Someone the loyal, if temperamental, Shashi too will adore, this time!'

It was late afternoon by the time we finally got to Taqdeer, what with Brij entertaining us for a bit at a local coffee shop, before he bid Parvati adieu.

Parvati's gift for RK sat in my lap as we approached the massive manor. The puppy was just too adorable, but I wondered if the cat-loving RK would take to the Labrador as much as we both had.

The study, RK's meeting room of choice, had its familiar gloomy air, much like on our first visit here.

He was already present, which was not always the case. Bollywood operated on its own sweet time more often than not, so we were glad that this moment once again favoured us.

I held out the basket as we entered, but the puppy had decided to take matters into his own paws. He jumped straight out of the basket into the arms of the very surprised superstar. And I realized immediately that I needn't have worried after all. RK's face lit up—he suddenly looked the most *alive* I had seen him, since we met.

'You brought company!' I could hear the smile in his voice.

'Thought you might need a friend,' Parvati, always quick at such times, responded easily. 'As all yours seem indisposed at present.'

The bit of irony in her words was not lost on any of us.

'Aman—who would have thought it would be so,' RK mused, setting himself and the puppy in his favourite leather armchair.

'That wasn't Aman,' Parvati reminded him gently. 'The real Aman died on his way to meet you.'

'I know,' RK's face crumpled a bit. 'But to me, this person was Aman. In my heart, it was like he was mine. I really believed it …'

'So too did his doctors, I take it? I asked curiously. 'How did he manage to fool them about his leg for so long?'

'Paid them to write things, I guess.' RK looked really down in the dumps. 'I used to give him money supposedly for his treatments. I never thought he would betray me like this …'

Then he seemed to revive a little.

'You know for a canny upstart, he actually is an excellent actor, whoever he is,' RK said. 'To be able to pull off that leg injury for so long. And such a vibrant personality, with such ease. I was so taken …'

'That's true,' Parvati agreed. 'And he does have movie-star good looks. Plus, he said he was a Bandra boy—he must've grown up wanting to act.'

'Don't forget the natural charm,' I said, a trifle ungraciously. I was still smarting from the way I had been taken in by him, at the beginning.

'And a fetish for the neck,' Parvati added. 'He liked to strangle. He held Alena by the throat on two occasions, one time with almost fatal results. He told us he would have preferred to strangle the cat, only it went for him so he had to defend himself by slashing at it. And he had wanted to strangle Amrut too, but couldn't find the opportune moment.'

'He did strangle Mohan Tawade though,' I said. 'And he actually kept the bell Mr Pickles wore around his neck as a souvenir. He told me it was "so pretty, to wear around the neck later" ...' I began feeling physically sick recalling Aman's expression when he said that.

'Yes, he had a thing for the neck, but he's with the police now, Aku,' Parvati said gently. 'Stress made him make silly mistakes towards the end, mistakes that proved costly—like limping on the wrong leg ...'

'He was so absolutely single-minded in getting what he wanted, though.' RK had gone back to his morose demeanour as he listened, staring moodily into the distance. 'It wasn't healthy in the end. He *killed* to get his way.'

'He actually told Alena it "wasn't personal" when he strangled her,' I recalled. 'That level of single-minded ...'

'Life is about the choices we make,' Parvati said. 'We become who we are, based on those.'

'Speaking of which, we hear your big life choice is on the anvil,' I spoke up, trying to lift the mood. 'Is it true, the rumours about a wedding sooner rather than later?'

RK looked at me, a trifle sheepish.

'I know I gave you the impression that I was going to marry Alena,' he said. 'And I believed I would too. But I realized during the course of all this, that she and I, we want different things.'

Parvati looked at me. Perhaps RK had actually seen Alena's true colours during the chequered course of this case, as Aman, her nemesis, had once hoped. Or perhaps he really did love this home, well enough not to give it up on the whim of a lady love he had barely known a few months.

Taqdeer's destiny might still go right after all. Whatever it was that had made RK reconsider, a little restraint wouldn't hurt either party; Parvati and I, we both instinctively felt this.

'We'll take it as it comes,' RK was saying, with typical Bollywood evasiveness. 'In any case, she has to recover first.'

'Yes, seems to me during the run of this case, it has been Alena taking the brunt, in hospital on two occasions, and attacked whilst there, a third time,' Parvati spoke up.

'But we all know she can take care of herself. And she's recovering well,' said a voice from the doorway. 'I checked just now. So is that extra, Amrut.' We looked up to find Shashi standing there.

'You were running a temperature,' said RK to him as he came into the room.

'I was, but I popped a few pills,' Shashi retorted. 'You wanted me to be here, so I am.'

Parvati met my eyes once again. We had suspected Shashi as the mastermind for his very gruffness and fixity, but really, he was an extremely loyal and true companion to RK, so doggedly committed to his friend that it was almost an anachronism.

'He *really* loves Mr Kamal,' Parvati would comment to me later, but it was evident regardless, for all to see.

And we knew now, that much like his idol, Shashi had never lied to us. He truly hadn't heard a single scream Aman had generated via the whistle, not once whilst visiting RK, nor the day we heard it either, possibly because he was crossing the soundproofed rooms when it happened. Also, his sudden, stealthy-seeming appearances were more a part of his unobtrusive, introspective character, than anything dark or sinister. We were relieved to understand the truth, that like RK, in this case, Shashi too, really was who he seemed to convey being, all along.

RK appeared childishly pleased to see his best friend. He pointed to his new puppy.

'See what they got me,' he said, happily.

'Wise choice,' said Shashi, looking at Parvati. He knew somehow that it was she who had made that decision, was thanking her without appearing to.

Parvati smiled that rare smile of hers. 'I thought so too.'

'What happened to Samuel?' I asked, suddenly curious.

'He hasn't been heard from since yesterday as far as I know,' Shashi said. 'But he'll be around, of that I'm certain. He won't stay far from Alena.'

'I just might though,' RK's eyes held mischief as he told Shashi, and we all noted a faint flicker of hope dance in Shashi's eyes then. Shashi might as yet retain his hold on RK as he had, before Alena. This was Bollywood after all, land of dreams, where things could change in an instant, sometimes for the worst, sometimes to serendipitously sweet moments!

'Why the change of heart?' Shashi asked RK quietly.

'I had a chat with Saddaq that night at the hospital, after we'd been to Alena's room,' RK said. 'I learnt a few things I didn't know about.'

He might well have learnt how Saddaq wasn't ever told how seriously RK and Alena were seeing each other, I guessed.

Whatever else was said, at least the blinkers about Alena were off, for good.

'Are you and Saddaq friends now?' Parvati asked.

'We were never enemies,' RK said, closing the chapter on that, classic Bollywood style—no permanent friends, no permanent enemies here, just business as usual.

'You should know,' Shashi spoke up, addressing us now. 'Roop will be paying for Amrut's care at the hospital and his return home, once he's better.'

RK's famed generosity to the rescue once again, I thought. Maybe it was this open-hearted giving nature of his that protected him time and again from evil, the universe's special thank you, even when evil housed in his own home and put a target on his loved one's back.

'That's generous of you,' Parvati thanked RK, gratitude in her eyes. I knew she meant it for me, she had seen how affected I had been by Amrut's condition.

Everything seemed to have tied up in the end. This seemingly ominous, baffling case sorted satisfactorily for all the concerned parties and RK had company now, in the form of both the new puppy and Shashi. Our work was done here.

'Akruti, Parvati,' RK began, as we said our goodbyes, 'Just one more thing ...'

We waited expectantly for the superstar to complete his sentence.

RK drew a breath, a pause followed, as if before imparting a great gift. 'From now on,' he said. 'You may call me Roop.'

We couldn't contain our laughter as we left his imposing gothic manor. Despite all that had transpired—two murders, a severe beating, a poisoning and two more harrowing attempts at murder—Bollywood would not lose its sense of self-importance anytime soon.

In fact, much like a movie-in-progress, this case had allowed us a glimpse into Tinseltown's varied and contrary facets up close, holding us captive to its singular magnetism through all its flamboyance and flaws. From the dazzling game face of its superstars to what lay just beneath that glitz, any manner of secrets and cover-ups.

Or then, its endless contradictions, in opposing extremes, like how much the near-isolated existence of a very public figure contrasted to the reverential groupies, the blinding adulation his on-screen presence commanded. Or then, the open-hearted expansiveness this most favourite luminary displayed, which was so at odds with the closeted, covetous darkness attempting to envelop and control him, a darkness we had managed to thwart, thankfully. Or then, Bollywood's strict code of conduct, closing ranks to outsiders, even as business dealings got right of way, over uncertain personal equations or enmity.

Parvati's off-the-cuff statement about this case actually also captured Bollywood's abiding ethos quite well—things were not always as they appeared to be here, and that was considered par for course in a profession based primarily on a nebulous, oft make-believe universe.

For all that, the sparkle of Tinseltown was undeniable, bouncing or then feeding off the energy of its many-hued strains as it did, vibrant, eternal, a magnet for all with dreams of technicolour stardom. And remarkably, despite all quirks or perhaps *because* of them, Tinseltown's omnipotent charm somehow endeared itself rather firmly to any that crossed its path.

And so we laughed as we took our leave, as much at ourselves for being so taken, as we did at Bollywood's unflagging sense of its own importance.

Our gaiety at successfully solving all the mystery behind this befuddling Bollywood affair was cut short though, as we arrived at the office. The phone was ringing off the hook.

'Aku,' I heard Jehaan's familiar voice at the other end, when I picked up. His tone sounded strained. 'Could you and Pari come to the office?'

'Right at this very minute?' I asked, a trifle petulant.

'There's a body in the newsroom,' was Jehaan's curt reply.

And just like that, almost immediately—another case! But that's a whole other book now, isn't it?

Acknowledgements

To say thank you (because the importance of gratitude cannot be underestimated—always, #strongertogether)

Chaitanya: For everything, naturally. How else? From long Sunday walks with the Direwolf, in the magic of the Mumbai monsoons (when not in lockdown), to homecooked meals from scratch that your singular culinary talent dreams up. I will always need your grace.

Tariecka: For helping me understand that love transcends breed—used to call myself a 'dog person' till your baby self-adopted stray Kitty Meow, and showed me so blindingly that there is always space in the world for a higher love, should you call upon it. The entire animal kingdom can reside in our hearts (and home if we can manage it, yes, including Larry the lizard!). And, in our books.

Jyotsna and Suresh: Papa and Ma, your unquestioning support buoys me at every step—I am so eternally grateful for you both.

Raphael ('Rafa'): For embodying the Direwolf I dreamt of (Be careful what you wish for—you might get it!). For getting me through the pandemic. For sharing my silences. For the fierceness and the simplicity of your love.

Simba and Caesar: For—just ever.

Manish Pachouly: For your crime reporting skills and knowledge, as ever, helping me understand law and order (in particular, related to pet killings) in the Nineties.

Ananth Padmanabhan: For faith in my writing. And for staunch support in this entire series, not just the one book—thank you so very much.

Diya Kar and the dynamic team at HarperCollins India: For backing my writing, unequivocally and always, through this series in all its meandering paths—a huge thank you.

Shabnam Srivastava: For making sure this series gets its due, despite all drama!

Paloma Dutta: For 'a light hand' in this book's copy edits, and for even subtler but significant 'suggestions'—so grateful our paths crossed. Your editing is what I have long sought, but seldom found in my craft—thank you!

And

The brilliant **Swati Daftuar:** For just unbelievably incisive primary edits/edits. For championing this series featuring women detectives in a primarily male-dominated sleuthing story scenario. For sensing my worries as the book's release continually delayed, keeping pace with the zeitgeist of lockdown in this interminable battle against the all-disruptive virus. For rock-solid support through this strange time we're all living through. For sharing journeys centred on animals.

For being there from the beginning. For being YOU—thank you and thank you!

Last, but not least,

Mumbai's iconic Glamour Industry (Tinseltown, Ramp Frat, TV World, High Society, Les Artistes, Popular Culture's Finest)—underbelly, warts and all: for enduring inspiration! From my debut in front of audiences as an insider, courtesy of my erstwhile catwalker career, to collating news, perspective and analysis on you as a journalist/Editor, to spinning stories around your compelling ethos as an author—it's been an epic ride!

About the Author

Gauri Sinh is the former Editor of some of India's biggest lifestyle and entertainment publications. Helming *Bombay Times*, the lifestyle and entertainment supplement of *The Times of India*, and, later, *DNA After Hrs*, gave her close insight into the workings of the country's glamour world, that also straddled fashion, film, television, art, books, theatre, travel, society, and the fitness and food industries.

Her writing also covers social issues and parenting—she has written numerous popular columns on the same for leading broadsheets and online journals. Having worked on issues concerning today's youth, her career includes former Editorship of the erstwhile national publication, *Femina Girl*, and young adult–focused *JLT*.

Gauri is the author of three previous books, including a non-fiction work. Her earlier books are *Dogsend: The Story of Simba* (2010), *The Garud Prophecies: Sitara's Story* (2015) and *Drop Dead Gorgeous* (2019). The last one introduced her current lady detective characters, though every book in this series is a stand-alone thriller. Gauri lives and works in Mumbai. Her website is www.gaurisinh.com.